ADDRESS: CENTAURI

By F. L. WALLACE

I0541602

ARMCHAIR FICTION
PO Box 4369, Medford, Oregon 97504

For more information about Armchair Books and products, visit our website at…

www.armchairfiction.com

Or email us at…
mailto:armchairfiction@yahoo.com
armchairfiction@yahoo.com

RACING THROUGH SPACE FOR A NEW HOME...

The accidentals were human...but not human enough for Earth. Humans had abolished nearly every disease, deformity, and defect; but there were still a few that couldn't be fixed by surgery or cures. Those people who couldn't be cured or repaired to reflect the perfection of the rest of the populace just didn't belong. They were called accidentals. Their home was an asteroid called Handicap Haven—the residents called it the Junkpile.

But there were those among the accidentals who longed for something better—a greater sense of freedom, and the vast reaches of space seemed to hold promise of that. So against the wishes of the Solar Committee, the Junkpile was piloted out of the solar system, toward the Centauri cluster. The only question remaining was whether or not the renegade asteroid could reach its new home before the long arm of the committee could reach out and stop them.

FOR A COMPLETE SECOND NOVEL, TURN TO PAGE 179

CAST OF CHARACTERS

DOCCHI
Docchi didn't have arms, and flashed like a firefly depending on his mood, but he was a leader who could get things done.

JORDAN
His lower half was missing, but powerful arms and a strong mind made him a coveted ally—or a deadly foe.

NONA
Deaf and mute, the medicouncil thought her less than a simpleton. But her intellect was incaluculable.

ANTI
Confined to a vat of acid, Anti was still a great friend to have around, with insight that would soon help her people.

JERIANN
This fantastic but flawed nurse raced against time to help those who—like her—were deficient in some way.

DOCTOR CAMERON
He didn't always agree with the Medicouncil—after all, his patients were imprisoned on an asteroid far removed from Earth.

GENERAL JUDD
He didn't relish the idea of being beaten by deficient sub-humans who were viewed as too sick to care for themselves.

CHAPTER ONE

LIGHT flickered. It was uncomfortably bright.

Doctor Cameron gazed intently at the top of the desk. It wasn't easy to be diplomatic. "The request was turned over to the Medicouncil," he said. "I assure you it was studied thoroughly before it was reported back to the Solar Committee."

Docchi edged forward, his face alight with anticipation.

The doctor kept his eyes averted. The man was damnably disconcerting—had no right to be alive. In the depths of the sea there were certain creatures like him and on a warm summer evening there was still another parallel, but never any human with such an infirmity. "I'm afraid you know what the answer is. A flat no for the present."

Docchi sagged and his arms hung limp. "That's the answer?"

"It's not as hopeless as you think. Decisions can be changed. It won't be the first time."

"Sure," said Docchi. "We'll wait and wait until it's finally changed. We've got centuries, haven't we?" His face was blazing. It had slipped out of control though he wasn't aware of it. Beneath the skin certain cells had been modified, there were substances in his body that the ordinary individual didn't have. And when there was an extreme flow of nervous energy the response was— light. His metabolism was akin to that of a firefly.

Cameron meddled with buttons. It was impossible to keep the lighting at a decent level. Docchi was a nuisance.

"Why?" questioned Docchi. "We're capable, you know that. How could they refuse?"

That was something he didn't want asked because there was no answer both of them would accept. Sometimes a blunt reply was the best evasion. "Do you think they'd take you? Or Nona, Jordan, or Anti?"

Docchi winced, his arms quivering uselessly. "Maybe not. But we told you we're willing to let experts decide. There's nearly a thousand of us. They should be able to get one qualified crew."

"Perhaps. I'm not going to say." Cameron abandoned the light as beyond his control. "Most of you are biocompensators. I concede it's a factor in your favor. But you must realize there are many things against you." He squinted at the desk top. Below the solid surface there was a drawer and in the drawer there was—that was what he was trying to see or determine. The more he looked the less clear anything seemed to be. He tried to make his voice crisp and professional. "You're wasting time discussing this with me. I've merely passed the decision on, I'm not responsible for it and I can't do anything for you."

Docchi stood up, his face colorless and bright. But the inner illumination was no indication of hope.

Doctor Cameron looked at him directly for the first time. It wasn't as bad as he expected. "I suggest you calm down. Be patient and wait. You'll be surprised how often you get what you want."

"You'd be surprised how we get what we want," said Docchi. He turned away, lurching toward the door which opened automatically and closed behind him.

Again Cameron concentrated on the desk, trying to look through it. He wrote down the sequence he expected to find, lingering over it to make sure he didn't force the pictures that came into his mind. He opened the drawer and compared the Rhine cards with what he'd written, frowning in disappointment. No matter how he tried he never got better than average results. Perhaps there was something to telepathy but he'd never found it. Anyway it was clear he wasn't one of the gifted few.

He shut the drawer. It was a private game, a method to keep from becoming involved in Docchi's problems, to avoid emotional entanglement with people he had nothing in common with. He didn't enjoy depriving weak and helpless men and women of what little hope they had. It was their lack of strength that made them so difficult to handle.

He reached for the telecom. "Get Medicouncilor Thorton," he told the operator. "Direct if you can; indirect if you have to. I'll hold on."

Approximate mean diameter thirty miles the asteroid was listed on tile charts as Handicap Haven with a mark that indicated except in emergency no one not authorized was to land there. Those who were confined to it were willing to admit they were handicapped but they didn't call it haven. They used other terms, none suggesting sanctuary.

It was a hospital, of course, but even more it was a convalescent home—the permanent kind. Healthy and vigorous humanity had reserved the remote planetoid, a whirling bleak rock of no other value, and built large installations there for less fortunate people. It was a noble gesture but like many gestures the reality fell short of the intentions. And not many people outside the Haven itself realized wherein it was a failure.

The robot operator broke into his thoughts. "Medicouncilor Thorton has been located."

An older man looked out of the screen, competent, forceful. "I'm on my way to the satellites of Jupiter. I'll be in direct range for the next half hour." At such distances transmission and reception were practically instantaneous. Cameron was assured of uninterrupted conversation. "It's a good thing you called. Have you got the Solar Committee reply?"

"This morning. I saw no reason to hold it up. I just finished giving Docchi the news."

"Dispatch. I like that. Get the disagreeable job done with." The medicouncilor searched through the desk in front of him without success. "Never mind. I'll find the information later. Now. How did Docchi react?"

"He didn't like it. He was mad clear through."

"That speaks well for his bounce."

"They all have spirit. Nothing to use it on," said Dr. Cameron. "I confess I didn't look at him often though he was quite presentable, even handsome in a startling sort of way."

Thornton nodded brusquely. "Presentable. Does that mean he had arms?"

"Today he did. Is it important?"

"I think so. He expected a favorable reply and wanted to look his best, as nearly normal as possible. In view of that I'm surprised he didn't threaten you."

Cameron tried to recall the incident. "I think he did, mildly. He said something to the effect that I'd be surprised how they got what they wanted."

"So you anticipate trouble. That's why you called?"

"I don't know. I want your opinion."

"You're on the scene, doctor. You get the important nuances," said the medicouncilor hastily. "However it's my considered judgment they won't start anything immediately. It takes time to get over the shock of refusal. They can't do anything. Individually they're helpless and collectively there aren't parts for a dozen sound bodies on the asteroid."

"I'll have to agree," said Dr. Cameron. "But there's something that bothers me. I've looked over the records. No accidental has ever liked being here, and that covers quite a few years."

"Nobody appreciates the hospital until he's sick, doctor."

"I know. That's partly what's wrong. They're no longer ill and yet they have to stay here. What worries me is that there's never been such open discontent as now."

"I hope I don't have to point out that someone's stirring them up. Find out who, and keep a close watch. As a doctor you can find pretexts, a different diet, a series of tests. You can keep the person coming to you every day."

"I've found out. There's a self-elected group of four, Docchi, Nona, Anti and Jordan. I believe they're supposed to be the local recreation committee."

The medicouncilor smiled. "An apt camouflage. It keeps them amused."

"I thought so too but now I'm convinced they're no longer harmless. I'd like permission to break up the group. Humanely of course."

"I always welcome new ideas."

In spite of what he'd said the medicouncilor probably did have an open mind. "Start with those it's possible to do the most with. Docchi, for instance. With prosthetic arms, he appears normal except for that uncanny fluorescence. Granted that the last is repulsive to the average person. We can't correct the condition medically but we can make it into an asset."

"An asset? Very neat, if it can be done." The medicouncilor's expression said it couldn't be.

"Gland opera," said Cameron, hurrying on. "The most popular program in the solar system, telepaths teleports pyrotics and so forth the heroes. Fake of course makeup and trick camera shots.

"But Docchi can be made into a real star. The death-ray man, say. When his face shines men fall dead or paralyzed. He'd have a tremendous following of kids."

"Children," mused the medicouncilor. "Are you serious about exposing them to his influence? Do you really want them to see him?"

"He'd have a chance to return to society in a way that would be acceptable to him," said Cameron defensively. He shouldn't have specifically mentioned kids.

"To him, perhaps," reflected the medicouncilor. "It's an ingenious idea, doctor, one which does credit to your humanitarianism. But I'm afraid of the public's reception. Have you gone into Docchi's medical history?"

"I glanced at it before I called him in." The man was unusual, even in a place that specialized in the abnormal. Docchi had been an electrochemical engineer with a degree in cold lighting. On his way to a brilliant career, he had been the victim of a particularly messy accident. The details hadn't been described but Cameron could supplement them with his imagination. He'd been badly mangled and tossed into a tank of the basic cold lighting fluid.

There was life left in the body; it flickered but never went entirely out. His arms were gone and his ribs were crushed into his spinal column. Regeneration wasn't easy; a partial rib cage could be built up, but no more than that. He had no shoulder muscles and only a minimum in his back and now, much later, that was why he tired easily and why the prosthetic arms with which he'd been fitted were merely ornamental, there was nothing which could move them.

And then there was the cold lighting fluid. To begin with it was semi-organic which, perhaps, was the reason he had remained alive so long when he should have died. It had preserved him, had in part replaced his blood, permeating every tissue. By the time Docchi had been found his body had adapted to the cold lighting substance. And the adaptation couldn't be reversed and it was self-perpetuating. Life was hardier than most men realized but occasionally it was also perverse.

"Then you know what he's like," said the medicouncilor, shaking his head. "Our profession can't sponsor such a freakish display of his misfortune. No doubt he'd be successful on the program you mention. But there's more to life than financial achievement or the rather peculiar admiration that would be certain to follow him. As an actor he'd have a niche. But can you imagine, doctor, the dead silence that would occur when he walks into a social gathering of normal people?"

"I see," said Cameron, though he didn't—not eye to eye. He didn't agree with Thorton but there wasn't much he could do to alter the other's conviction at the moment. There was a long fight ahead of him. "I'll forget about Docchi. But there's another way to break up the group."

The medicouncilor interrupted. "Nona?"

"Yes. I'm not sure she really belongs here."

"Every young doctor thinks the same," said the medicouncilor kindly. "Usually they wait until their term is nearly up before they suggest that she'd respond better if she were returned to normal society. I think I know what response they have in mind." Thorton smiled in a fatherly fashion. "No offense, doctor, but it happens so often I'm thinking of inserting a note in our briefing program. Something to the effect that the new medical director should avoid the beautiful and self-possessed moron."

"Is she stupid?" asked Cameron stubbornly, "It's my impression that she's not."

"Clever with her hands," agreed the medicouncilor. "People in her mental classification, which is very low, sometimes are. But don't confuse manual dexterity with intelligence. For one thing she doesn't have the brain structure for the real article.

"She's definitely not normal. She can't talk or hear, and never will. Her larynx is missing and though we could replace it, it wouldn't help if we did. We'd have to change her entire brain structure to accommodate it and we're not that good at the present."

"I was thinking about the nerve dissimilarities," began Cameron.

"A superior mutation, is that what you were going to say? You can forget that. It's much more of an anomaly, in the nature of cleft palates, which were once common—poor prenatal nutrition or traumas. These we can correct rather easily but Nona is surgically beyond us. There always is something beyond us, you know." The medicouncilor glanced at the chronometer beside him.

Cameron saw the time, too, but continued. It ought to be settled. It would do no good to bring up Helen Keller; the medicouncilor would use that evidence against him. The Keller techniques had been studied and reinterpreted for Nona's benefit. That much was in her medical record. They had been tried on Nona, and they hadn't worked. It made no difference that he, Cameron, thought there were certain flaws in the way the old techniques had been applied. Thorton would not allow that the previous practitioners could have been wrong. "I've been wondering if we haven't tried to force her to conform. She can be intelligent without understanding what we say or knowing how to read and write."

"How?" demanded the medicouncilor. "The most important tool humans have is language. Through this we pass along all knowledge."

Thorton paused, reflecting. "Unless you're referring to this Gland Opera stuff you mentioned. I believe you are, though personally I prefer to call it Rhine Opera."

"I've been thinking of that," admitted Cameron. "Maybe if there was someone else like her she wouldn't need to talk the way we do. Anyway I'd like to make some tests, with your permission. I'll need some new equipment."

The medicouncilor found the sheet he'd been looking for from time to time. He creased it absently. "Go ahead with those tests if it will make you feel better. I'll personally approve the requisition. It doesn't mean you'll get everything you want. Others have to sign too. However you ought to know you're not the first to think she's telepathic or something related to that phenomenon."

"I've seen that in the record too. But I think I can be the first one to prove it."

"I'm glad you're enthusiastic. But don't lose sight of the main objective. Even if she is telepathic, and so far as we're concerned she's not, would she be better suited to life outside?"

He had one answer—but the medicouncilor believed in another. "Perhaps you're right. She'll have to stay here no matter what happens."

"She will. It would solve your problems if you could break up the group, but don't count on it. You'll have to learn to manage them as they are."

"I'll see that they don't cause any trouble," said Cameron.

"I'm sure you will." The medicouncilor's manner didn't ooze confidence. "If you need help we can send in reinforcements."

"I don't anticipate that much difficulty," said Cameron hastily. "I'll keep them running around in circles."

"Confusion is the best policy," agreed the medicouncilor.

He unfolded the sheet and looked down at it. "Oh yes, before it's too late I'd better tell you I'm sending details of new treatments for a number of deficients—"

The picture collapsed into meaningless swirls of color. For an instant the voice was distinguishable again before it too was drowned by noise. "Did you understand what I said, doctor? If it isn't clear contact me. Deviation can be fatal."

"I can't keep the ship in focus," said the robot. "If you wish to continue the conversation it will have to be relayed through the nearest main station. At present that's Mars."

It was inconvenient to wait several minutes for each reply. Besides the medicouncilor couldn't or wouldn't help him. He wanted the status quo maintained; nothing else would satisfy him. It was the function of the medical director to see that it was. "We're through," said Cameron.

He sat there after the telecom clicked off. What were the deficients the medicouncilor had talked about? A subdivision of the accidentals of course, but it wasn't a medical term he was familiar with. Probably a semi-slang description. The medicouncilor had been associated with accidentals so long that he assumed every doctor would know at once what he meant.

Deficients. Mentally Cameron turned the word over. If it was used accurately it could indicate only one thing. He'd see when the medicouncilor's report came in. He could always ask for more information if it wasn't clear.

The doctor got heavily to his feet—and he actually was heavier. It wasn't a psychological reaction. He made a mental note of it. He'd have to investigate the gravity surge.

In a way accidentals were pathetic, patchwork humans, half or quarter men and women, fractional organisms which masqueraded as people. The illusion died hard for them harder than that which remained of their bodies, and those bodies were unbelievably tough. Medicine and surgery were partly to blame. Techniques were too good or not good enough, depending on the viewpoint—doctor or patient.

Too good in that the most horribly injured person, if he were found alive, could be kept alive. Not good enough, because a certain percent of the injured couldn't be returned to society completely sound and whole. The miracles of healing were incomplete.

There weren't many humans who were broken beyond repair, but though the details varied in every respect, the results were monotonously the same. For the most part disease had been eliminated. Everyone was healthy—except those who'd been hurt in accidents and who couldn't be resurgeried and regenerated into the beautiful mold characteristic of the entire population. And those few were sent to the asteroid.

They didn't like it. They didn't like being *confined* to Handicap Haven. They were sensitive and they didn't want to go back. They knew how conspicuous they'd be, hobbling and crawling among the multitudes of beautiful men and women who inhabited the planets. The accidentals didn't want to return.

What they did want was ridiculous. They had talked about, hoped, and finally embodied it in a petition. They had requested rockets to make the first long hard journey to Alpha and Proxima Centauri. Man was restricted to the solar system and had no way of getting to even the nearest stars. They thought they could break through the barrier. Some accidentals would go and some would remain behind, lonelier except for their share in the dangerous enterprise.

It was a particularly uncontrollable form of self-deception. They were the broken people, without a face they could call their own, who wore their hearts not on their sleeves but in a blood-pumping chamber, those without limbs or organs—or too many. The categories were endless. No accidental was like any other.

The self-deception was vicious precisely because the accidentals were qualified. Of all the billions of solar citizens they alone could make the long journey there and return. But there were other factors that ruled them out. It was never safe to discuss the first reason with them because the second would have to be explained. Cameron himself wasn't sadistic and no one else was interested enough to inform them.

CHAPTER TWO

Docchi sat beside the pool. It would be pleasant if he could forget where he was. It was pastoral though not quite a scene from Earth. The horizon was too near and the sky was shallow and only seemed to be bright. Darkness lurked outside.

A small tree stretched shade overhead. Waves lapped and made gurgling sounds against the banks. But there was no plant life of any kind, and no fish swam in the liquid. It looked like water but wasn't— the pool held acid. And floating in it, all but submerged, was a shape. The records in the hospital said it was a woman.

"Anti they turned us down," said Docchi bitterly.

"What did you expect?" rumbled the creature in the pool. Wavelets of acid danced across the surface, stirred by her voice.

"I didn't expect that."

"You don't know the Medicouncil very well."

"I guess I don't." He stared sullenly at the fluid. It was faintly blue. "I have the feeling they didn't consider it that they held the request for a time and then answered no without looking at it."

"Now you're beginning to learn. Wait till you've been here as long as I have."

Morosely he kicked an anemic tuft of grass. Plants didn't do well here either. They too were exiled, far from the sun removed from the soil they originated in. The conditions they grew in were artificial. "Why did they turn us down?" said Docchi.

"Answer it yourself. Remember what the Medicouncil is like. Different things are important to them. The main thing is that we don't have to follow their example. There's no need to be irrational even though they are."

"I wish I knew what to do," said Docchi. "It meant so much to us."

"We can wait, outlast the attitude," said Anti, moving slowly. It was the only way she could move. Most of her bulk was beneath the surface.

"Cameron suggested waiting." Reflectively Docchi added. "It's true we are biocompensators."

"They always bring in biocompensation," muttered Anti restlessly. "I'm getting tired of that excuse. Time passes just as slow."

"But what else is there? Shall we draw up another request?"

"Memorandum number ten? Let's not be naive. Things get lost when we send them to the Medicouncil. Their filing system is in terrible shape."

"Lost or distorted," grunted Docchi angrily. The grass he'd kicked already had begun to wilt. It wasn't hardy in this environment. Few things were.

"Maybe we ought to give the Medicouncil a rest. I'm sure they don't want to hear from us again."

Docchi moved closer to the pool. "Then you think we should go ahead with the plan we discussed before we sent in the petition? Good. I'll call the others together and tell them what happened. They'll agree that we have to do it."

"Then why call them? More talk, that's all. Besides I don't see why we should warn Cameron what we're up to."

Docchi glanced at her worriedly. "Do you think someone would report it? I'm certain everyone feels as I do."

"Not everyone. There's bound to be dissent," said Anti placidly. "But I wasn't thinking of people."

"Oh that," said Docchi. "We can block that source any time we need to." It was a relief to know that he could trust the accidentals. Unanimity was important and some of the reasons weren't obvious.

"Maybe you can and maybe you can't," said Anti. "But why make it difficult, why waste time?"

Docchi got up awkwardly but he wasn't clumsy once he was on his feet. "I'll get Jordan. I know I'll need arms."

"Depends on what you mean," said Anti.

"Both," said Docchi, smiling. "We're a dangerous weapon."

She called out as he walked away. "I'll see you when you leave for far Centauri."

"Sooner than that, Anti. Much sooner." Stars were beginning to wink. Twilight brought out the shadows and tracery of the structure that supported the transparent dome overhead. Soon controlled slow rotation would bring near darkness to this side of the asteroid. The sun was small at this distance but even so it was a tie to the familiar scenes of Earth. Before long it would be lost.

Cameron leaned back and looked speculatively at the gravity engineer, Vogel. The engineer could give him considerable assistance. There was no reason why he shouldn't but anyone who voluntarily had remained on the asteroid as long as Vogel was a doubtful quantity. He didn't distrust him, the man was strange.

"I've been busy trying to keep the place running smoothly. I hope you don't mind that I haven't been able to discuss your job at length," said the doctor, watching him closely.

"Naw, I don't mind," said Vogel. "Medical directors come and go. I stay on. It's easier than getting another job."

"I know. By now you should know the place pretty well. I sometimes think you could do my work with half the trouble."

"Ain't in the least curious about medicine and never bothered to learn," grunted Vogel. "I keep my stuff running and that's all, I don't interfere with nobody and they don't come around and get friendly with me."

Cameron believed it. The statement fit the personality. He needn't be concerned about fraternization. "There are a few things that puzzle

15

me," he began. "That's why I called you in. Usually we maintain about half Earth-normal gravity. Is that correct?"

The engineer nodded and grunted assent.

"I'm not sure why half gravity is used. Perhaps it's easier on the weakened bodies of the accidentals. Or there may be economic factors. Either way it's not important as long as half gravity is what we get."

"You want to know why we use that figure?"

"If you can tell me without getting too technical, yes. I feel I should learn everything I can about the place."

The engineer warmed up, seeming to enjoy himself. "Ain't no reason except the gravity units themselves," Vogel said. "Theoretically we can get anything we want. Practically we take whatever comes out, anything from a quarter to full Earth gravity."

"You have no control over it?" This contradicted what he'd heard. His information was that gravity generators were the product of an awesome bit of scientific development. It seemed inconceivable that they should be so haphazardly directed.

"Sure we got control," answered the engineer, grinning. "We can turn them off or on. If gravity varies, that's too bad. We take the fluctuation or we don't get anything."

Cameron frowned; the man knew what he was doing or he wouldn't be here. His position was of only slightly less importance than that of the medical director—and where it mattered the Medicouncil wouldn't tolerate incompetence. And yet—

The engineer rumbled on. "You were talking how the generators were designed especially for the asteroid. Some fancy medical reason why it's easier on the accidentals to have a lesser gravity plus a certain amount of change. Me, I dunno. I guess the designers couldn't help what was built and the reason was dug up later."

Cameron concealed his irritation. He wanted information, not a heart to heart confession. Back on Earth he had been told it was for the benefit of the accidentals. He'd reserved judgment then and saw no reason not to do so now. "All practical sciences try to justify what they can't escape but would like to. Medicine, I'm sure, is no exception."

He paused thoughtfully. "I understand there are three separate generators on the asteroid. One runs for forty-five minutes while two are idle. When the first one stops another one cuts in. The operations are supposed to be synchronized. I don't have to tell you that they're not. Not long ago you felt your weight increase suddenly. I know I did. What is wrong?"

"Nothing wrong," said the engineer soothingly. "You get fluctuations while one generator is running. You get a gravity surge when one generator is supposed to drop out but doesn't. The companion machine adds to it, that's all."

"They're supposed to be that way? Overlapping so that for a time we have Earth or Earth and a half gravity?"

"Better than having none," said Vogel with heavy pride. "Used to happen quite often, before I came. You can ask any of the old timers. I fixed that though."

He didn't like the direction his questions were taking him. "What did you do?" he asked suspiciously.

"Nothing," said the engineer uncomfortably. "Nothing I can think of. I guess the machines just got used to having me around."

There were people who tended to anthropomorphize anything they came in contact with and Vogel was one of them. It made no difference to him that he was talking about insensate machines. He would continue to endow them with personality. "This is the best you can say, that we'll get a wild variation of gravity, sometimes none?"

"It's not *supposed* to work that way but nobody's ever done better with a setup like this," said Vogel defensively. "If you want you can check the company that makes these units."

"I'm not trying to challenge your knowledge and I'm not anxious to make myself look silly. I do want to make sure I don't overlook anything. You see, I think there's a possibility of sabotage."

The engineer's grin was wider than the remark required.

Cameron swiveled the chair around and leaned on the desk, "All right," he said tiredly, "tell me why the idea of sabotage is so funny."

"It would have to be someone living here," said the big engineer. "He wouldn't like it if it jumped up to nine G, which it could. I think he'd let it alone. But there are better reasons. Do you know how each gravity unit is put together?"

"Not in detail."

The gravity generating unit was not a unit. It was built in three parts. First there was a power source, which could be anything as long as it supplied ample energy. The basic supply on the asteroid was a nuclear pile, buried deep in the core. Handicap Haven would have to be taken apart, stone by stone, before it could be reached.

Part two were the gravity coils, which actually originated and directed the gravity. They were simple and very nearly indestructible. They could be destroyed but they couldn't be altered and still produce the field.

The third part was the control unit, the real heart of the gravity generating system. It calculated the relationship between the power flowing through the coils and the created field in anyone microsecond. It used the computed relationship to alter the power flowing in the next microsecond to get the same gravity. If the power didn't change the field died instantly. The control unit was thus actually a computer, one of the best made, accurate and fast beyond belief.

The engineer rubbed his chin. "Now I guess you can see why it doesn't always behave as we want it to."

He looked questioningly at Cameron, expecting a reply. "I'm afraid I can't," said the doctor.

"If it was one of your patients you'd understand," said Vogel. "Fatigue. The gravity control unit is an intricate computer and it gets tired. It has to rest an hour and a half to do forty-five minutes work. It can't keep running all the time any more than any delicate machine can. It has to be shut down to clear the circuits.

"Naturally they don't want anyone tinkering with it. It's sealed and non-repairable. Crack the case open and it disintegrates. But first you've got to open it. Now I know that it can be done, but not without a lot of high-powered equipment that I could detect if it was anywhere on the asteroid."

In spite of the engineer's attitude it didn't seem completely foolproof. But Cameron had to admit that it was probable none of the accidentals could tamper with it. "I'll forget about gravity," he said. "Next, what about hand weapons? What's available?"

"Nothing. No knives even. Maybe a stray bar or so of metal." Vogel scratched his head. "There is something that's dangerous though. I dunno whether you could classify it as a weapon."

Cameron was instantly alert. "If it's dangerous someone can find a way to use it. What is it?"

"The asteroid itself. Nobody can physically touch any part of the gravity system. But I've often wondered if an impulse couldn't be squeezed into the computer. If anybody can do that he can change direction of the field." Vogel's voice was grave. "Somebody could pick up Handicap Haven and throw it anywhere he wanted. At Earth, say. Thirty miles in diameter is a big hunk of rock."

This was the kind of information Cameron had been looking for, though the big engineer seemed to regard the occasion as merely a long overdue social call. "What's the possibility?"

Vogel grinned. "Thought I'd scare you. Used to wake up sweating myself. Got so bad I had to find out about it."

"Can or can't it be done?" demanded the doctor.

"Naw. It's too big to take a chance with. They got monitors set up all over, moons of Jupiter, Mars, Earth, Venus. This or any other gravity computer gets dizzy, the monitor overrides it. If that fails they send a jammer impulse and freeze it up tight. It can't get away until the monitor lets loose."

Cameron's mind was already busy elsewhere. Vogel was loquacious and would talk all night if encouraged. It wasn't that he lacked information but he had no sense of what was important. "You don't know how you've helped me," the doctor said, standing up. "We'll have to get together again."

He watched the engineer depart for the gravity generating chamber below the surface of the asteroid. The day had started badly and wasn't getting better. Docchi to Thorton to Vogel. All the shades of shortsightedness, the convalescent's, authority's, and finally the technician who refused to see beyond his dials. A fine progression, but somewhere the curve ought to turn upward.

The post on Handicap Haven wasn't pleasant but there were advantages—advancement was proportional to the disagreeableness of the place. After shepherding accidentals for a year any other assignment would be a snap. Ten months to go before the year was over and if Cameron could survive with nothing to mar his administration he was in line for something better, definitely better. This was where the Medicouncil sent promising young doctors.

Cameron flipped on the telecom. "Connect me with the rocket dome. Get the pilot." When the robot answered it wasn't encouraging. "There's no answer. I'm sorry. I'll notify you when he comes in."

"Trace him," he snapped. "If he's not near the rocket he's somewhere in the main dome. I don't care how you do it, get him."

A few seconds of silence followed. The answer was puzzling, "There's no record that the pilot has left the rocket dome."

His heart skipped and his breathing was constricted. He spoke carefully. "Scan the whole area. Look every place, even if you think he can't be there. I've got to have the pilot."

"Scanning isn't possible. The system is out of operation in that area. I'm trying to check why."

That was bad. He could feel muscles tighten that he didn't know he had. "All right. Send out repair robots." They'd get the job done— they always did. But they were intolerably slow and just now he needed speed.

"Mobile repair units were dispatched as soon as scanning failed to work. Is this an emergency? If so I can alert the staff."

He thought about it. He needed help, plenty of it. But was there anyone he could depend on? Vogel? He'd probably be ready for action. But to call on him would leave the gravity generating plant unprotected. And if he told the engineer what he suspected, Vogel would insist on mixing in with it. He was too vital where he was.

Who else? The sour middle-aged nurse who'd signed up because she wanted quick credits toward retirement? She slept through most of her shift and considering her efficiency perhaps it was just as well she did. Or the sweet young trainee—her diploma said she'd completed her training, but you couldn't lie to a doctor—who had bravely volunteered because someone ought to help poor unfortunate men? Not a word about women of course. She always walked in when Cameron was examining a patient, male, but she had the deplorable habit of swooning when she saw blood. Fainting was too vulgar for her and, as Cameron had once told her, so was the profession of her choice.

These were the people the emergency signal would alert. He would do better to rely on robots. They weren't much help but at least they wouldn't get hysterically in his way. Oh yes, there was the pilot too, but he couldn't be located.

The damned place was undermanned and always had been. Nobody wanted to be stationed here except those who were mildly psychotic or inefficient and lazy. There was one exception. Ambitious young doctors had been known to ask for the position. Mentally Cameron berated himself. Ambition wasn't far from psychosis, or at times it could produce results as bad. If anything serious happened here he'd begin and end his career bandaging scratches at a children's playground.

"This is not an emergency," he said. "However leave word in gravity with Vogel. Tell him to put on his electronic guards. I don't want him to let anyone get near the place."

"Is that all?"

"Send out six geepees. I'll pick them up near the entrance to the rocket dome."

"Repair robots are already in the area. Will they do as well?"

"They won't. I want general purpose robots for another reason. Send the latest huskiest models we have." They were not bright but they were strong and could move fast. He clicked off the picture. What did he have to be afraid of? For the most part they were a beaten ragged bunch of humans. He would feel sorry for them if he wasn't apprehensive about his future.

CHAPTER THREE

Docchi waited near the rocket dome. He wasn't hiding but he did make himself inconspicuous among the carefully nurtured shrubbery. Plants failed to give the illusion of an Earth landscape—in part because some of them were Venusian or Martian imports—but at least the greenery added to the oxygen supply of the asteroid.

"That's a good job," commented Docchi. "I thought Nona could do it."

Jordan could feel him relax as he watched the event. "A mechanical marvel," he agreed. "But we can gab about that later. I think you ought to get going."

Docchi glanced around and then went boldly into the passageway that connected the main dome with the much smaller rocket dome that was adjacent to it. Normally it was never completely dark in the inhabited part of the asteroid; modulated twilight was considered more conducive to the slumber of the grievously infirm. It was the benevolent Medicouncil's theory that a little light would keep away bad dreams. But this wasn't twilight as they neared the rocket dome. It was a full scale rehearsal for the darkness of interstellar space.

Docchi stopped at the emergency airlock which loomed formidably solid in front of them. "Let's hope," he said. "We can forget about it if Nona didn't manage to cut this out of the circuit."

"She seemed to understand, didn't she? What more do you want?" Jordan twisted around Docchi and reached out. The great slab moved easily in the grooves. It was open. "The trouble with you is that you lack confidence, in yourself and in genius."

Docchi didn't answer. He was listening intently, trying to interpret the faint sounds ahead of him.

"Okay, I hear it," whispered Jordan. "Let's get way inside before he comes near us."

Docchi went cautiously into the darkness of the rocket dome, feeling his way. He'd never recover in time if he stumbled and fell. He tried to force the luminescence into his face. Occasionally he could control his altered metabolism, and now was the time he needed it.

He was nervous and that hindered his accuracy. He couldn't be sure the light was right, enough so that he'd be noticed, not so much that the details of his appearance would be plain. He wished he could ask Jordan, but Jordan was in no position to tell him.

The footsteps came nearer and so did profanity, rich in volume but rather meager in imaginative symbolism, Docchi flashed his face once, as bright as he could manage, and then lowered the intensity immediately.

The footsteps stopped. "Docchi?"

"No. Just a lonely little light bulb out for an evening stroll."

The rocket pilot's laughter wasn't altogether friendly. "Sure it's you. I'd recognize you at the bottom of the sea. What I mean was what are you doing here?"

"I saw the lights go out in the rocket dome. The airlock at the entrance was open so I came. I thought I might be able to help."

"The lights are off all right. Everything. Even the standby system. First time in my life even the hand beams wouldn't go on." The pilot moved closer. The deadly little toaster was in his hand. "Thanks, but you can't help. You'd better get out. It's against regulations for patients to be in here. You might steal a rocket or something."

Docchi ignored the weapon. "What was the cause, a high velocity meteor strike?"

The pilot grunted. "I'd have heard if it was."

"And you didn't hear a thing?"

"Nothing." The pilot peered intently at Docchi, a barely visible silhouette. "Well, I see you're getting smart these days. You should do it all the time. Wear your arms. You look better that way even if you can't use them. You look hundred percent better, almost..." His voice faded.

"Almost human?" asked Docchi kindly. "Nothing like, say a pair of legs and a very good if slightly used spinal column with a lightning bug face stuck on top? You didn't have this in mind?

"I didn't say it. I'm used to you. I can't help it if you're overly sensitive. I don't suppose it's your fault." His voice got higher. "Anyway, I told you to get going. You don't belong in here."

"But I don't want to go," said Docchi. "I'm not afraid of the dark. Are you? I'm looking for some corner to brighten. Can I let a little light in your life?"

"I'm supposed to report psycho talk, Docchi, and damned if I won't. Personally I always suspected you. Get out of here before I take your fake hand and drag you out."

"Now you've hurt my feelings," said Docchi reproachfully stepping nimbly away.

"Don't say you didn't try to make me mad," growled the pilot, lunging after him. What he took hold of wasn't an imitation hand, delicately molded and colored to duplicate skin. The hand he touched was real and the muscles in it were more than a match for his own. It was surprise, at first that caused him to scream.

Docchi bent double and the dark figure on his back came over his head like a knife from a sheath. The pilot was lifted off his feet and slammed to the floor.

"Jordan," gurgled the pilot.

"It's me," said Jordan. He wrapped one arm around the pilot's throat and clamped tight. With the other he felt for the toaster the pilot still held but hadn't time to use. Effortlessly he tore it away and hammered the man unconscious with the butt. He stopped just short of smashing the skull. Docchi stood ineffectually by, kicking where he could, but the action was fast and he had no arms.

But Jordan didn't need help. "Let there be light," he said when he was finished, and there was—a feeble flickering illumination from Docchi.

Jordan balanced himself with his hands. He had a strong head and massive powerful arms and shoulders. His body stopped below his chest, there was no more. A round metal capsule contained his digestive organs. Accidentals were indeed the odds and ends of creation, and of Jordan one end was missing. But the part that remained made up for the loss.

"Dead?" Docchi glanced down at the pilot.

Jordan rocked forward and listened for the heartbeat. "Nah," he said, "I was going to clout him again but I remembered we can't afford to kill anybody."

"See that you don't forget," said Docchi. He stifled an exclamation as something coiled around his leg. Jumping forward he broke loose from the thing that caught him.

"Repair robot," chuckled Jordan, looking around. "The place is lousy with them."

Docchi blinked on and off in confusion and the robot rolled clumsily toward him.

"Friendly creature," commented Jordan. "I think it wants to tinker with your lighting system."

Docchi shook off the squat contrivance which, after it touched his flesh whirred puzzledly to itself. The job was beyond its capacity but it didn't leave. "What'll we do with him?" asked Docchi, staring at the pilot.

"He needs attention," said Jordan. "Not the kind I gave him." He balanced the toaster in his hand and burned a small hole in the little wheeled monster. Extensibles emerged from the side of the machine and carefully explored the damaged area. The extensibles slid back into the machine and presently came out again with a small torch. It began welding the hole.

Meanwhile Jordan pulled the unconscious man toward him. He leaned against the machine for leverage and raised the inert pilot over his head and laid him gently on the top flat surface. The reaction from the robot was immediate. Another extensible reached out to investigate the body. Jordan welded the joints solid. Three times he repeated the process until the pilot was securely fastened to the robot.

"It doesn't know when it's licked," said Jordan. "It'll stay there repairing itself until it's completely sound. However I can do something about that." He adjusted the toaster beam to an imperceptible thickness and deftly sliced through the control case removing a circular section. He thrust his hand inside and ripped out circuits. "No further self-repair," he said cheerfully. "Docchi, I'll need your help. I think it's a good idea to route the robot around the main dome a few times before it delivers the pilot to the hospital. No point giving ourselves away before we're ready."

Docchi bent over to help him and with some trouble the proper sequence was implanted. The robot stood motionless as the newest commands shuttled erratically through damaged but not inoperative circuits. Finally it screeched softly and began to roll drunkenly away.

"Get on my back," said Docchi doggedly. "You know we've got to hurry."

"You're tired," said Jordan. "Half gravity or not, you can't carry me farther." He worked swiftly and the harness that had supported him on Docchi's back fell to the floor. "Stay down and listen," growled Jordan as Docchi attempted to get up.

Docchi listened. "Geepees."

"Yeah," said Jordan. "I wonder who they're after. You'll have to move fast to get to the rocket."

"What can I do when I get there? By myself nothing. You'll have to help me."

"Get on your back and neither of us get there?" said Jordan. "You can figure out something later. Start moving."

"I'm not leaving you," said Docchi.

A huge paw clamped on the back of his head. "Now you listen," said Jordan fiercely. "Together we were a better man than the pilot— your legs and my arms. Now we got to separate but we can still prove we're better than Cameron and all his geepees."

"We're not trying to *prove* anything," said Docchi. "It's a question of urgent principle. Right now there are men who can go to the stars and it's up to us to let the rest of mankind know it."

A brilliant light sliced through the darkness and swept around the rocket dome, revealing beams and columns of the structure. "Maybe you're not trying to prove anything personal," said Jordan. "I am. The rest of us are. Otherwise why shouldn't we let them go on spoon feeding us, rocking us to sleep every night?" Impatiently he hitched himself along the ground until he came to a column.

"You can't hide behind that," said Docchi.

"Not behind it. On top I can. With no legs that's where I belong." He grasped the steel member in his great hands and in the light gravity ascended rapidly.

"Careful," called Docchi.

"What have I got to be careful about?" Jordan's voice floated down from the lacy structure. And it was no longer directly overhead. Jordan was moving away along the beams that stretched from column to column. For those who knew of it there was an unsuspected roadway above. Jordan had it to himself and the geepees would never find him.

It was foolish to become elated over such a trivial thing. Jordan wasn't there yet and what he'd do when he arrived was problematical. But it did prove—yes, there was already proof, of some sort for him. Docchi set out, walking faster and faster until he was running. He wouldn't have thought it possible but he was able to increase the distance between himself and the pursuing robots.

Even so he didn't have much time to look around when he reached the rocket. The first glimpse of the ship was disheartening. Passenger and freight locks were still closed. Nona either hadn't understood their instructions completely or she hadn't been able to carry them out. Probably the first. She'd disrupted the circuits, light and scanning, with no tools except her hands. Her skill with machines she couldn't have known about previously was sometimes uncanny. But it was too much to expect that she'd have the rocket ready for them to walk into.

It was up to Docchi to get in by himself. If he was ever going to it would have to be by his own efforts. Momentarily he wished for the toaster they'd taken from the pilot, and then dropped the wish before it was fully formed. With the toaster he might have managed to soften the inside catch at the entrance. And the thought itself was an indication of how his mind rebelled at reality—he had no arms and he couldn't have used the toaster. It was right and proper that Jordan had kept the weapon. It was of value to him.

Docchi searched frantically, trying to comprehend the complex installation around him in a glance. There had to be some provision made for opening the ship when no one was inside, a device which would send an impulse to actuate the catches. He'd be lucky if he could operate it, but luck had been with him so far.

But if there was an external control he failed to find it. And the approaching lights warned that his chances were diminishing. That there was any time left was Cameron's mistake—he'd ordered the geepees to look too thoroughly as they came along. They were capable of faster pursuit. This mistake was on Cameron and he might make more.

From the sounds that drifted to him Docchi surmised that Jordan was still at large, perhaps nearby. Did the doctor know this? Probably not—he'd tend to underestimate the accidentals.

Docchi descended into the shallow landing pit. It was remarkably ill suited for concealment. The walls were smooth, glazed with a faintly green substance, and there were no doors or niches anywhere. Yet he had to be somewhere near the ship and this was as close as he could get. It wouldn't do to wander away—Cameron would post a robot guard around the ship and he wouldn't be able to get back through. He had to hide at once.

He leaned against the stem tube cluster, the metal pressing hard into the thin flesh that covered his back. Seconds passed before he realized that the tubes were the answer. He turned around to look at them. A small boy could climb inside and crawl out of sight. So could a grown man who had no shoulders or arms to get wedged in the narrow cylinder.

It was difficult to get into them. He tried a lower tube, bending down and thrusting his head in. He wriggled and shoved with his feet until he was almost entirely in. His feet were still out and so he bent his knees to get better purchase and forced himself further in. He didn't stop until he was certain he couldn't be seen by anyone who didn't specifically peer into the tube.

He waited there, listening. A geepee came down noisily into the landing pit. The absence of any other sound indicated to Docchi that it probably was radio controlled. The robot clambered around, searching. The noise abated soon but it became apparent that the geepee wasn't going to leave. It had been stationed to watch the pit.

Docchi couldn't get out. He was caught in the pit. He fought back the claustrophobia that swirled through his mind. It was nothing to be afraid of; he could assure his rescue, or capture, by shouting. The robot would drag him out instantly.

But that was not the only way. The tube extended forward as well as back. The inner end of the tube was closed with a combustion chamber which was singed and would swing away. The ship hadn't been used for months and there was a distinct possibility that the tubes were open at the other end. He might get through.

He stopped to catch his breath. The metal conducted sound well, almost magnifying it. In the interval, over his own breathing, he heard the characteristic sputter, like frying, that the toaster beam made when it struck metal. A great clatter followed.

"Get him," shouted Cameron. "He's up there."

Jordan had arrived and succeeded in disabling a geepee. And Cameron would find out that he wasn't easily captured. The diversion came when Docchi needed it.

"Don't use heat," ordered Cameron. "Get lights on him. Drive him up higher. Corner him and go up and get him."

Docchi had been wrong; the geepees were voice controlled, not by radio. It would make it easier once he got inside. If he ever did get in the ship. But he had to hurry. Jordan couldn't elude the robots forever.

Docchi shoved on less cautiously. The robot in the pit had joined the others and he needn't fear detection. It became harder to advance, though. He had expected it but he didn't know it would be this hard to push through the narrowing tube.

His legs slipped and it didn't matter, somehow he inched along. Blood pounded furiously but his head slid out of the end of the tube— and he was looking at the inside of the ship.

He gazed longingly at the combustion cap a few feet away. If he had hands he could grasp it and pull himself out. But if he had, he'd never have gotten this far. He closed his eyes to rest for a moment and then continued wriggling, his back arching with the effort. He was nearly through now, only his legs were in the tube. He kicked once, hard, and fell to the floor.

He lay there until his head cleared and his breath came back. He rolled ever, bent his knees, and stood up, staggering forward through the corridor to the control compartment. The rocket was his but he didn't want it for himself, and by himself he couldn't use it.

He studied the instrument panel carefully. It had been a long time since he'd operated a ship. A long time and two arms ago. When he thought he understood he bent down and thrust his chin against a dial. Laboriously he rotated his head, turning the dial to the setting he wanted. Then he sat down and kicked on a switch. The ship rocked- and rose a few inches.

He was betting that Cameron wouldn't notice it. The doctor ought to be too busy trying to capture Jordan. But if Cameron did see what was happening, he had thirty seconds in which to stop Docchi. It wasn't enough. Things looked good for their plan.

"Rocket landing," said Docchi when the allotted thirty seconds had passed. "Emergency instructions. Repeat, emergency instructions. Stand by." Technically the ship was in flight, though by very little, and the frequency he was using was assurance that the message would be heard, and heeded.

"All energized geepees lend assistance. This order supersedes any previous command. Additional equipment is necessary to prepare for a possible crash landing." After listing what equipment was needed Docchi sat down and chuckled.

He waited for another few minutes and then flicked on the external lights with his knee. He got up and went to the passenger entrance, brushing against the switch on the way. The passenger ramp swung down and he stood boldly at the entrance, looking out. The whole rocket dome was floodlighted by the ship, beams and columns standing out in sharp detail. It was an impressive structure now, even beautiful, though he remembered hating it once, coming in.

"All right, Jordan, it's safe to come down," he called.

Jordan dangled overhead. He swung along until he reached a column and slid down. Awkwardly he propelled himself across the floor and up the ramp. Balancing himself with his hands he looked up at Docchi.

"Well, monster," he grinned. "How did you do it?"

"Monster yourself," said Docchi, "I crawled through the rocket tube."

"I saw you start in," said Jordan. "I wasn't sure you'd make it. Even when the ship rose I wasn't certain until you came out." Jordan scratched his cheek. "What I meant was: how did you get rid of Cameron?"

"Doctors usually aren't mechanically inclined," said Docchi, "Cameron was no exception. He forgot an emergency rocket landing cancels any verbal orders. So I took the ship up a few inches. Geepees aren't very bright and it wouldn't matter if they were. As long as the ship was in the air and I said I was coming in for a landing they had to obey."

Jordan nodded delightedly. "Poor doc," he said. "It wasn't that he was dumb. There was nothing he could do when you outsmarted him."

"He should have anticipated it," said Docchi. "He could have splashed heat against a gravity generator. This would have created an emergency condition in the main dome, artificial of course, but it would have outweighed the one I set up. He'd have had priority, not me, and he could have directed the robots from gravity center."

"*I* wouldn't have thought of it," said Jordan. "Anyway, how did you get the robots to rush off, carrying Cameron with them?"

"I didn't have to do anything. As long as the pilot of the incoming ship declares he may crash, the geepees must remove all humans from the danger zone, willing or not. They'd have taken you too if they could have reached you but they had to abandon that idea when I ordered crash equipment."

"Glad they did," said Jordan. "Wouldn't want to hear what Cameron's saying. Besides it's safer inside the ship." He swung himself in, touching the hull fondly, peering down the corridor with grave wonder. "It's ours now," he said. "But what about the others? How do we get them?"

"Anti's taken care of. Geepees aren't built to question anything and in their mind she's listed as emergency landing material. They'll bring her. And Nona is supposed to be waiting with Anti." Docchi's face showed misgiving. "I think we made it clear she was supposed to stay there."

"What if she didn't understand?"

"I'm sure she did," said Docchi, "It wasn't complicated. Meanwhile you'd better get ready to lift ship."

Jordan disappeared, heading toward the control compartment. Docchi stationed himself at the passenger lock. He had said the instructions weren't hard to understand, and they weren't—for anyone else. But to Nona the world was upside down, the simplest things often she didn't comprehend—and the reverse was true. He hoped she hadn't got mixed up.

He had little time to dwell on it. The geepees were coming back. He heard them first and saw them seconds later. They came into sight half carrying, half pushing a huge rectangular tank. With ingenuity that was unexpected in robots they had mounted it on four of their smaller brethren, the squat repair robots. This served to support the tremendous weight.

The tank was filled with blue liquid. Twisted pipes dangled from the ends—it had been torn from the pit in the ground, lifted up from the foundation. Broken plants still clung to a narrow ledge on top and moist soil adhered to the sides. Wracked out of shape and askew, the tank was intact and did not leak. Five geepees pushed it rapidly toward the ship, mechanically oblivious to the disheveled man who shouted and struck at them, incoherent with frustrated rage.

"Jordan, open the freight lock."

In response the ship rose a few more inches and hung quivering. To the rear a section of the ship hinged outward and downward to form a ramp. The ship was ready and the cargo had arrived.

Docchi remained at the passenger entrance. Cameron was an idiot. He should have stayed in the main dome once the geepees had released him. His presence was unwelcome, more than he may have realized. Still, they'd gotten rid of him once and it ought to work again.

It was Nona who worried Docchi. She hadn't accompanied the robots and she wasn't to be seen. It didn't look as if Cameron had found her there and managed to confine her to the hospital. It had happened too fast; the doctor was lucky to have kept up with the geepees. Docchi started uncertainly down the ramp and came back. She wasn't around, he could see that, and it was too late to go back to the main dome.

The tank neared the ship, the forward section sliding onto the ramp. The motion slowed as the geepees' effort slackened. Then the robots stopped altogether, straightening up in bewilderment.

The tank rolled backward. The geepees got out of the way, shaking and buzzing, looking questioningly around. Simultaneously, it seemed, they saw Docchi. Their intentions were obvious but he forestalled them, leaping back in the ship. "Close the passenger entrance," he shouted.

Jordan appeared at the far end of the corridor. "Sure. What's wrong?"

"Vogel, the engineer. He must have seen the geepees on scanning when they entered the main dome. He's trying to do what Cameron should have thought of but didn't have sense."

Jordan went away and the passenger ramp rose with ponderous slowness, clamping shut with metallic finality. As soon as he saw there was no danger there Docchi hurried to the control compartment.

"Now we can't see what to do," complained Jordan.

"Maybe," said Docchi. "Try to get something on the telecom."

From the angle it was difficult to see anything. The receptor tubes were close to the hull, and the ship curved backward, filling most of the screen. By rotating the view they managed to pick up a corner of the tank. Apparently it was resting where Docchi had last seen it. He couldn't be sure but he thought it hadn't been moved.

"I don't know whether we can bring it in," said Jordan nervously. "Maybe we should leave it. We'll make out by ourselves."

"Leave without the tank? Not a chance. Vogel hasn't got complete control of the robots yet." It seemed to be true. They were huddled away from the ship, looking alternately at the rocket and the tank nearly motionless paralyzed.

"Yeah, but he'll have them soon. Look at them."

"I am, which is why I think he's having trouble. Give me full power on the emergency radio."

"What good will it do? He's got priority."

"He's got it, but can he push it through to them? It's my idea that he can't, that he's at the wrong angle to put much power in his signal. There's a lot of steel between him and the robots and that's weakening his beam."

"Maybe you've got something," said Jordan. "I'll burn the emergency stuff out. If it doesn't work we won't need it again anyway." He flipped the dials until the lights above them were blazing fiercely.

"Energized geepees are requested to lend assistance. This is an emergency. Place the tank in the ship. At once. At once."

Geepees were not designed to sift contradictory commands at nearly the same level of urgency. Their reasoning ability was feeble but the mechanism that enabled them to think at all was complicated. In one respect they resembled humans: borderline decisions were difficult. A ship in distress—an asteroid in danger. Both called for the robot to destroy itself if necessary. It seemed as if that was all that would be accomplished.

"More power," whispered Docchi.

"There ain't more," answered Jordan, but somehow he coaxed an extra trickle out of the reserves.

Marionettes. But they were always that, puppets on invisible wires. And now this string led toward one action. Another, intrinsically more important but suddenly less powerful, pulled for something else. Circuits burned in electronic brains. Microrays fluttered under the stress. They didn't know. They just didn't know.

But there had to be a choice.

Stiffly the geepees moved in and grasped the tank. The quality of their decision was strained. They were pushing themselves more than the tank but inch by inch the huge twisted structure rolled up the ramp.

"When it's completely on, raise the ramp." Docchi wasn't aware that he could hardly be heard.

The cargo ramp began to lift up. The tank gained speed as it rolled forward into the ship. "Geepees, the job is finished. Save yourselves," shouted Docchi. He saw a swirl of metallic bodies as they leaped from the ramp.

Jordan breathed deeply, "That did it. I don't think they can hurt us now."

"It's not over. Get ship-to-station communication, if there's any radio left."

"I'll be surprised if there is," muttered Jordan, but his skepticism was without basis. The radio was still functioning. He made the adjustments.

Docchi was matter of fact. "Vogel, we're going out. Don't try to stop us. Give us clearance and save the dome some damage."

There was no reply.

"He's bluffing," said Jordan. "He knows the airlocks in the main dome will close automatically if we break through."

"Sure," said Docchi. "Everyone in the main dome is safe—*if* everyone is in there. Vogel, do you know where Cameron is? Are you certain a nurse or an accidental hasn't wandered in here to see what's wrong? We'll give you time to think about it."

Again they waited and waited. Each second was tangible, the precious duration that lives and events were measured with—and the measure was exceedingly slow. Meanwhile Jordan flipped on the telecom and searched the rocket dome. They saw nothing; there was not even a geepee in sight. Docchi watched the screen impassively; what he thought didn't show on his face.

And still there was no reply from the engineer in the gravity station.

"All right. We've given you a chance," said Docchi. His voice was brittle. "You know what we're going to do. If anybody gets hurt you can take the credit." He turned away from the screen. "Jordan, let's go. Hit the shell with the bow."

Jordan grasped the levers. The ship hardly quivered as it tilted upward and leaped away. It roared in the air and then fell silent as it passed into space. And the silence was worse than any sound—it was tilled with the imagined hiss of air escaping from a great hole in the transparent covering of the dome.

Jordan sat at the controls. "Did he?"

"He had to. He wouldn't risk killing some innocent person."

"I don't know," said Jordan. "If you'd said he wouldn't want his pretty machinery banged up it would be easier to believe."

"I didn't hear anything. We would have if we'd hit."

"It was fast. Could we tell? Maybe Vogel played it safe and had the inner shell out of the way even if he didn't give us the automatic signal. In that event it's all right because it would close as soon as we got out of the way even if we did rip through the outer shell. All the air wouldn't escape." Jordan sat there for a moment, silently reviewing his own arguments.

He twisted the lever and the ship leaped forward. "Cameron I don't mind. He had time to get away and he knew what we were going to do. I keep thinking Nona *might* have been there."

"He opened it," said Docchi harshly. "We didn't hit the dome. I didn't hear anything. Nona wasn't there." His face was gray; there was no light at all in it. "Come on," he said, walking away.

Jordan rocked back and forth. The hemisphere that held what remained of his body was suited for it. He set the autocontrols and reduced the gravity to quarter normal. He bent his arms and shoved himself into the air, deftly catching a guide rail, swinging along it.

It was pure chance that he glanced toward the back of the ship instead of forward as he entered the corridor after Docchi. There was a light blinking at a cabin door.

It was occupied.

CHAPTER FOUR

JORDAN caught up before Docchi reached the cargo hold. In lesser gravity he was more active and could move freely. Now his handicap was almost unnoticeable, seemed to have disappeared. The same was not true of Docchi. It required less effort to walk, but there was also a profound unsettling effect that made him cautious and uncertain.

Docchi heard him coming and waited, bracing himself against the wall in case the gravity should momentarily change. Jordan still carried the weapon he'd taken from the pilot. It was clipped to the sack-like garment, dangling from his midsection which, for him, was just below his shoulders. Down the passageway he came, swinging from the guide rails with easy grace though the gravity on the ship was as erratic as on the asteroid.

Jordan halted, hanging on with one hand. "We have a passenger. Someone we didn't know about."

Docchi stiffened. "Who?" he asked. But the answer was already on Jordan's face. "Nona," he said in relief. He slumped forward. "How did she get on?"

"A good question," said Jordan. "But there isn't any answer and never will be. It's my guess that after she jammed the lights and scanners in the rocket dome she went to the ship and it looked inviting. So she went in. She wouldn't let a little thing like a lock that couldn't be opened stop her."

"It's a good guess," agreed Docchi. "She's exceedingly curious."

"We may as well make the picture complete. Once in the ship she felt tired. She found a comfortable cabin and fell asleep. She can't hear anything so our little skirmish with the geepees didn't bother her."

"I can't argue with you. It'll do until a better explanation comes along."

"But I wish she'd waited a few minutes to take her nap. She'd have saved us a lot of trouble. She didn't know you'd be able to crawl through the tubes—and neither did you until you'd actually done it."

"What do you want?" said Docchi. "She did more than we did. We depend too much on her. Next thing we'll expect her to escort us personally to the stars."

"I wasn't criticizing her," protested Jordan.

"Maybe not. You've got to remember her mind works differently. It never occurred to her that we'd have difficulty with something that was so simple to her. At the same time she's completely unable to grasp our concepts." He straightened up. "We'd better get going if we don't want Anti to start yelling."

The cargo hold was sizable. It had to be to hold the tank, which was now quite battered and twisted. But the tank was sturdily built and looked as if it would hold together for ages to come. There was some doubt as to whether the ship would. The wall opposite the ramp was badly bent where the tank had plowed into it and the storage racks were demolished. Odds and ends of equipment lay in scattered heaps on the floor.

"Anti," called Docchi.

"Here."

"Are you hurt?"

"Never felt a thing," came the cheerful reply. It was not surprising; her surplus flesh was adequate protection against deceleration.

Jordan began to scale the side of the tank, reaching the top and peering over. "She seems to be all right," he called down, "Part of the acid's gone. Otherwise there's no damage."

"Of course not," replied Anti. "What did I say?"

It was perhaps more serious than she realized. She might personally dislike it, but acid was necessary to her life. And some of it had been splashed from the tank. Where it had spilled metal was corroding rapidly. By itself this was no cause for alarm. The ship was built for a multitude of strange environments and the scavenging system would handle acid as readily as water, neutralizing it and disposing of it where it would do no harm. But the supply had to be conserved. There was no more.

"What are you waiting for?" Anti rumbled with impatience. "Get me out of here. I've stewed in this disgusting soup long enough."

"We were thinking how we could get you out. We'll figure out a way."

"You let me do the thinking. You just get busy. After you left I decided there must be some way to live outside the tank and of course when I bent my mind to it there was a way. After all, who knows more about my condition than me?"

"You're the expert. Tell us what to do."

"Oh I will. All I need from you is no gravity and I'll take care of the rest. I've got muscles, more than you think. I can walk as long as my bones don't break from the weight."

Light gravity was bad, none at all was worse for Docchi. Having no arms he'd be helpless. The prospect of floating free without being able, to grasp anything was terrifying. He forced down his fear. Anti had to have it and so he could get used to null gravity.

"We'll get around to it," he promised. "Before we do we'll have to drain and store the acid."

"I don't care what you do with it," said Anti. "All I know is that I don't want to be in it."

Jordan was already working. He swung off the tank and was busy expelling water from an auxiliary compartment into space. As soon as the compartment was empty he led a hose from it to the tank. A pump vibrated and the acid level in the tank began to fall.

Docchi felt the ship lurch familiarly. The ship was older than he thought, the gravity generator more out of date. "Hurry," he called to Jordan.

In time they'd cut it off. But if gravity went out before they were ready they were in for rough moments. Free floating globes of highly corrosive acid, scattered throughout the ship by air currents, could be as destructive as high velocity meteor clusters.

Jordan tinkered with the pump and then jammed the lever as far as it would go, holding it there. "I think we'll make it," he said above the screech of the pump. The machinery gasped, but it won. The throbbing broke into a vacant clatter that betokened the tank was empty. Jordan had the hose rolled away before the gravity generator let the feeling of weight trickle off into nothingness.

As soon as she was weightless Anti rose out of the tank.

In all the time Docchi had known her he had seen no more than a face framed in blue acid. Where it was necessary periodic surgery had trimmed the flesh away. For the rest, she lived submerged in a corrosive fluid that destroyed the wild tissue as fast as it grew. Anyway, nearly as fast.

"Well, junkman, look at a real freak," snapped Anti.

He had anticipated—and he was wrong in what he thought. It was true humans weren't meant to grow so large, but Jupiter wasn't repulsive merely because it was the bulging giant of planets. It was unbelievable and overwhelming when seen close up but it was not obscene. It took getting used to but he could stand the sight of Anti.

"How long can you live out of the acid?" he stammered.

"Can't live out of it," said Anti loftily. "So I take it with me. If you weren't as unobservant as most men you'd see how I do it."

"It's a robe of some kind," said Docchi carefully after studying it.

"Exactly. A surgical robe, the only thing I have to my name. Maybe it's the only garment in the solar system that will fit me. Anyway, if you've really examined it you'll notice it's made of a sponge-like substance. It holds enough acid to last at least thirty-six hours."

She grasped a rail and propelled herself toward the passageway. For most people it was spacious enough but not for Anti. However she could squeeze through. And satellites, one glowing and the other swinging in an eccentric orbit, followed after the Jupiter of humans.

Nona was standing in front of the instrument panel when they came back. It was more or less like all panels built since designers first got the hang of what could really be done with seemingly simple components. There was a bewildering array of lights, levers, dials, and indicators in front of her but Nona was interested in none of these. There was a single small switch and dial, separate from the rest, that held her complete attention. She seemed disturbed by what she saw or failed to see. Disturbed or excited, it was difficult to guess which.

Anti stopped. "Look at her. If I didn't know she's as bad as the rest of us, in fact the only one who was born that way, it would be easy to hate her. She's disgustingly normal."

There was truth in what Anti said—and yet there wasn't. Surgical techniques that could take bodies apart and put them together with a skill once reserved for machines had made beauty commonplace. There were no more sagging muscles, discolored skin, or wrinkles. Even the aged were attractive and youthful seeming until the day they died, and the day after too. There were no more ill-formed limbs, misshapen bodies, unsightly hair. Everyone was handsome or beautiful. No exceptions.

The accidentals didn't belong, of course. In another day most of them would have been employed by a circus—if they had first escaped the formaldehyde of the specimen bottle.

And Nona didn't belong—doubly. She couldn't be called normal, and she wasn't a repair job as the other accidentals were. Looked at closely she was an original as far from the average in one direction as Anti was in the other.

"What's she staring at?" asked Anti as the others slipped past her into the compartment. "Is there something wrong with the little dial?"

"That dial has a curious history," said Docchi. "It's not useless, it just isn't used. Actually it's an indicator for the gravity drive which at one time was considered fairly promising. It hasn't been removed because it might come in handy during an extreme emergency."

"But all that extra weight—"

"There's no weight, Anti. The gravity drive is run from the same generator that supplies passenger gravity. It's very interesting that Nona should spot it at once. I'm certain she's never been in a control room before and yet she went straight to it. She may even have some inkling of what it's for."

Anti dismissed the intellectual feat. "Well, why are you waiting here? You know she can't hear us. Go stand in front of her."

"How do I get there?" Docchi had risen a few inches now that Jordan had released his grip. He was free floating and helpless, sort of a plankton of space.

"A good engineer would have sense to put on magnetics. Nona did." Anti grasped his jacket. How she was able to move was uncertain. The tissues that surrounded the woman were too vast to permit the perception of individual motions. Nevertheless she proceeded to the center of the compartment and with her came Docchi.

Nona turned before they reached her. "My poor boy," sighed Anti. "If you're trying to conceal your emotions, that's a very bad job. Anyway, stop glowing like a rainbow and say something."

It was one time Anti missed. He almost *did* feel that way and maybe if she weren't so competent in his own specialty he might have. It was irritating to study and work for so many years as he had—and then to be completely outclassed by someone who did neither, to whom certain kinds of knowledge came so easily it seemed to be inborn. She was attractive but for him something was missing. "Hello," he said lamely.

Nona smiled at him though it was Anti she went to.

"No, not too close, child. Don't touch the surgery robe unless you want your pretty face to peel off when you're not looking."

Nona stopped; she was close but she may as well have been miles away. She said nothing.

Anti shook her head hopelessly. "I wish she'd learn to read lips or at least recognize words. What can you say to her?"

"She knows facial expressions and actions, I think," said Docchi. "She's pretty good at emotions too. She falls down when it comes to words. I don't think she knows there is such a thing."

"Then how does she think?" asked Anti, and answered her own question. "Maybe she doesn't."

"Let's not be as dogmatic as psychologists have been. We know she does. What concepts she uses is uncertain. Not verbal, nor mathematical anyway—she's been tested for that." He frowned puzzledly. "I don't know what concepts she uses in thinking, I wish I did."

"Save some of the worry for our present situation," said Anti. "The object of your concern doesn't seem to need it. At least she isn't interested."

Nona had wandered back to the instrument panel and was staring at the gravity drive indicator again. There was really nothing there to hold her attention but her curiosity was insatiable and childlike.

And in many ways she seemed immature. And that led to an elusive thought: what child was she? Not whose child—what child. Her actual parents were known, obscure technicians and mechanics, descendants themselves of a long line of mechanics and technicians. Not one notable or distinguished person among them, her family was decently unknown to fame or misfortune in every branch—until she'd come along. And what was her place, according to heredity? Docchi didn't know but he didn't share the official medical view.

With an effort Docchi stopped thinking about Nona. "We appealed to the medicouncilor," he said, "We asked for a ship to go to the nearest star, a rocket, naturally. Even allowing for a better design than we now have the journey will take a long time—forty or fifty years going and the same time back. That's entirely too long for a normal crew, but it wouldn't matter to us. You know what the Medicouncil did with that request. That's why we're here."

"Why rockets?" interrupted Jordan. "Why not some form of that gravity drive you were talking about? Seems to me for travel over a long distance it would be much better."

"As an idea it's very good," said Docchi. "Theoretically there's no upper limit to the gravity drive except the velocity of light and even that's questionable. If it would work the time element could be cut in fractions. But the last twenty years have proved that gravity drives don't work at all outside the solar system. They work very well close to the sun, start acting up at the orbit of Venus and are no good at all from Earth on out."

"Why don't they?" asked Jordan. "You said they used the same generator as passenger gravity. Those work away from the sun."

"Sure they do," said Docchi impatiently. "Like ours is working now? Actually ship internal gravity is more erratic than we had on the asteroid, and that's hardly reliable. For some reason the drive is always worse than passenger gravity. Don't ask me why. If I knew I wouldn't be on Handicap Haven. Arms or no arms, biocompensator or not, I'd be the most important scientist on Earth."

"With multitudes of women competing for your affections," said Anti.

"I think he'd settle for one," suggested Jordan.

"Poor unimaginative man," said Anti. "When I was young I was not so narrow in my outlook."

"We've heard about your youth," said Jordan. "I don't believe very much of it."

"Talk about your youth and love affairs privately if you want but spare us the details. Especially now, since there are more important things to attend to." Docchi glowered at them. "Anyway the gravity drive is out," he resumed. "At one time they had hopes for it but no longer. The present function of, the generator is to provide gravity inside the ship, for passenger comfort. Nothing else.

"So it is a rocket ship, slow and clumsy but reliable. It'll get us there. The Medicouncil refused us and so we'll have to go higher."

"I'm all for it," said Anti. "How do we get higher?"

"We've discussed it before," answered Docchi. "The Medicouncil is responsible to the Solar Government, and in turn Solar has been known to yield to devious little pressures."

"Or not so devious great big pressures. Fine. I'm in favor," said Anti. "I just wanted to be sure."

"Mars is close," continued Docchi. "But Earth is more influential. Therefore I recommend it." His voice trailed off and he stopped and listened...listened...

Anti listened too but the sound was too faint for her hearing. "What's the matter?" she said. "I think you're imagining things."

Jordan leaned forward in his seat and examined the instrument panel carefully before answering. "That's the trouble, Anti. You're not supposed to hear it, but you should be able to feel vibrations as long as the rocket's on."

"I don't feel it either."

"I know," said Jordan, looking at Docchi. "I can't understand. There's plenty of fuel."

The momentum of the ship carried it along after the rockets stopped firing. They were still moving but not very fast and not in the direction they ultimately had to go. Gingerly Docchi tried out the magnetic shoes. He was clumsy but no longer helpless in the gravityless ship. He stared futilely at the instruments as if he could wring out more secrets than the panel had electronic access to.

"It's mechanical trouble of some sort," he said uneasily. "I don't know where to begin."

Before he could get to it Anti was in the passageway that led from the control compartment. "Course I'm completely ignorant," she said. "Seems to me we ought to start with the rocket tubes and trace the trouble from there."

"I was going to," said Docchi. "You stay here, Anti. I'll see what's wrong."

She reached nearly from the floor to the ceiling. She missed by scant inches the sides of the corridor. Locomotion was easy for her, turning around wasn't. So she didn't turn. "Look, honey," her voice floated back. "You brought me along for the ride. That's fine. I'm grateful but I'm not satisfied with just that. Seems to me I've got to earn my fare. You stay and run the ship. You and Jordan know how. I don't. I'll find out what's wrong."

"But you won't know what to do."

"I don't have to. You don't have to be a mechanic to see something's broken. I'll find it, and when I do you can come and fix it."

He knew when it was useless to argue with her. "We'll both go," he said. "Jordan will stay at the controls."

It was a dingy poorly lighted passageway in an older ship. Handicap Haven didn't rate the best equipment that was being produced, and even when it was new the ship had been no prize. On one side of the corridor was the hull of the ship; on the other a few small cabins. None were occupied. Anti stopped. The long hall ended in a cross corridor that led to the other side of the ship where a return passage led back to the control compartment.

"We'll check the stern tubes," he said, still unable to see around her. "Open the door and we'll look in."

"Can't," said Anti. "Tried to but the handle won't turn. There's a red light too. Does it mean anything?"

He'd expected something like this but nevertheless his heart sank now that he was actually confronted with it. "It does. Don't try again. With your strength you might be unlucky enough to open the door."

"There's a man for you," said Anti. "First you tell me to open it and then you don't want me to."

"There's no air in the rear compartment, Anti. The combustion chamber's been retracted—that's why the rockets stopped firing. The air rushed out into space as soon as it happened. That's what the red light means."

"We'd all die if I opened it now?"

"We would."

"Then let's get busy and fix it."

"We will. But we've got to make sure it doesn't happen again. You see, it wasn't accidental. Someone, or something, was responsible."

"Are you sure?"

"Very sure. Did you see anyone while we were loading your tank in the ship?"

"Nothing. How could I? I heard Cameron shouting, other noise. But I couldn't see a thing that wasn't directly overhead, and there wasn't anything."

"I thought so. A geepee could have got in without anyone seeing him. I didn't count them but I was certain all of them had dropped outside. I was mistaken; one of them didn't."

"Why does it have to be a geepee?"

"It just does, Anti. The combustion chamber was retracted while we were all in the control compartment. We didn't do it and therefore it had to be someone back here.

"No man is strong enough to retract the cap, but if he somehow exerted superhuman effort, as soon as the chamber cleared the tubes rocket action would cease and the air in the compartment would exhaust into space."

"So we have a dead geepee in the rocket compartment."

"A geepee doesn't die or even become inactive. Lack of air doesn't hinder it in the least. Not only that, a geepee might be able to escape from the compartment. It's strong and fast enough to open the door against the pressure and get out and close it again in less than a second. We wouldn't notice it because the ship would automatically replenish the small amount of air that would escape."

Anti settled down grimly. "Then there's a geepee on the loose, intent on wrecking us?"

"I'm afraid so."

"Then what are we standing around for? All we have to do is go back to the controls and pick up the robot on the radio. We'll make it go in there and repair the damage it's done."

She partly turned around and saw Docchi's face. "Don't tell me," she said. "I should have thought of it. The radio doesn't work inside the ship."

Docchi nodded reluctantly. "It doesn't. Robots are never used aboard and so the emergency band is broadcast by the bow antenna. The hull of the ship is a pretty good insulation."

"Ain't that nice?" said Anti happily. "We've got a robot hunt ahead of us."

"And our bare hands to hunt it with."

"Oh come. It's not as hopeless as that. Look, the robot was back here when the rockets stopped. It couldn't get by the control compartment without our seeing it."

"That's right. There are two corridors leading through the compartment, one on each side of the ship."

"That's what I mean. We came down one and there wasn't any geepee. So it's got to be in the other. If it goes in a cabin a light will shine outside. It can't hide from us."

"I don't doubt we'll find it. But what'll we do then?"

"I was thinking," said Anti. "Can you get past me when I'm standing like this?"

"No."

"That's what I thought. Neither can a geepee. All I need is a toaster, or something that looks like it. I'll drive the robot forward and Jordan can burn it down." Determinedly she began to move toward the far corridor. "Hurry back to Jordan and tell him. There ought to be another weapon on the ship. Should be one for the pilot to use. Bring it back to me."

Docchi bit his lip and stared at the back of the huge woman.

He knew Anti, and when it was useless to argue with her. "All right," he answered. "Stay here though. Don't try anything until I get a toaster for you."

The magnetics on his feet were no substitute for gravity, Docchi couldn't move fast, no human could. He had time to think as he went along but nothing better suggested itself. A toaster for Jordan and another for Anti—if there was another.

And Anti would block the passageway. A geepee might go through her but it could never squeeze past. The robot would try to get away. If it came toward Anti she might disable it. But she would be firing directly into the control compartment. And if she missed even partially—well, the instruments were delicate.

But Jordan might get the chance to bring down the robot. Then Anti would be in the line of fire. No matter how he looked at it, Docchi was sure the plan was unworkable. They'd have to devise something else.

"Jordan," called Docchi as soon as he got there; but Jordan wasn't in sight. Nona was, still gazing serenely at the gravity indicator. Nothing seemed capable of breaking through the shell that surrounded her.

Light was streaming from the opposite corridor. Docchi hurried over. Jordan was just inside the entrance, the toaster clutched grimly in his hand. He was hitching his truncated body slowly toward the stern.

Coming to meet him was Anti—unarmed enormous Anti. She hadn't meant to wait for the weapon—she was pretty certain there wasn't any—she had merely wanted to get him out of the way. And she wasn't walking; somehow it seemed more like swimming, a bulbous huge sea animal moving through the air. She waved what resembled fins against the wall, with them propelling herself forward. "Melt it down," she cried.

It was difficult to make out the vaguely human form of the geepee. The powerful shining body blended in with the structure of the ship— unintentional camouflage, though the robot wasn't aware of it. It crouched at the threshold of a cabin, hesitating between approaching dangers.

Jordan raised the weapon and lowered it with the same motion. "Get out of the way." He gestured futilely to Anti.

There was no place she could go. She was too big to enter a cabin, too massive to let the robot squeeze by even if she wanted. "Never mind. Get him," she called.

The geepee wasn't a genius even by robot standards. But it did know that heat is deadly and that a human body is a fragile thing. And so it ran toward Anti. Unlike humans it didn't need special magnetics; such a function was built into it and the absence or presence of gravity disturbed it not at all. It moved very fast.

Docchi had to watch though he didn't want to. The robot exploded into action, launching its body at Anti. But it was the robot that was thrown back. It had calculated swiftly but incorrectly—relative mass favored the enormous woman.

The electronic brain obeyed the original instructions, whatever they were. It got up and rushed Anti again. Metal arms shot out with dazzling speed and crashed against the flesh of the huge woman. Docchi could hear the rattle of blows. No ordinary person could take that punishment and live.

But Anti wasn't ordinary. Even for an accidental she was strange, living far inside a deep armor of flesh. It was possible she never felt the crushing force of those blows. And she didn't turn away, try to escape. Instead she reached out and grasped the robot, drawing it to her. And the geepee lost another advantage, leverage. The bright arms didn't flash so fast nor with such lethal power.

"Gravity," cried Anti. "Give me all you've got."

Her strategy was obvious; she was leaning against the struggling machine. And here at least Docchi could help her. He turned and took two steps before the surge hit him. Gravity came in waves, each one greater than that before. The first impulse staggered him, and at the second his knees buckled and he sank to the floor. After that his eardrums hurt and he thought he could feel the ship quiver. He knew dazedly that an artificial gravity field of this magnitude had never been attained—but the knowledge didn't help him move. He was powerless in the force that held him.

And it vanished as quickly as it had come. Painfully his lungs expanded, each muscle aching individually. He rolled over and got up, lurching past Jordan.

Anti wasn't the inert broken flesh he expected. Already she was moving and was standing up by the time he got to her. "Oof," she grunted, gazing with satisfaction at the twisted shape at her feet. It was past repair, the body dented and arms and legs bent, the head smashed, the electronic brain in it completely useless.

"Are you hurt?" asked Docchi in awe.

She waggled the extremities and waited as if for the signal to travel through the nerves. "Nope," she said finally. "Can't feel anything broken. Would have been if I'd tried to stand." She moved back to get a better view of the robot. "That's throwing my weight around," she said with satisfaction. "At the right time in the right way. The secret's timing. And I must say you took the cue well." Her laughter rolled through the ship.

"I didn't have anything to do with the gravity," said Docchi.

"Who? Jordan—no, he's just getting up."

46

"Nona," said Docchi. "She was the only one who wasn't doing anything else. She saw what had to be done and got to it before I did. But I can't figure out how she got so much gravity."

"Ask her," said Anti.

Docchi grimaced, limping into the control room, followed by Anti and Jordan. Nona was at the gravity panel, her face pleasant and unconcerned.

The unprecedented power of the gravity field could be accounted for, of course. The ship was old and had seen much use. Connections were loose or broken and had somehow crossed, circuiting more power into the gravity generator than it was designed for. Miraculously it had held up for a brief time—and that was all there was to it. And yet the explanation failed to be completely satisfactory. "I wonder if you had anything to do with it," he said to her. Nona smiled questioningly.

"Had to, didn't she?" said Jordan. "She was the only one who could have turned it on."

"Started it, yes. Increased the power of the field, I don't know," said Docchi. He outlined what he thought had taken place.

"That sounds logical," agreed Jordan. "But it doesn't matter how it was done. Gravity engineers would find it interesting. If we had time I'd like to see how the circuits are crossed. We might discover something new."

"I'm sure it's interesting," said Anti irritably. "Interesting to everybody but me. And I'm pragmatic. All I want to know is: when do we start the rockets? We've got a long way to go."

"There's something that comes before that, Anti," said Jordan. "A retracted combustion cap in flight generally means at least one burned out tube." He made his way to the instruments, checking them glumly. "This time it's three."

"You forgot something yourself, Jordan," said Docchi. "I was thinking of the robot."

"I thought we'd settled *that,*" said Anti impatiently.

"We have. But let's follow it through. Where did the robot get instructions? Not from Vogel via the radio. The ship's hull cuts off that band. And the last we knew it was in our control."

"Voice," said Jordan. "We freed it. Someone else could take it over."

"Who?" said Anti. "None of us."

"No. But think back to when we were loading the tank. We saw it through the telecom and the angle of vision was bad. You couldn't see anything that wasn't directly overhead. Not only the robot but Cameron also managed to get inside."

Jordan hefted the weapon. "So we've got another hunt on our hands. Only this time it's in our favor. Nothing I like better than aiming at a nice normal doctor."

Docchi glanced at the weapon. "Take it along. But don't use it. A homicide would ruin us. We could forget what we're going for. Anyway, you won't actually need it. The ship's temporarily disabled and he'll consider that damage enough. He'll be ready to surrender."

He was.

CHAPTER FIVE

THE DOCTOR was at ease, confident. "You've got the ship and you've caught me. How long do you think you can keep either of us?"

Docchi regarded him levelly. "I don't expect active cooperation but I'd like to think you'll give us your word not to hinder us hereafter."

Cameron glared at the toaster. "I won't promise anything."

"We can chain him to Anti," suggested Jordan. "That will keep him out of trouble."

"Don't wince, Cameron," said Docchi. "She was a woman once. An attractive one too."

"We can put him in a spacesuit and lock his hands behind his back," said Jordan. "Like the old-fashioned straitjacket."

Cameron laughed loudly, "Go ahead."

Jordan juggled the toaster. "I can use this to weld with. Let's put him in a cabin and close the door, permanently. I'll cut a slot to shove food in—a very narrow slot."

"Excellent. That's the solution. Cameron, do you want to reconsider your decision?"

Cameron shrugged blithely. "They'll pick you up in a day or less anyway. I'm not compromising myself if I agree."

"It's good enough for me," declared Anti. "A doctor's word is as good as his oath—Hippocratic or hypocritic."

"Don't be cynical, Anti. Doctors have an economic sense as well as the next person," said Docchi. He turned to Cameron. "You see, after Anti grew too massive for her skeletal structure, doctors reasoned she'd be most comfortable in the absence of gravity. That was in the early days, before successful ship gravity units were developed. They put her on an interplanetary ship and kept transferring her before each landing.

"But the treatment was troublesome—and expensive. So they devised a new method—the asteroid and the tank of acid. Not being aquatic by nature, Anti resented the change. She still does."

"Don't blame me for that," said Cameron. "I wasn't responsible."

"It was before your time," agreed Docchi. He frowned speculatively at the doctor. "I noticed it at the time but I had other things to think about. Tell me, why did you laugh when Jordan mentioned spacesuits?"

Cameron grinned broadly. "That was my project while you were busy with the robot."

"To do what? Jordan—"

But Jordan was already on his way. He was gone for some time, minutes that passed slowly.

"Well?" asked Docchi on Jordan's return. The question was hardly necessary; his face told the story.

"Cut to ribbons."

"All of them? Even the emergency pack?"

"That too. He knew where everything was. Nothing can be repaired."

"So who cares?" rumbled Anti. "We don't need spacesuits unless something happens and we have to go outside the ship."

"Exactly, Anti. How do we replace the defective tubes? From the outside, of course. By destroying the spacesuits Cameron made sure we can't."

Anti glowered at the doctor. "And I suppose you merely had our welfare at heart. Isn't that so, Cameron?"

"You can think anything you want. I did and I do," said Cameron imperturbably. "Now be reasonable. We're still in the asteroid zone. In itself that's not dangerous. Without power to avoid stray rocks it can be very unpleasant. My advice is to contact the Medicouncil at once. They'll send a ship to take us in."

"Thanks, no. I don't like Handicap Haven as well as you," Anti said brusquely. She turned to Docchi. "Maybe I'm stupid for asking but what's so deadly about being in space without a spacesuit?"

"Cold. Lack of pressure. Lack of oxygen."

"Is that all? Nothing else?"

His voice was too loud; it seemed thunderous to him. "Isn't that enough?"

"Maybe not for me. I just wanted to be sure." She beckoned to Nona and together they went forward, where the spacesuits were kept. "Don't do anything drastic until I get back," she said as she left.

Cameron scowled puzzledly and started to follow until Jordan waved the toaster in front of him, "All right, I see it," he growled, stopping and rubbing his chin. "There's nothing she can do. You know it as well as I do."

"Do I? Well, for once I'm inclined to agree with you," said Docchi. "But you never can tell with Anti. Sometimes she comes up with surprising things. She's not scientifically trained but she has a good mind, as good as her body once was."

"And how good was that?" asked Cameron ironically.

"Look it up in your records," said Jordan shortly. "We don't talk about it ourselves."

The women didn't come back soon, and when they did Cameron wasn't sure that the weird creature that floated into the control compartment with Nona was Anti. He looked again and saw shudderingly what she had done to herself. "You do need psychotherapy," he said bitingly. "When we get back it's the first thing I'll recommend. Can't you understand how foolhardy you're being?"

"Be quiet;" growled Jordan. "Anti, explain what you've rigged up. I'm not sure we can let you do it."

"Any kind of pressure will do as far as the outside of the body is concerned," answered Anti, flipping back the helmet, "Mechanical pressure is as satisfactory as air. I had Nona cut the spacesuit in strips and wind them around me, very hard. That will keep me from squishing out. Then I found a helmet that would cover my head when the damaged part was cut away. It won't hold much air pressure even taped tight to my skin. It doesn't have to as long as it's pure oxygen."

"So far it makes sense," admitted Docchi. "But what can you do about temperature?"

"Do you think I'm going to worry about cold?" asked Anti.

"Me? Way down below all this flesh? Mountains and mountains of it?"

"I've heard enough," said Cameron, standing in front of Anti. "Now listen to me. Stop this nonsense and take off that childish rig. I can't permit you to ruin my career by deliberate suicide."

"You and your stinking career," said Jordan disgustedly. "You don't know what success is and what it means to give it up. Stay out of this. We don't have to ask your permission to do anything." Cameron retreated from the toaster and Jordan turned to Anti. "Do you understand what the risk is, Anti? You know that it may not work at all?"

"I've thought about it," said Anti. "On the other hand I've thought about the asteroid. I don't want to go back."

"We should have viewers outside," said Docchi. "One directly in back, one on each side. At least we'll know what's happening."

At the control panel Jordan began flipping levers. "They're out and working," he said at last. "Anti, go to the freight ramp. Close your helmet and wait. I'll let the air out slowly. If everything doesn't work perfectly let me know on the helmet radio and I'll yank you in immediately. Once you're outside I'll give you further instructions. You'll find the tools and equipment that opens to space."

Anti waddled away. Huge, but she wasn't any bigger than her determination.

Once she was gone Jordan looked down at his legless body. "I hate to do this but we've got to be realistic about it."

"It's the only way we've got a chance," answered Docchi. "Anti's the only one who can do the job. And I think she'll survive."

Jordan adjusted a dial. "Cameron had better hope she will," he muttered. "He'll join her if she doesn't."

Docchi glanced hastily at the screen. Anti was hanging free in space, wrapped and strapped in strips torn from the supposedly useless spacesuits. And she was also enclosed in more flesh than any human had borne. The helmet was taped jauntily to her head and the oxygen cylinder was fastened to her back. And she lived.

"How is she?" he asked anxiously, unaware that the microphone was open.

"Fine," came the reply, faint and reedy. "The air's thin but it's pure."

"Cold?"

"Don't know. Don't feel it yet. Anyway it can't be worse than the acid. What do I do?"

Jordan gave her directions while the others watched. It required considerable effort to find the tools and examine the tubes for defectives, to loosen the tubes in the sockets and pull them out, sending them spinning into space. It was still more difficult to replace them, though there was no gravity and Anti was held firmly to the hull by magnetics.

Anti had never been a technician of any kind, Cameron was sure of it. She was ignorant of the commonest terms, the simplest tool. She shouldn't have been able to do it. And yet she managed nicely, though she didn't know how. The explanation must be that she did know, that somewhere in her remote past, of which he was totally uninformed, she had had training which prepared her for this. Such contradiction was ridiculous. But there was rhythm to her motions, this giant shapeless creature whose bones would break with weight if she tried to stand at half gravity.

The whale plowing through the deeps and waves has the attraction of beauty. It can't be otherwise for any animal in an environment which it is suited to live in. And the human race had produced, haphazardly, one unlikely person to whom interplanetary space was not alien. Anti was at last in her element.

"Now," said Jordan, keeping tension out of his voice though it was trembling in his hand. "Go back to the outside tool compartment. You'll find a lever near it. Pull. This will set the combustion cap in place."

"Done," said Anti when it was.

"That's all. Come in now."

She went slowly over the hull to the cargo ramp and while she did Jordan reeled in the viewers. The lock was no sooner closed to the outside and the air hissing into the intermediate space than he was there, waiting for the inner lock to open.

"Are you all right?" he asked gruffly.

She flipped back the helmet. There was frost on her eyebrows and her face was bright and red. "Why shouldn't I be? My hands aren't cold." She stripped off the heated gloves and waggled her fingers.

"I can't believe it," protested Cameron with more vehemence than he intended. "You should be frozen through."

"Why?" said Anti with gurgling laughter. "It's merely a matter of insulation and I have plenty of that. More than I want."

Shaking his head Cameron turned to Docchi. "When I was a boy I saw a film of a dancer. She did a ballet. I think it was called: Free Space-Free Life. Something like that. I can't say why but it came to my mind when Anti was out there. I hadn't thought of it in years."

He rubbed his hand over his forehead. "It fascinated me when I first saw it. I went to it again and again. When I grew older I found out a tragic thing had happened to the dancer. She was on a tour of Venus when the ship she was in was forced down. Searching parties were sent out but they didn't find anyone except her. And she had been struggling over a fungus plain for a week. You know what that meant. The great ballerina was a living spore culture medium."

"Shut up," said Jordan. "Shut up."

Cameron was engrossed in the remembrance and didn't seem to hear. "Naturally she died. I can't recall her name but I can't forget the ballet. And that's funny because it reminded me of Anti out there—"

"I told you to shut up!" Jordan exploded a fist in the doctor's face. If there had been more behind the blow than shoulders and a fragment of a body Cameron's jaw would have been broken. As it was he floated through the air and crashed against the wall.

Angrily he got to his feet. "I gave my word I wouldn't cause trouble. I thought the agreement worked both ways." He glanced significantly at the weapon Jordan carried. "Better keep that around all the time."

"I told you," said Jordan. "I told you more than once." After that he ignored the doctor, thrusting the weapon securely into his garment. He turned to Anti. "Very good," he said, his anger gone and his voice courtly. "An excellent performance. One of your best, Antoinette."

"You should have seen me when I was good," said Anti. The frost had melted from her eyebrows and was trickling down her cheek. She left with Jordan.

Cameron remained behind. It was too bad about his ambition. He knew now he was never going to be the spectacular success he'd once envisioned—not after this escape from Handicap Haven. He'd done all he could to prevent it but it wouldn't count with the Medicouncil that he had good intentions. Still, he'd be able to practice somewhere; doctors were always necessary. There were worse fates—suppose he had to abandon medicine altogether?

Think of the ballerina he'd been talking about—she hadn't died as the history tapes indicated. That much was window dressing; people were supposed to believe it because it was preferable to the truth. It would have been better for that woman if she hadn't lived on. By now he had recalled her name: Antoinette.

And now it was Anti. He could have found it out by checking the records—if Handicap Haven kept that particular information on file. He was suddenly willing to bet that it wasn't there. He felt his jaw, which ached throbbingly. He deserved it. He hadn't really been convinced that they were people too.

"We'll stick to the regular lanes," decided Docchi. "I think we'll get closer. They've no reason to suspect we're heading toward Earth. Mars is more logical, or one of the moons of Jupiter, or another asteroid. I'm sure they don't know what we're trying to do."

Jordan shifted uneasily. "I'm against it. They'll pick us up before we have a chance to do anything."

"There's nothing to distinguish us from an ordinary Earth to Mars rocket. We have a ship's registry on board. Use it. Take a ship that's in our general class and thereafter we'll be that ship. If Traffic blips us, and I don't think they will unless we try to land, we'll have a recording ready. Something like this: 'ME 21 zip crackle 9 reporting. Our communication is acting up. We can't hear you, Traffic.'

"That's quite believable in view of the age and condition of our ship. Don't overdo the static effects but repeat it with suitable variations and I don't think they'll bother us."

Shaking his head dubiously Jordan swung away toward the tiny fabricating shop.

"You seem worried," said Anti as she came in.

Docchi didn't turn around. "Yeah."

"What's the matter, won't it work?"

"Sure. There are too many ships. They can't pick us out among so many. Anyway they're not looking for us around Earth. They don't really know why we took the rocket and escaped."

"Then why so much concern? Once we're near Earth we won't need much time."

His face was taut and tired. "I thought so too, in the beginning. Things have changed. The entire Solar Police force has been alerted for us."

"So the Solar Police really want us? But I still don't understand why that changes a thing."

"Look, Anti. We planned to bypass the Medicouncil and take our case directly to the Solar Government. But if they want us as badly as the radio indicates they're not going to be sympathetic. Not at all.

"And if they're not, if the Solar Government doesn't support us all the way, we'll never get another chance. Hereafter there'll be guards everywhere on the asteroid. They'll watch us even when we sleep."

"Well?" said Anti. She seemed trimmer and more vigorous, "We considered it might turn out this way, didn't we? Let's take the last step first."

Docchi raised his head. "Go to the ultimate authority? The Solar Government won't like it."

"They won't, but there's nothing they can do about it."

"Don't be sure. They can shoot us down. When we stole the ship we automatically became criminals."

"I know, but they'll be careful, especially after we make contact. How would it look if we were blown to bits in front of their eyes, in a billion homes?"

Docchi chuckled grimly. "Very shrewd. All right, they'll be careful. But is it worth it to us?"

"It is to me."

"Then it is to me," said Docchi. "I suggest we start getting ready."

Anti scrutinized him carefully. "Maybe we ought to fix you up."

"With fake arms and a cosmetikit? No. They'll have to take us as we are, unpretty, even repulsive."

"That's a better idea. I hadn't thought of the sympathy angle."

"Not sympathy—reality. It means too much to us. I don't want them to approve of us as handsome unfortunates and then have them change their minds when they discover what we're really like."

Sitting in silence, Docchi watched her go. She at least would benefit. Dr. Cameron apparently hadn't noticed that the exposure to extreme cold had done more to inhibit her unceasing growth than the acid bath. She probably would never get back to her former size but some day, if the cold treatment were properly investigated, she might be able to stand at normal gravity. For her there was hope. The rest of them had to keep on pretending that there was.

He examined the telecom. They were getting closer. No longer a point of light, Earth was a perceptible disc. He could see the outline of oceans, the shapes of land and the shadows of mountains, the flat ripple where prairies and plains were; he could imagine people. This was home—once.

Jordan came in. "The radio tape is rigged up. I haven't had to use it yet. But we have a friend trailing along behind us, an official friend."

"Has he blipped at us?"

"When I left he hadn't. He keeps hanging on."

"Is he overtaking us?"

"He'd like to."

"Don't let him."

"With this bag of bolts?"

"Shake it apart if you have to," said Docchi impatiently. "How soon can you slide into a broadcast orbit?"

Jordan furrowed his forehead. "I didn't think we'd planned on that this time. It was supposed to be our last resort."

"Anti and I have talked it over. We agree that this is our last chance. Now's the time to speak up if you've got any objections."

"I've been listening to the police calls," said Jordan thoughtfully. "No, I guess I haven't got any objection. Not with a heavy cruiser behind us. None at all."

They came together in the control compartment. "I don't want a focus exclusively on me," Docchi was saying. "Nor on Nona either, though I know she's most acceptable. To a world of perfect and beautiful people we may look strange but they must see us as we are. We have to avoid the family portrait effect."

"Samples," suggested Anti.

"In a sense we are, yes. A lot depends on whether they accept those samples."

For the first time Cameron began to realize what they were attempting. "Wait," he said urgently. "You're making a mistake. You've got to listen to me."

"We've got to do this and we've got to do that," said Jordan. "I'm getting tired of it. Can't you understand we're giving orders now?"

"That's right," said Docchi. "Jordan, see that Cameron stays out of the transmitting angle and doesn't interrupt. We've come too far to let him influence us."

"Sure. If he makes a sound I'll melt the teeth out of his mouth." Jordan held the toaster against his side, away from the telecom but aimed at Cameron.

The doctor wanted to break in but the weapon, though small, was very real. And Jordan was ready to use it. That was the only justification for his silence, that and the fact they'd learn anyway.

"Ready?" said Docchi.

"Flip the switch and we will be. I've hooked everything on. They can't help themselves. They've got to listen."

The rocket slipped out of the approach lanes. It spun down, stem tubes pulsing brightly, falling toward Earth in a tight trajectory. Down, down; the familiar planet was very large.

"Citizens of the solar system, everyone on Earth," began Docchi. "This is an unscheduled broadcast. We're using the emergency bands because for us it is an emergency. I said we, and you want to know who we are. Look at us. Accidentals—that's all we can be.

"We're not pretty. We know it. But there are other things more important. Accomplishment, contribution to progress. And though it may seem unlikely to you there are contributions we can make—if we're permitted to do so.

"But shut away on a little asteroid we're denied our rights. All we can do is exist in frustration and boredom, kept alive whether we want to be or not. And yet we can help you as you've helped us—if we're allowed to. You can't go to the stars yet, but we can. And ultimately, through what we learn, you'll be able to.

"You've listened to experts who say it can't be done, that rockets are too slow and that the crew would die of old age before they got back. They're almost right, but accidentals are the exception. Ordinary people would die but we won't. The Medicouncil has all the facts—they know what we are—and still they refuse us."

At the side of the control compartment Cameron moved to protest. Jordan glanced at him, imperceptibly waggling the weapon. Cameron stopped, the words unspoken.

"Biocompensation," continued Docchi evenly as if nothing had occurred. "Let me explain what it means in case information on it has been suppressed. The principle of biocompensation has long been a matter of conjecture. This is the first age in which medical techniques are advanced enough to explore it. Every cell and organism tends to survive as an individual and a species. Injure it and it strives for survival according to the extent of damage. If it can it will heal the wound and live on in its present state. Otherwise it propagates almost immediately.

You can verify this by forgetting to water the lawn and watch how soon it goes to seed.

"Humans aren't plants, you say. And yet the principle applies. Accidentals are people who have been maimed and mutilated almost past belief. And our bodies have had the assistance of medical science, *real* medical science. Everyone knows how, after certain illnesses, immunity to that disease can be acquired. And more than blood fractions are involved in the process. For us blood was supplied as long as we needed it, machines did our breathing, kidneys replaced, hearts furnished, glandular products in exact minute quantities, nervous and muscular systems regenerated—and our bodies responded. They had to respond or none of us would be here today. And such was the extremity of the struggle—so close did we come to it that we gained practical immunity to death."

Sweat ran down Docchi's face. He longed for hands to wipe it away.

"Most accidentals are nearly immortal. Not quite of course; we may die four or five hundred years from now. Meanwhile there is no reason why we can't be explorers for you. Rockets are slow. You'd die before you got to Alpha Centauri and back. We won't. Time means nothing to us.

"Perhaps better faster rockets will be devised after we leave.

You may get there before we do. We don't mind. We will have tried to repay you the best way we know how and that will satisfy us."

With an effort Docchi smiled. The instant he did so he felt it was a mistake, one he couldn't call back. Even to himself it seemed more like a snarl.

"You know where we're kept—that's more polite than saying imprisoned. We don't call it Handicap Haven. Our name for it is: *Junkpile*. And we're junkmen. Do you know how we feel?

"I don't know how you can persuade the Medicouncil to let us man an expedition to the stars. We've appealed and appealed and they've always turned us down. Now that we've let you know it's up to you. Our future as humans is at stake. Settle it with your conscience. When you go to sleep think of us out there on the junkpile."

He nudged the switch and sat down. His face was gray and his eyes were rimmed and burning.

"I don't want to bother you," said Jordan. "What'll we do about these?"

Docchi glanced at the telecom. The ships were uncomfortably close and, considerably more numerous than the last time he had looked. "Take evasive action," he said wearily. "Swing close to Earth and use the planet's gravity to give us a good fast sendoff. We can't let them take us until people have a chance to make their feelings known."

"Now that you've finished I want to discuss it with you," said Cameron. There was an odd tone to his voice.

"Later," said Docchi. "Save it. I'm going to sleep. Jordan, wake me if anything happens. And remember you don't have to listen to this fellow if you don't want to."

Jordan nodded contemptuously, "I know what he's like. He's got nothing to say to me."

Nona, leaning against the panel, paid no attention to any of them. She seemed to be listening to something nobody else could hear, she, to whom sound had no meaning. Docchi's body sagged as he went out. Her perpetual air of wondering search for something she could never have was not new but it was no more bearable because of that.

And while Docchi slept the race went on against a slowly changing backdrop of stars and planets. Only the darkness remained the same; it was immutable. The little flecks of light that edged nearer hour after hour didn't seem cheerful to Jordan. His lips were fixed in a thin hard line. His expression didn't alter. Presently, long after Earth was far behind, he heard Docchi come in again.

"I've been thinking about it," said Cameron. "Nice speech."

"Yeah." Docchi glanced at the screen. The view didn't inspire comment.

Cameron was standing at the threshold. "I may as well tell you," he said reluctantly. "I tried to stop the broadcast as soon as I found out what was going on. You wouldn't listen."

He came on into the control compartment. Nona was huddled in a seat, her face blankly incurious. Anti was absent, replenishing the acid for her robe. "Do you know why the Medicouncil refused to let you go?"

"Get to the point."

"Damn it, I am," said Cameron, sweating. "The Centauri group contains several planets, just how many we're not sure. From what we know of cosmology there's a good chance intelligent life exists there, probably not far behind us in technical development. Whoever goes there will be our representatives to an alien race. What they look like isn't important; it's their concern. But our ambassadors have to meet certain minimum standards. It's an important occasion, our future relations rest on. Damn it—don't you see our ambassadors must at least *appear* to be human beings?"

"You're not telling us anything new. We know how you feel." Jordan was rigid with disgust.

"You're wrong," said Cameron. "You're so wrong. I'm not speaking for myself. I'm a doctor. The medicouncilors are doctors. We graft on or regenerate legs and arms and eyes. The tools of our trade are blood and bones and intestines. We know very well what people look like from the inside. We're well aware of the thin borderline that separates normal men and women from accidentals.

"Can't you still understand what I'm saying? They're perfect, everybody's perfect. Too much so. They can't tolerate small blemishes. More money is spent for research on acne than to support the whole asteroid. They rush to us with wrinkles and dandruff. Health, or the appearance of it, has become a fetish. You may think the people you appealed to are sympathetic but what they feel is something else."

"What are you driving at?" said Docchi in a low voice.

"Just this: if it were up to the Medicouncil you'd be on your way to the Centauris. It isn't. The decision wasn't made by us. Actually it came directly from the Solar Government. And the Solar Government never acts contrary to public opinion."

Docchi turned away, his face wrinkled in distaste. "I didn't think you had the nerve to stand there and say that."

"I didn't want to. But you've got to know the truth." Cameron twisted his head uncomfortably. "You're not far from Earth. You can still pick up the reaction to your broadcast. Try it and see."

Jordan looked at Docchi who nodded imperceptibly. "We may as well," said Docchi. "It's settled now, one way or the other. Nothing we can do will change it."

Jordan searched band after band, eagerly at first. His enthusiasm died and still the reaction never varied. Private citizen, or public figure, man or woman, the indignation was concealed but nevertheless firm and unmistakable. There was no doubt accidentals were unfortunate but they were well taken care of. There was no need to trade on deformity; the era of the freak show had passed and it never would return.

"Turn it off," said Docchi at last. Numbly Jordan complied.

"Now what?" he said.

"Why fight it?" said the doctor, "Go back to the asteroid. It'll be forgotten."

"Not by us," said Docchi dully. "But there doesn't seem to be any choice. It would have been better if we had tried to work through the Medicouncil. We misjudged our allies."

"We knew you had," said Cameron. "We thought we'd let you go on thinking as you did. It gave you something to hope for, allowed you to feel you weren't alone. The trouble was that your discontent carried you further than we thought it could."

"We did get somewhere," Docchi said. His, lethargy seemed to lift somewhat as he contemplated what they'd achieved. "And there's no reason we have to stop. Jordan, contact the ships behind us. Tell them we've got Cameron on board. A hostage. Play him up as their man. Basically he's not bad. He's not against us as much as the rest are."

Anti came into the compartment. Cheerfulness faded from her face. "What's the matter?"

"Jordan'll tell you. I want to think."

Docchi closed his eyes and his mind to the whispered consultation of Anti and Jordan, to the feeble ultimatum to the ships behind them. The rocket lurched slightly though the vibration from the exhaust did not change. There was no cause for alarm, the flight of a ship was never completely steady. Minor disturbances no longer affected Docchi.

When he had it straightened out in his mind he looked around. "If we were properly fueled and provisioned I would be in favor of heading for Alpha or Proxima. Maybe even Sirius. Distance doesn't matter since we don't care whether we come back." It was plain he wasn't expending much hope. "But we can't make it with the small fuel reserve we have. If we can lose the ships behind us we may be able to hide until we can steal fuel and food."

"What'll we do with doc?" said Jordan. He too was infected with defeat.

"We'll have to raid an unguarded outpost, a small mining asteroid is our best bet. We'll leave him there."

"Yeah," said Jordan listlessly. "A good idea, *if* we can run away from our personal escort. Offhand I don't think we can. They hesitated when I told them we had Cameron but they didn't drop back. Look."

He looked himself and, unbelievingly, looked again. He blinked rapidly but the screen could report only what there was.

"They're gone," he said, his voice breaking with excitement.

Almost instantly Docchi was at his side. "No, they're still following but they're very far behind." Even as he looked the pursuing ships shrank visibly, steadily losing ground.

"What's the relative speed?" said Jordan. He looked at the dials, tapped them, pounded on them, but the speed wouldn't change. If it hadn't been confirmed by the screen he'd have said that the needles were stuck or the instruments were completely unreliable.

"What did you do with the rockets?" demanded Docchi.

"That's a foolish question. What could I do? We were already at top speed for this piece of junk."

And there was no way to explain the astonishing thing that had happened. They were all in the control compartment, Cameron, Anti, Jordan and himself. Nona was there too, sitting huddled up, head resting in her arms. There was no explanation at all, unless— Docchi scanned all the instruments again. That was when he first noticed it:

Power was pouring into the gravity drive. The useless, or at least long unused dial was indicating unheard of consumption. "The gravity drive is working," Docchi said.

"Nonsense," said Anti. "I don't feel the weight."

"You don't and won't," said Docchi. "The gravity drive was installed to propel the ship. When it was proved unsatisfactory for that purpose it was converted, which was cheaper than removing it.

"The difference between the drive and ordinary gravity is slight but important. An undirected general field produces weight effects inside the ship. That's for passenger comfort. A *directed* field, outside it, will drive it. You can have one or the other but not both."

"But I didn't turn on the drive," said Jordan in bewilderment. "It wouldn't work for more than a few seconds if I did. That's been proven."

"I'd agree with you except for one thing. It is working, has been working and shows no sign of stopping." Docchi stared speculatively at Nona. She was curled up but she wasn't resting. Her body was too tense. "Get her attention," he said.

Jordan gently touched her shoulder. She opened her eyes but she wasn't looking at them. On the panel the needle of a once useless dial rose and fell.

"What's the matter with the poor dear?" asked Anti. "She's shaking."

"Let her alone," said Docchi. "Let her alone if you don't want to return to the asteroid." No one moved. No one said anything. Minutes passed and the ancient ship creaked and quivered and ran away from the fastest rockets in the system.

"I think I can explain it," said Docchi at last, frowning because he couldn't quite. There were things that still eluded him. "Part of the gravity generating plant—in a sense the key component—is an electronic computer, capable of making all the calculations and juggling the proportion of power required to produce directed or undirected gravity continuously. In other words a brain, a complex mechanical intelligence. But it was an ignorant intelligence and it couldn't see why it should perform ad infinitum a complicated and meaningless routine. It couldn't see why and because it couldn't very simply it refused to do so.

"It was something like Nona. She's deaf, can't speak, can't communicate in any way. Like it she has a very high potential intelligence and also, in the very same way, she's had difficulty grasping the facts of her environment. Differently though, she does have some contact with people and she has learned something. How much she knows is uncertain but it's far beyond what psychologists credit her with. They just can't measure her type of knowledge."

"Yeah," said Jordan dubiously. "I'll agree about Nona. But what is she doing?"

"If there were two humans you'd call it telepathy," said Docchi. It upset his concepts too. A machine was a machine—a tool to be used. How could there ever be rapport? "One intelligence is electronic, the other organic. You'll have to dream up your own term because the only thing I can think of is extra sensory perception. It's ridiculous but that's what it is."

Jordan smiled and flexed his arms. Under the shapeless garment muscles rippled. "To me it makes sense," he said. "The power was always there but they didn't know what to do with it." The smile broadened. "It couldn't have fallen into better hands. We can use the power, or rather Nona can."

"Power?" said Anti, rising majestically. "If you mean by that what it sounds like, I don't care for it. All I want is just enough to take us to Centauri."

"You'll get there," said Docchi. "A lot of things seem clearer now. In the past why did the drive work so poorly the further out it got? I don't think anyone investigated this aspect but if they had I'm sure they'd have found that the efficiency was inversely proportional to the square of the distance from the sun.

"It's what you'd expect from a deaf, blind, mass sensitive brain, the gravity computer. It wouldn't be aware of the stars. To it the sun would seem the center of the universe and it would no more leave the system than our remote ancestors would think of stepping off the edge of a flat world.

"And now that it knows differently the drive ought to work anywhere. With Nona to direct it, even Sirius isn't far."

"What are you thinking about, doc?" said Jordan carelessly. "If I were you I'd be figuring a way to get off the ship. Remember we're going faster than man ever went before." He chuckled. "Unless, of course, you like our company and don't want to leave."

"We've got to do some figuring ourselves," said Docchi. "There's no use heading where there are no stars. We'd better determine our destination."

"A good idea," said Jordan, hoisting himself up to the charts. He busied himself with intenninable calculations. Gradually his flying fingers slowed and his head bent lower over the work. Finally he stopped, his arms hanging slack.

"Got it?"

"Yeah," said Jordan. "There." Dully he punched the telecom selector and a view took shape on the screen. In the center glimmered a tiny world, a fragment of a long exploded planet. The end of their journey was easily recognizable.

It was Handicap Haven.

"But why are we going there?" asked Anti. She looked at Docchi in amazement.

"We're not going voluntarily," he said, his voice flat and spent. "That's where the Medicouncil wants us. We forgot about the monitor system. When Nona activated the gravity drive it was indicated at some central station. All the Medicouncil had to do was take the control away from Nona."

"We thought we were running away from the ships," said Anti, "We were, but only to beat them back to the junkpile."

"Yeah," said Docchi. "Nona doesn't know it yet."

"Well, it's over. We did our best. There's no use crying about it." Yet she was. Anti passed by the girl, patting her gently. "It's all right, darling. You tried to help us."

Jordan followed her from the compartment. Cameron remained, coming over to Docchi. "Everything isn't lost," he said awkwardly. "The rest of you are back where you started but at least Nona isn't."

"Do you think she'll benefit?" asked Docchi. "Someone will, but it won't be Nona."

"You're wrong. Suddenly she's become important."

"So is a special experimental machine. Very valuable but totally without rights or feelings. I don't imagine she'll like her new status."

Silence met silence. It was the doctor who turned away. "You're sick with disappointment," he said thickly. "Irrational, you always are when you glow. I thought we could talk over what was best for her but I can see it's no use. I'll come back when you're calmer."

Docchi glared sightlessly after him. Cameron was the only normal who was aware that it was Nona who controlled the gravity drive. All the outside world knew was that it was in operation—that at last it was working as originally intended. If they should dispose of Cameron—

He shook his head. It wouldn't solve anything. He could fool them for a while, pretend that he was responsible. But in the end they'd find out. Nona wasn't capable of deception—and they'd be very insistent with a discovery of this magnitude.

She looked up and smiled. She had a right to be happy. Until now she'd been alone as few people ever are. But the first contact had been made and however unsatisfactory—what could the limited electronic mind say? In other circumstances it might have presaged better days. She didn't know she was no less a captive than the computer.

Abruptly he turned away. At the telecom he stopped and methodically kicked it apart, smashing delicate tubes into powder. Before he left he also demolished the emergency radio. The ship was firmly in the grip of the monitor and it would take them back. There was nothing they had to do. All that remained for him was to protect Nona as long as he could. The Medicouncil would start prying into her mind soon enough. He hoped they'd find what they were after without too much effort. For her sake he hoped they would.

CHAPTER SIX

PERFECTLY synchronized to their speed the outer shell of the dome opened, closing behind them before they reached the inner shell. It too gaped wide to swallow them, snapping shut like a quickly sprung trap. Jordan set the controls in neutral and dropped his hands, muttering to himself. They glided to a stop over the landing pit, thereafter settling slowly. Homecoming.

"Cheer up," said Cameron jauntily. "You're not prisoners." Nona alone seemed not to mind. Docchi hadn't said anything for hours and the light was gone from his face. Anti wasn't with them; she was back floating in the acid tank. The re-entry into the gravity field of the asteroid made it necessary.

The ship scraped gently; they were down. Jordan mechanically touched a lever, flicked a switch. Passenger and freight locks swung open. "Let's go," said Cameron. "I imagine there's a reception committee for us."

Even he was surprised at what was waiting. The little rocket dome held more ships than normally came in a year. The precise confusion of military discipline was everywhere. Armed guards lined either side of the landing ramp and more platoons were in the distance. It was almost amusing to see how dangerous the Medicouncil considered them.

Near the end of the ramp a large telecom had been set up. If size indicated anything someone thought this was an important occasion. From the screen, larger than life, Medicouncilor Thorton looked out approvingly.

"A good job, Dr. Cameron," said the medicouncilor as the procession from the ship halted. "We were quite surprised at the escape of our accidentals and your disappearance which coincided with it. From what we were able to piece together, you followed them deliberately. A splendid example of quick thinking, doctor. You deserve recognition."

"I thought it was my fault for letting them get so far. I had to try to stop them."

"No doubt it was. But you atoned, you atoned. I'm sorry I can't be there in person to congratulate you but I'll arrive soon." The medicouncilor paused discreetly. "At first the publicity was bad, very bad. We thought it unwise to try to conceal it. Of course the broadcast made it impossible to hide anything. Fortunately the discovery of the gravity drive came along at just the right time. When we announced it opinion began swinging in our direction. I don't mind telling you the net effect is now in our favor."

"I hoped it would be," said Cameron. "I don't want them to be hurt. They're all vulnerable, Nona especially, because of what she is. I've thought quite a bit about how she should be approached—"

"I'm sure you have." The medicouncilor smiled faintly, "Don't let your emotions run away with you. In due time we'll discuss her. For the present see that she and the other accidentals are returned to their usual places. Bring Docchi to your office at once. He's to be questioned privately."

It was a strange request and mentally Cameron retreated.

"Wait. Are you sure you want Docchi? He's the engineer but—"

"No objections, doctor," said Thorton sternly. "Important people are waiting. Don't spoil their good opinion of you." The telecom snapped into darkness.

"I think you heard what he said, Dr. Cameron." The officer at his side was very polite, perhaps because it emphasized the three big planets on his tunic.

"I heard," said Cameron irritably. "I don't want to argue with authority but since I'm in charge of this place I demand that you furnish a guard for this girl.

"So you're in charge?" drawled the officer. "You know I've got a funny feeling I'm commander here. My orders said I was to replace you until further notice. I haven't got that notice." He looked around at his men and crooked a finger. "Lieutenant, see that the little fella—Jordan, I think his name is—gets a lift back to the main dome. And you can walk the pretty lady to her room, or whatever it is she lives in. Don't get too personal though unless she encourages it." He smiled conde-scendingly at Cameron. "Anything else I can do to oblige a fellow commander?"

Cameron glanced at the guards. They were everywhere he looked, smartly uniformed, alert. There was no indication of amusement in the expressions of those near enough to have heard the conversation. They were well disciplined. "Nothing else, general," he said stonily. "Keep her in sight. You're responsible."

"So I am," remarked the officer pleasantly, winking at the lieutenant. "Let's go."

Medicouncilor Thorton was waiting impatiently on the screen in Cameron's office. The attitude suited him well, as if he'd tried many and found slightly concealed discourtesy best for the personality of the busy executive. "We'll arrive in about two hours," he said immediately. "By this I mean a number of top governmental officials, scientists, and some of our leading industrialists. Their time is valuable so let's get on with this gravity business."

He caught sight of the commander. "General Judd, this is a technical matter. I don't think you'll be interested."

"Very well, sir. I'll stand guard outside."

The medicouncilor was silent until the door closed. "Sit down, Docchi," he said with unexpected solicitude, pausing to note the effect. "I can sympathize with you. Everything within your reach—and then to return here. Well, I can understand how you feel. But since you did come back I think we can arrange to do things for you."

Docchi stared at the screen. A spot of light pulsed in his cheek and then flared rapidly over his face. "You probably will," he said casually. "But what about theft charges? We stole a ship."

"A formality," declared the medicouncilor with earnest simplicity. "With a thing like the discovery, or rediscovery, of the gravity drive, no one's going to worry about an obsolete ship. How else could you test your theories except by trying them out in actual flight?"

The medicouncilor was dulcet, coaxing. "I don't want to mislead you. Medically we can't do any more for you than we have. However you'll find yourself the center of a more adequate social life. Friends, work, whatever you want. In return for this naturally we'll expect your cooperation."

"Wait," said Cameron, walking to the screen and standing squarely in front of it. "I don't think you realize Docchi's part—"

"Don't interrupt," glowered Thorton. "I want to reach an agreement at once. It will look very good for us if we can show these famous people how well we work with our patients. Now, Docchi, how much of the drive can you have on paper by the time we land?"

"He can't have anything," Cameron started shouting. "I tried to tell you—he doesn't know—"

"Look out," cried Thorton too late.

Cameron's knees buckled and he clutched his legs in pain. Again Docchi kicked out and the doctor fell down. Docchi aimed another savage blow with his foot that grazed the back of Cameron's head. Blood trickled from his mouth and he stopped trying to get up.

"Docchi," screeched Thorton, but there was no answer.

Docchi crashed through the door. The commander was lounging against the wall, looking around vacantly. Head down Docchi plunged into him. The toaster fell from his belt to the floor. With scarcely a pause Docchi stamped on it and continued running.

The commander got up, retrieving the weapon. He aimed it at the retreating figure and would have triggered it except that it didn't feel right in his hand. He lowered it and quickly examined the damaged mechanism. Sweating, he slipped it gingerly into a tunic pocket.

Muffled shouts were coming from Cameron's office, growing in vehemence. The general broke in.

The medicouncilor glared at him from the screen. "I see that you let him get away."

The disheveled officer straightened his uniform. "I'm sorry, sir. I didn't think he had that much life in him. I'll alert the guards immediately."

"Never mind now. Revive that man."

The general wasn't accustomed to resuscitation; saving lives was out of his line. Nevertheless in a few minutes Cameron was conscious, though somewhat dazed.

"Now, doctor, who does know something about the gravity drive if it isn't Docchi?"

Cameron shook his head groggily. "It was an easy mistake," he said. "Cut off from communication with us the drive began to work. How, why, who did it? Mostly who. Not me, I'm a doctor, not a physicist. Nor Jordan; he's at best a mechanic. Therefore it had to be Docchi because he's an engineer." He stopped to wipe the blood from his cheek.

"For God's sake tell me," said Thorton. "It couldn't be—"

"No," said Cameron with quiet satisfaction, "It wasn't Anti either. The last person you'd think of. The little deaf and dumb girl the psychologists wouldn't bother with."

"Nona?" said Thorton incredulously.

"I told you," said Cameron and proceeded to tell him more, filling in the details.

"I see. We overlooked that possibility," said the medicouncilor gravely. "Not the mechanical genius of an engineer. Instead the strange telepathic sense of a girl. That puts the problem in a different light."

"It's not so difficult though." Cameron rubbed the lump on the back of his head. The hair was bristling, clotted with blood. "She can't tell us how she does it. We'll have to find out by experiment, but it won't involve any danger. The monitor can always control the drive."

The medicouncilor laughed shakily, teetering backward. "The monitor is worth exactly nothing. We tried it. For a microsecond it seemed to take over as it always has on other units—but this gravity generator slipped away. We thought Docchi found a way to disengage the control circuit."

"But it wasn't Docchi who told the computer how to do it."

"We figured it out when we thought it was Docchi," growled the medicouncilor wearily. "He was sensible, that's all. It was the only reasonable thing a man could do, come back and take advantage of his discovery." He shook his head in perplexed disgust. "Why the girl returned is beyond me."

"Do you think—" said Cameron and then wished he'd left it unsaid.

"Yes, by God, I do think." The medicouncilor's fist crashed down. "Docchi knows why. He found out in this room and we told him. As soon as he knew he escaped."

Panic slipped into Thorton's face and then was gone, covered over almost at once by long habits of sudden decisions. "She could have taken the ship anywhere she wanted and we couldn't stop her. Since she's here voluntarily it's obvious what she wants—the asteroid."

The medicouncilor tried to shove himself out of the screen. "Don't you ever think, general? There's no real difference between gravity generators except size and power. What she did on the ship she can do as easily here."

"Don't worry," said the startled officer. "I'll get her. I'll find the girl and Docchi too."

"Never mind him," choked the medicouncilor. "I don't care how you do it. Take Nona at once, without delay."

The time had passed for that command. The great dome overhead trembled and creaked in countless joints. But the structure held though unexpected stresses were imposed on it. And the tiny world shivered, groaning and grumbling at the orbit it had lain too long in. Already that was changing—the asteroid began to move.

VAGUE shapes were stirring. They walked if they could, crawled if they couldn't—fantastic and near-fantastic creatures were coming to the assembly. Large or tiny, on their own legs or borrowed ones they arrived, with or without arms, faces. The news had spread fast, by voice or written message, sign language, lip reading, all the conceivable ways that humans communicate, not the least of which was the vague intuition that something was going on that the person should know about. The people on Handicap Haven sensed the emergency.

"Remember it will be hours or perhaps days before we're safe," said Docchi. His voice was hoarse but he hadn't noticed it yet. "It's up to us to see that Nona has all the time she needs."

"Where is she hiding?" asked someone in the crowd.

"I don't know. I wouldn't tell you if I did. They might pry it out of you. Right now our sole job is to keep them from finding her."

"How?" demanded someone else near the front. "Do you expect us to fight the guards?"

"Not directly," said Docchi. "We have no weapons for that—no armament. Many of us have no arms in another sense. All we can do is to obstruct their search. Unless someone can think of something better, this is what I plan:

"I want all the men, older women and the younger ones who aren't suitable for reasons I'll explain later. The guards won't be here for half an hour—it will take that long to get them together and give them orders. When they do come the first group will attempt to interfere in every possible way with their search.

"How you do it I'll leave to your imagination. Appeal to their sympathy as long as they have any. Put yourself in dangerous situations. They have ethics and at first they'll be inclined to help you. When they do, try to steal their weapons. Avoid physical violence as much as you can. We don't want to force them into retaliation—they'll be so much better at it. Make the most of this phase of their behavior. It won't last long."

Docchi paused to look over the crowd. "Each of you will have to decide for himself when to drop passive resistance and start the real battle. Again, you may be able to think of more things than I can tell you but here are some suggestions. Try to disrupt the light, scanning and ventilation systems. They'll be forced to keep them in repair. Perhaps they'll even attempt to guard all the strategic points. So much the better for us—there'll be fewer guards to contend with."

"What about me?" called a woman from far in back. "What can I do?"

"You're in for a rough time," Docchi promised. "Is Jeriann here?"

Jeriann elbowed her way through the crowd to his side. Docchi glanced at her. He'd seen her many times but never so close. It was hard to believe that she should be here with the rest of them. "Jeriann," said Docchi to the accidentals, "is a normal pretty woman—outwardly. However she has no trace of a digestive system. The maximum time she can go without food and fluid absorption is ten hours. That's why she's with us and not on Earth."

Docchi scanned the group. "I'm looking for a miracle. Is there a cosmetechnician who thinks she can perform one? Bring your kit."

A legless woman propelled herself forward. Docchi conferred at length with her. At first she was startled, reluctant to try but after persuasion she consented. Under her deft fingers Jeriann was transformed. When she turned around and faced the crowd she was no longer herself—she was Nona.

"She can get away with the disguise longer and therefore she'll be the first Nona they find," explained Docchi. "I think—hope—that they'll call off the search for a few hours after they take her. Eventually they'll find out she isn't Nona when they can't get her to stop the drive. Fingerprints or x-rays would reveal it at once but they'll be so sure they have her that it won't occur to them. Nona is impossible to question as you know and Jeriann will give as good an imitation as she can.

"As soon as they discover that the girl they have is Jeriann they won't bother to be polite. Guards will like the idea of finding attractive girls they can manhandle in the line of duty especially if they think it will help them find Nona. It won't, but I think they'll get too enthusiastic and that in itself will hold up the search."

No one moved. The women in the crowd were still, looking at each other in silent apprehension, Jordan started them. He twisted his head, grimacing. "Let's get busy," he said somberly.

"Wait," said Docchi. "I have one Nona. I need more volunteers, at least fifty. It doesn't matter whether the person is physically sound or not, we'll raid the lab for plastic tissue. If you're about her size and can walk and have at least one arm come forward."

And slowly, singly and by twos and threes, they came to the platform. There were few indeed who wouldn't require liberal use of camouflage. It was primarily on these women their hopes rested.

The other group followed Jordan out, looking at Docchi for some sign. When he gave them none they hurried on determinedly. He could depend on them. The sum total of their ingenuity would produce some results.

Mass production of an individual. Not perfect in every instance—good enough to pass in most. Docchi watched critically, suggesting occasional touches that improved the resemblance. "She can't speak or hear," he reminded the volunteers. "Remember it at all times no matter what they do. Don't scream for help, we won't be able to. Hide in difficult places. After Jeriann is taken and the search called off and then resumed, let yourselves be found, one at a time. We can't communicate with you and so you'll just have to guess when it's your turn. You should be able to tell by the flurry of activity. That will mean they've discovered the last person they captured wasn't Nona. Every guard that has to take you in for examination is one less to search for the girl they really want. They'll have to find Nona soon or get off the asteroid."

The cosmetechnicians were busy and they couldn't stop. But there was one who looked up. "Get off?" she asked. "Why?"

He thought he'd told everyone. She must have arrived late. It was satisfying to repeat it. "Handicap Haven is leaving the solar system," he said.

Her fingers flew, molding the beautiful curve of a jaw where there had been none. Next, plastic lips were applied that were more life-like than any this woman had ever created.

Soon Nona was hiding in half a hundred places.

And one more.

The orbit of Neptune was behind them, far behind, and still the asteroid accelerated. Two giant gravity generators strained at the crust and core of the asteroid. The third clamped an abnormally heavy gravity field around the fragment of an isolated world. Prolonged physical exertion was awkward and doubly exhausting, it tied right in; the guards were not and couldn't be very active. Hours turned into a day and the day passed too—and the generators never faltered. It seemed they never would.

"Have you figured it out precisely? It's your responsibility you know," said Docchi ironically. "You share our velocity away from the sun. You'll have to overcome it before you start going back. If you wait too long you might not be able to reach Earth."

Superficially the general seemed to ignore him but the muscles in his jaw twitched. "If we could only turn off that damned drive."

"That's what we're trying to do," said Vogel placatingly.

"I know. But if we could do it without finding her."

The resident engineer shrugged sickly. "Go ahead. Try it. I don't want to be around when you do. I know, it sounds easy, just a couple of gravity generators. But remember there's also a good sized nuclear pile involved."

"I know, I know," muttered the general morosely. "Damned atomics not worth inventing. Nothing you can do with them, always too touchy." He glowered at the darkness overhead. "On the other hand we can take off and blow this rock apart from a safe distance."

"And lose all hope of finding her?" taunted Docchi.

"We're losing her anyway," commented Vogel sourly.

"You're getting way from the perspective. It's not as bad as that," counseled Docchi. "Now that you know where the difficulty is you can always build other computers and this time furnish them with auxiliary senses. Or maybe give them the facts of elementary astronomy."

"Now why didn't I think of that?" said Vogel disgustedly. "You don't need me here, do you, general? If not I'd like to go back to my ship." The general grunted consent and the engineer left, lurching under the massive gravity.

"There's even another solution though it may not appeal to you," said Docchi cautiously. "I can't believe Nona is altogether unique. There must be others like her, so-called 'born mechanics' whose understanding of machinery is a form of intelligence we haven't suspected. Look hard and you may find them, perhaps in the most unlikely or unlovely bodies." It didn't show but inwardly he was smiling. He was harassing them effectively from this end. Hope was sometimes the most demoralizing agent.

General Judd growled wearily. "If I thought you knew where she is—"

Docchi stiffened, glowing involuntarily.

"Forget the dramatics, general," said Cameron with distaste. "Resistance we'd have had in any event. He's responsible merely for making it more effective."

He frowned heavily, continuing. "At the moment what he's trying to do is obvious. He needn't bother tearing down our morale though—it's already collapsed. I can't think of a thing we can do that will help us." He wished the medicouncilor had been able to land; he needed further instructions. His own role wasn't clear and he kept thinking, thinking... He should stop thinking. Of course the ship that carried the medicouncilor couldn't actually touch on the asteroid— there were too many important people aboard and they couldn't risk being taken out of the system. Still, the medicouncilor might have spared a few minutes to discuss things with him. He knew what he ought to do.

The sun was high in the center of the dome. Sun? It was much more like a very bright star. It cast no shadows; it was the lights in the dome that did. They flickered and with monotonous regularity went out again. Each time the general swore constantly and emotionlessly until service was restored.

A guard approached, walking warily behind his captive. He saluted negligently. "I think I've found her, sir."

Cameron looked at the girl. "I don't think you have. And it seems to me you were unnecessarily rough."

The guard smirked with bland insolence. "Orders, sir."

"Whose orders?"

"Yours, sir. You said she couldn't talk or make any kind of a sound. It was the easiest way to make sure. She didn't say a thing."

Cameron turned to the general but saw he'd get no support there. Judd was scowling, completely indifferent to the guard's behavior.

The doctor snapped open the sharp scalpel and thrust it savagely deep in the girl's thigh. She looked at him with a tear-stained face but didn't complain or move a muscle.

"Plastic tissue as any fool can plainly see," said Cameron dourly. His rage was growing.

The guard stared, twisting his lips. "Let her go," snapped the doctor.

The girl darted away. The guard saluted stiffly and left rubbing his hands against his uniform. He'll go and scrub his hands, because he touched her, Cameron thought wearily.

"I have a request to make," said Docchi.

"Sure, sure," said the general cholerically. "We're apt to give you what you want. If you don't see it, just ask. We'll send out and get it."

"You might at that." Docchi was smiling openly. "You're going to leave without Nona, and very soon. When you go, don't take all the ships. You won't need them but we will, when we get to another system."

The general started to reply but his anger was greater than his epithets. There was nothing left to use, and so he remained silent.

"Don't say anything you'll regret," cautioned Docchi. "When you get back, what will you report? Can you tell your superiors that you left in good order, while there was still time to continue the search? Or will they like it better if they know you stayed until the last minute—so late that you had to transfer your men and abandon some ships? Think it over. I have your interests at heart."

The general swallowed with difficulty, his face reddening at first and then becoming quite white. Wordlessly he stamped away. Cameron looked after the retreating officer and in a few minutes followed. But he walked slower and the distance between doctor and officer grew greater. Docchi was beginning to relax at the nearness of victory and didn't notice where either of them went.

The last rocket disappeared, leaving a trail behind that over-whelming darkness soon extinguished. The sun was now one bright star among many, which one was sometimes difficult to say. And the asteroid itself seemed subtly to have been transformed more spacious than it had been and not so dingy—and it was not hard to find a reason—it had become a miniature world, a tiny system complete in itself.

"I think we can survive," said Docchi. "We've got power and we can replenish the oxygen. We'll have to grow or synthesize our food but actually the place was set up originally to do just that. It will take work to make everything serviceable again—but we've always wanted something more than meaningless routine."

They were sitting beside the tank, which had been returned to the usual place. A tree rustled in the artificial breeze and the grass around them had been torn and trampled by the guards. It seemed more peaceful because of the violence which had lately swept over them. Now it had ebbed and it would never come back.

Jordan teetered beside the tree. "We'll find some way to get Anti out of the tank," he said. "When Nona comes back maybe we can rig up a null gravity place—something to make Anti more comfortable. And of course we've got to continue the cold treatment."

"I can wait," said Anti. "I've already waited a long time."

Docchi glanced around; his eyes were following his mind which was wandering and searching.

"Now there's no need to worry," said Anti. "The guards were rough with some of the women but plastic tissue doesn't feel pain and so they escaped with fewer injuries than you'd believe. As for Nona, well, she can look out not only for herself but the rest of us as well."

It was almost true; she seemed fragile ethereal even but she wasn't. And her awareness began where that of normal humans left off. And where her perceptions ended no one knew—least of all herself. Right there was a source of trouble. "I think we should start looking," said Docchi. "At the last moment, upset at leaving and not knowing or caring who she was, one of the guards might have—" The enormity of the thought was too great to complete.

"Listen," said Anti. The ground vibrated, felt rather than heard. "As long as the gravity is functioning can there be any doubt?"

In his mind there could be. Nona had started it but once the gravity computer was informed of the nature of the universe there was no reason to suppose that it wouldn't keep running indefinitely. It existed to perform such tasks. It didn't actually have volition—but that applied to stopping as well.

"I think I can convince you," said Jordan. "First you'll have to turn around."

Docchi scrambled to his feet and there she was coming toward them, fresh and rested. There was a smudge on her cheek but she might have got that from some machine she'd stopped to investigate on the way here. Her curiosity was not limited and there was nothing mechanically so insignificant that it escaped her attention.

"Where were you?" asked Docchi, expecting no reply. She smiled and for a moment he thought she knew what he asked. He was relieved that she was safe—and that was all. Something was missing in the reactions he expected from himself but he couldn't say where. At one time he had thought—and now he no longer did. Perhaps it was an expression of the new freedom they had all achieved.

Jordan looked at him quizzically, half penetrating the screen he'd thrown over his lack of emotions. "It's not as bad as you think. She understands some things. Machines."

And a machine he was not. He wasn't even a complete human. Perhaps that was where the difference was.

"She's a born mechanic, such as never existed. It's about time one appeared in the human race. We've worked with machines long enough to evolve someone who understands them without having to study and learn. I'm that way myself, a little. Nothing like her."

They all knew that. Even on Earth they were probably busy revising their intelligence ratings. "That doesn't change our problem— her problem."

Jordan hesitated. "The idea's pretty vague but we've made one advance: we know she can think."

"We always did," said Anti.

"Sure, we did. But doctors and psychologists weren't convinced and they were the ones who were studying her. Now it's up to us."

There was a difference. No matter what they'd thought, previously they'd been patients, and it was axiomatic that the patient's ideas were largely ignored. Now they had stepped into a dual role, patient and doctor, subject and experimenter, the eye at the microscope and the object on the slide.

They all had second-hand medical training—with long association some of it had rubbed off on them. There wasn't one of them who didn't know his own body far better than the average man. That knowledge, subjective though it was, could be pooled. Fortunately they had a well-equipped hospital to work with.

"We'll have to get busy on Nona," continued Jordan. "Where are we going? She knows but we don't. There's got to be some way to find out."

It hadn't mattered before—it was enough that they were leaving. But once they had achieved that, new problems were thrusting up every direction they looked. "What do you suggest?" asked Docchi.

"An oscillograph," said Jordan triumphantly.

Docchi shook his head. "No good. She's been around them often enough to show an interest if she really feels any."

"Maybe she could learn to write, actually, on the screen."

"She hasn't changed and I doubt if her interests have. From what we know she doesn't use words; she thinks directly in terms of mechanical function. The gravity computer was the first thing she found complex enough to arouse her interest."

"But she's always been near the computer."

"That's not so. She came here years ago and though there was a computer in the ship that brought her she wasn't mature enough to use it. Since then she's been kept away from the main computers the same as the rest of us have been."

Jordan leaned on his hands and rocked thoughtfully. "She learned all that during the few hours we were on the ship?"

"It was days," said Docchi. "Yes, she did. It was the only opportunity she had." It was a strange language she'd learned, the code a complex computer used inside itself, the stop, go; current and no current; the electron stream; the mechanical memory rocked back and forth magnetically—and all the while the whisper of a steel tape as it coiled and uncoiled. It was possible that only a computer would ever be able to understand the girl. And yet she was a creature of flesh, bones, glands, nerves, and blood flowing through her veins in response to the intangible demands of life.

Anti stirred restlessly. Waves of acid spilled over the sides and where the fluid touched, grass curled and blackened. "I said I'd wait but I didn't say I liked waiting. Why don't you two get busy?"

"I was thinking where to begin," said Jordan. He hoisted himself onto a repair robot he'd taken for himself. It was an uncomfortable vehicle for anyone else but it seemed just right for him.

Docchi got up; there was no question where to start. Anything they considered needed something done. In the struggle for freedom, in their resistance to the guards, they'd overlooked it. They'd have to re-orient their outlook. Perhaps that was the biggest thing that confronted them.

"Goodbye," Anti called out as they left. The picture Docchi looked back to was unforgettable—the tank and Anti in it, Nona sitting in blank pensiveness under the tree. One was capable of near miracles with seemingly little effort, but at times she seemed inert. The other was raw vitality with an urge to live—but there was hardly any time she could stand upright.

Docchi hurried along, trying to keep up with Jordan. He lengthened his pace but still the gap grew. After a while he slowed down, attempting to assess the damage the guards had done as he passed by evidence of their destructiveness.

Visibly they seemed to have torn everything apart but actually not much had been destroyed. Mostly the repairs would consist in reassembling machines and structures that had been dismantled. This wasn't the result of consideration. Until the last moment the general had been certain he'd find Nona and hence retain possession of the asteroid. If he had, the unnecessary violence would have been hard to explain. Lucky—because the guards *could* have wrecked the place.

They'd still have difficulty; even able-bodied men would, and they were far from that. They were not equipped for an expedition of this nature and somehow they'd have to build what they lacked. Light and heat, the function of power, was automatic, and the oxygen supply was nearly so. It was with the lesser things they'd have trouble. Some food had always been brought in, and now that supply was gone. It would have to be replaced. They could do without other luxuries now that they had the biggest one—freedom to do what they wanted.

Docchi himself was a good engineer and Nona couldn't be too highly evaluated. Between them they could convert unnecessary equipment into something they needed. Two geepees and a repair robot taken apart and properly reassembled might equal some inconceivable machine that would go a long way toward solving problems of food, air, meteor detection or what have you. It was a thought.

Jordan clung perilously to the robot as it rumbled along. "Where is everyone?" he called back.

"Asleep, I guess," said Docchi.

"Sleeping, when there's so much to be done?"

Habit had taken over. The mechanisms of the asteroid were still operating as they were set to function. The lighting in the dome indicated it was time and so they slept. But there were no hours, days, weeks, and moments any more, nothing but necessity to guide them.

"We'll change this," said Docchi, "Most of us have been treated as invalids so long we believe it. We'll divide up in groups and from now on somebody will always be awake, working or watching, or both."

It was obvious what the watch would be for. Empty space—but how empty? The region near Sol had been explored but what lay beyond? Between the sun and Alpha Centauri there might be many interstellar masses large enough to smash the asteroid. They'd have to take precautions.

Jordan sent the machine along faster as if to compensate for others' inactivity. Presently he stopped abruptly, waiting for Docchi to catch up. He glanced down in front of his machine. "Here's one of them who was very sleepy," he said. "Unless—"

Docchi looked at her. It was one of the Nonas who hadn't yet removed the disguise. The cosmetechnicians had done their work well and it was difficult to say who she was. There was a startling resemblance to the girl they'd just left with Anti. She was curled up in an uncomfortable position and it was obvious she wasn't there by choice.

Jordan swung off the machine and felt her pulse. "There is one," he muttered, carefully looking her over. "Can't see anything," he said at last. "At first I thought the guards had done it but there's no broken bones nor, as far as I can tell, internal injuries. She ought to have a medical examination."

Startled, Docchi glittered. Medical care was one of the luxuries they'd have to do without. They needn't fear epidemics, they were isolated and their bodies were phenomenally resistant to disease and anyway the antibiotics they had would quell any known infections. But here was something they hadn't accounted for. "There are a few people around who used to be nurses," said Docchi. "We'd better get them."

"Where?" grunted Jordan. "She needs attention now."

Jordan was right; the girl couldn't wait. Part of the difficulty was that there were so many accidentals with peculiarities. What was safe for one accidental might be deadly to another. They had to know who the girl was before they could decide whether to do anything. The disguise had helped them get away but it was hurting them now. "Can you pry off the makeup?" he asked.

"Without the goop they carry in the cosmetic kit? Hardly, I'd tear her own face off."

It could mean her death to move her before something was done— but what was that something? She would know; everyone did. They were all experts on their own ailments and could give down to the last item on their prescription, diet or exercise, a concise analysis of what they had to do to maintain their health.

Jordan shook her gently, harder when that failed. Presently she stirred, her eyes fluttered and she whispered something.

"Ask her who she is," said Docchi, but that was impossible. It had taken strength to respond at all and after she'd used it the girl had lapsed back in the coma.

"She didn't say," said Jordan helplessly. "She whispered one word—food. That was all."

Food. Docchi knelt beside her to check his conclusions. Now that he was close he could see that her skin was extraordinarily smooth and lustrous. Her face, arms, legs, even her hands, and if they removed her clothing the rest of her body would be the same. Her skin and the mention of food told him what he needed to know. It was Jeriann, the first volunteer Nona—and the first real casualty.

He could reconstruct with some accuracy what had happened. After Cameron discovered who she was she'd been kept in custody and given medical care. As the search wore on and more guards were sent out to search she had managed to escape, hiding from the guards. But she had remained hidden too long and had collapsed trying to get to the hospital.

Hunger shock, simply that, but with her hunger was a traumatic experience. Having no digestive system at all she was always close to starvation. "Pick her up. It won't hurt her," said Docchi. "Let's rush her to the dispensary."

Jordan hoisted the limp girl to the top of the repair robot, wrapping extensibles around her, adjusting them so they held her. He got on beside hero, reaching into the controls and squeezing extra speed out of the makeshift ambulance.

Docchi was not far behind, arriving at the hospital not long after Jordan and his passenger did. The dispensary was on the first floor and so Jordan wheeled the robot directly to the door. He dismounted and lifted Jeriann off.

Inside the dispensary there was little that had actually been broken. This was remarkable considering how thoroughly the guards had ransacked the hospital. But someone with a grim sense of humor had seen to it that the medical preparations were hopelessly intermixed, scattered over the floor in complete confusion. For the present emergency it couldn't have been worse if everything *had* been broken.

Docchi stared down at the litter, his face twitching as he glanced back at Jeriann.

"It's in here somewhere," said Jordan. "How do we find it in a hurry?"

"See if there are names or symbols on them."

Jordan was close to the floor anyway; he leaned down and began pawing hastily but with extreme care through the confusion of medicals. Every bit of it was precious even though they didn't know what it was. Someone could use it, had to have it, and eventually they'd be able to place whom it was intended for. "No names," said Jordan as he continued to look.

Docchi was afraid of that, but it was a thought for the future. Hereafter there would be names on everything so that even if it got displaced they'd be able to identify it. The medical administration must have been exceedingly lax. "What about symbols?" he said quickly.

"There seem to be some. Don't know what they mean." Jordan brightened. "We can look in the files."

Docchi bent his body. He'd observed that when he entered, "Won't do any good. The files are scattered too." And that was an act of wanton hatred. It hadn't helped the guards find Nona.

Jordan stopped scrabbling through the piles of miscellaneous bottles, capsules, and vials. "Then we've got to go for help," he said slowly. "There's got to be somebody who knows what she takes looks like."

He couldn't condemn her so easily and that's what it would mean if she wasn't attended to in the next few minutes. There was a line beyond which the body couldn't pass without extreme damage, perhaps death. And she'd been close to it when they found her. Docchi began to review desperately what he knew of Jeriann. It wasn't much. There were too many accidentals for him to know all of them.

First, she never ate or drank. Her needs in this respect were supplied medically. That was why her skin was so soft and evenly beautiful. It was not a reflection of inner health. If anything it was due to the method of intake. *And that told him what he had to know.*

Another accidental might have guessed it instantly, but there were various kinds of accidentals, groups within groups, and their peculiarities varied so widely that few knew what all of them were. In one sense Jeriann was a deficient.

"I think we can find it. Look for the largest capsule," said Docchi.

"I know what you're thinking, but it won't work," said Jordan, sweeping his arm around to indicate how impossible the request was. "She gets all her food and water that way so it has to be the largest. But which one? Some of the preparations are supposed to last for weeks. They might be bigger than hers."

"It's simpler than you suppose. I don't know what her schedule is but it must be at least five times daily, and massive at that. It would be exceedingly painful, not to say inconvenient, if she got all her food and fluid needs by injection."

"Absorption capsules," exclaimed Jordan. "Why didn't I think of that? That makes it easy."

"Don't be so sure. There are other deficients," cautioned Docchi.

Jordan had cleared a space around him and was already separating the preparations. At first glimpse the absorption capsules were like any other container—and then they weren't. The shape was not quite regular and the outside was soft to the touch, almost like human flesh. That's what it was, almost. And in time, when properly applied, that's what it did become.

Further, there was a thin film on one side. When this was peeled off and the exposed surface was pressed against the body, only surgery could remove it.

Jordan gazed in indecision at the absorption capsules he'd assembled in the cleared space near Jordan. "Which one is hers?" he said doubtfully. "They're all alike."

Actually they weren't. There were subtle differences in size and shape that would enable anyone who was familiar with it to distinguish his preparation from any other. Another deficient might say which was Jeriann's since generally they'd be more observant of these matters. But it did no good to wish that the girl's friends were here. "We'll have to keep looking," said Jordan, hitching himself over to the heap of medicals he'd just gone through.

It hadn't worked out as well as he'd expected. Reflection should have shown it wouldn't. The capsules were expensive and difficult to make and so they wouldn't be used except where the sheer volume and the repetitive nature of the injection required it. There was probably no case on the asteroid as extreme as Jeriann's, but once a day instead of five was still repetition. "There's nothing in that pile," said Docchi harshly. "You've gone through it and I watched."

Jordan paused; he knew it too. "What'll we do?"

"Simplify it. Toss out the smaller ones until only fifteen are left." There was no real reason for selecting that figure, none but this: in her dazed condition she'd have time for one glance. If it wasn't there, it just wasn't.

Jordan complied, exceedingly dexterous when he had to be, though more than dexterity was involved. Visual comparison had to suffice and it was never harder to make. "That look about right?" asked Jordan when he finished.

"It should be one of them," said Docchi. He was guessing. They both knew they were. The capsules were set near Jeriann, about the size of a man's fist. One of them, the one for Jeriann, was remarkably small considering it had to supply the total needs of a human body. For a fraction of a day only, a fourth or a sixth, but even so it was little. She must be always hungry. It would never do to mention food to her.

Jordan raised her up gently, tilting her limp body so she could see what she had to choose from. He glanced at Docchi for confirmation and then began to slap her. Still the consciousness was buried deep. He hit her harder until breath ran shudderingly into her lungs. "Which one?" he asked quickly, as soon as her eyes flickered open, running over the array of capsules.

He grabbed the one she seemed to indicate, holding it closer, "Is this it?" Her eyes dropped shut and she couldn't answer. Jordan laid her down. He wiped his hands on the sack-like garment. "She recognized this one," he said, not looking at Docchi.

So she had, but was it recognition of something that was *hers*? "I could see that. We'll give it to her."

"Should I sterilize it or something?"

Jordan wanted to delay because he wasn't sure. And they couldn't delay, even if it was the wrong thing. It might be like giving sugar to a person in a diabetic coma, the certain way of finishing him off faster. And yet with Jeriann it had to be done. Actually very little time had elapsed since they found her, five or ten minutes. What they didn't know was how long she'd lain there.

Docchi shook his head. "The absorption capsule was meant to be administered under any condition. Outside of puncturing it and squirting in a virus culture there's no way to harm it. It's self-sterilizing."

"I forgot," said Jordan. "Where'll I give it to her?"

"Anywhere. Oh, I guess maybe her thigh. It may sink in faster since she's gone so long without."

Jordan brushed her skirt up and carefully peeled off the film on one side, making certain the exposed surface didn't come in contact with his hand. The capsule contracted as the film came off rhythmically writhing. The shape changed too; it was like nothing so much as a giant amoeba. Quickly Jordan thrust the raw surface of the squirming thing on Jeriann's thigh. It was not alive but it was capable of motion and it moved a quarter of an inch before it adhered.

It stuck there. It was one with the girl, it was her; and the correct injection or not it couldn't be removed. The fluid in that pseudo-body was being injected into Jeriann through the countless pores it covered—through her skin without a puncture. It was no wonder her skin was radiantly beautiful—five times a day an area of ten to fifteen square inches. In a short time her body would be covered, and she never could use the same place on successive days. She achieved clarity and flawlessness of complexion, but at a price. At a price.

Jordan wiped his forehead. "Shouldn't we be seeing some results?" he said anxiously.

"It has a long way to go," Docchi assured him. "Into her bloodstream and to her muscles and glands, to her brain. In a minute now if we don't see some results we'll know we've failed."

They waited.

CHAPTER EIGHT

DOCCHI slumped in the chair, looking the place over with some satisfaction. The medical inventory was proceeding quite well; one by one each preparation was being identified and the local source checked. It wasn't nearly as bad as he had assumed at first; they were nearly self-sufficient.

One of the checkers came in. Docchi recognized her vaguely; he'd seen her around but that was all. He didn't know who she was nor what she did. Unless he was mistaken her arms and legs were her own, a trifle heavy but shapely enough. If there was anything about her that was camouflaged with plastic tissue it was her face—the sullen glamour was an exaggeration of nature and moreover her expression didn't change at all as she came nearer. There must be something with her face that couldn't be corrected surgically and so she'd overcompensated.

"We've got it all done," she said in a flat throaty voice. Glamour there too, in about the same degree.

"What?" he said. "Oh yes, the check of the biologicals. All identified?" He recalled her name, Maureen something or other.

"Everything that people claimed. There was some that no one knew what it was. Useless I suppose, or worse. It ought to be destroyed."

That was a logical assumption any time save now. Medicine was precious and had to be hoarded even if they didn't know what it was. "Save it, Maureen. Sooner or later someone will be in for it."

"They've all been in. You don't know how they rushed here when they learned the dispensary had been ransacked by the guards." She smiled with faint disdain.

He was beginning to doubt whether her expression came out of the cosmetic kit; it was applied with extraordinary skill if it had, flexible enough to allow her to smile without seeming strained. But if it actually was her face it was monotonous. How long could she keep up the glamour? "Don't be condescending, Maureen. Of course they were concerned. There are people who need those preparations to live comfortably, some in order to live at all."

"I know," she said. "I've personally contacted all the regular deficients."

She seemed to know more about it than he did. There was a fraternity of the ailing and degrees of confraternity. Within the accidentals there were special groups, allied by the common nature of their infirmity. It was possible she belonged to some such group or knew someone who did. The latter probably; there seemed to be nothing seriously wrong with her. "What do you suppose happened? Why is there some left?" said Docchi. "If everyone's been here all of it ought to be accounted for."

"They're always experimenting," said Maureen.

"Who?"

"Doctors," she said. "They try the latest ideas out on us and if we survive they use it on normal people."

There was some truth in it—not much, but the bitterness was there though Earth and all it stood for was far behind. "Don't blame them. They've got to make improvements," he said in mild reproof.

"You don't know," said Maureen. "Anyway, what I was saying is that there is some stuff we can't place. In each case it substitutes for one or more substances that have been in use up to now. We don't know who it's for."

It was more serious than he thought, if only in a negative sense. He straightened up, "How many are missing biologicals?"

"I didn't keep track accurately. Thirty or forty."

A small number compared to the total. *But thirty or forty invalids?* And some would be affected seriously, depending on the nature of the preparation that couldn't be traced to the person who should have it. The man whose unaided body couldn't utilize calcium would certainly be in for trouble but not as soon as he who couldn't make use of, say, iron. "We'll find out," he said with a confidence he didn't altogether feel. "There are records around and we'll look into them." There were records but it was uncertain how complete they were after the guards had scattered them. "Do you know where they're kept?"

She shook her head, the sullen glamorous smile transfixing her face. "I wish I did," she said.

He was struck by the intensity. "Why?" he asked. He wanted to know too but it wasn't an emotional thing.

"Don't you know? I'm one of them."

One of what, he was about to ask before he realized she meant she was a deficient whose salvaged body lacked certain physiological elements. More, she was one whose preparation couldn't be identified. "Don't worry. It'll take us a little while to trace everything but we'll have it straightened out in a matter of days."

"You'd better," she said, and it was not exactly a threat. There were overtones he couldn't account for.

Before he could stop her she began loosening her dress and for the first time he saw that she wasn't breathing, that she never did. Her dress fluttered as the air went in and out, sleeping or waking, without volition, responding mechanically to the needs of her bloodstream. The breathing mechanism was hidden in her body, replacing her lungs. Moreover it was probably connected to her speech centers in such a way to release a certain amount to her throat when the nervous system demanded. Perhaps it accounted for the peculiar vibrant quality of her voice.

She pointed to the tube that was showing. "It's not just lungs I lack," she said. "Everyone, man or woman, manufactures both male and female hormones, in different proportions of course. Except me. I don't produce a single male hormone." She stared at him intently.

"Do you know what that means?" Her voice was rising, terror mingled with something else. "Without injections in a few months I'll be completely female. One hundred percent woman and nothing else."

He thought he saw her grow more feminine before his eyes; reluctantly he turned away. Theoretically the completely female person should be repulsive, yet she wasn't. If anything, pathetic features dominated.

Pure femininity could destroy her, but how long would it take? He could discount her own estimate as arbitrary. She had decided on it in an attempt at self-dramatization.

"You're fortunate," he said, and he couldn't keep his eyes from straying back to her. "There are plenty of people around, both men and women, who can be donors. There must be some way to extract the hormones you need from the bloodstream. Our medical techniques may be crude but we'll manage. Keep that in mind."

"I will—will you?" she asked, her lips parted, and it wasn't to breathe because she couldn't.

He had the uncomfortable feeling that he knew exactly what she meant and it didn't have anything to do with what he'd said. Had she even been listening? Probably she hadn't. A pure male or female creature didn't exist but if one should come into being it would scarcely be human. To a human, life mattered—or death did. But to the pure abstract creature there was only one thing of importance.

He looked up to see her coming toward him. "I'm afraid," she said, clasping him to her, carefully keeping the tube free and open. And she was afraid—it was not dramatization. The studied glamour slipped from her face. "I don't want to be like this," she whispered. "But if it happens—help me, please." Her nearness was overpowering, and deadly.

At length she drew away. Terror left her eyes—and it had been there, real though with other factors. Even in fear, and he was conscious of that and her deeper design, she had planned ahead against the time she might not be wholly human. It was something like to death to change drastically from a thinking reasoning person to someone who could react only to one stimulus.

"We'll see that nothing happens to you," he said with weak assurance. "There may be a delay but it won't be long. We'll work it out."

She was regarding him fixedly and he could see she was reverting. What he said wasn't penetrating. He cleared his throat. "You're as familiar with the place as any of us. Look around and see if you can find duplicate records. There may be a clue in them as to what the new preparations are for." Clarity returned to her face as he spoke. It would leave again and come back at decreasing intervals unless or until the hormone deficiency was corrected. How far she could descend and remain mentally unscathed he didn't know, nor did he want to find out. "Don't leave until I come back. Do you understand?"

She smiled invitingly to show that perhaps she did understand what he said. He knew now that the sullen glamour was real, and terrifying. She couldn't help any of her responses. Docchi hurried out; so little time had elapsed she must be nearly normal.

He thought of locking the door but there was no way to do that. The essence of a hospital was free access at all times, and so it was built. Besides, it wasn't a good idea to try to keep her in. Constraint might produce violent reaction.

Docchi slanted the louvers so that the place looked vacant and let it go at that. The best he could hope for was that Maureen wouldn't think of leaving.

He walked away. There were villages. Planned or otherwise, over the years, dwellings and dormitories had gradually grown around three main centers. Externally there was not much to distinguish one village from the other except the distance from the hospital. The buildings nearest were little more than very large machines which fed, bathed, and tried to anticipate the intellectual stimulation of the almost helpless tenants. The houses in the farthest village, except for certain peculiarities; were much like any comfortable dwelling on Earth.

At the third village he found the house, glancing at the tiny light on the door. It was glowing; the occupant was at home. The numbered positions flashed on, indicating further that the person was awake and in bed. This information was necessary on the asteroid where many people suffered from some disability which might strike suddenly, leaving them helpless and unattended, Docchi leaned against the button and the light blinked him in.

Jeriann was sitting up in the middle of the bed; she seemed healthy and alert. "How do you feel?" he asked as he caught a chair with his foot and slid it near her.

She made a wry face and smiled, "Fine."

"No polite answers, please. Do you feel like work?"

"Now that you're here, no." She laughed outright at his dis-comfiture. "Maybe now you'll believe me when I say I'm all right. Do you?"

She didn't wait for his answer but smoothed the covers around her. "You're the one who found me, aren't you?"

"Jordan really. I was there."

She didn't attempt to thank him; help was expected. No one knew when his turn would come. "I guess you're wondering what I was doing there without my capsules."

He wasn't but he'd listen if she felt she had to talk. "It seemed strange you'd forget something like that. But everyone was confused then."

"Not me. I knew exactly what I was doing. I was running from some big lunk who kept chasing me all over the dome. He knew I wasn't Nona because I yelled for him to leave me alone. He didn't pay any attention and I guess I lost the absorbics just before he caught me."

"You don't have to talk about it if it's painful," he said impassively.

"What do you think?" she said scornfully, "You think I'd let *him* bother me? I told him to go away or I'd slip my face off. He got sick right there and let go."

He smiled at her vigor. "It's a good thing he didn't take you at your word and let you remove the disguise."

"Thank you, kind sir. Now I know I'm pretty too." Her manner overcame the apparent sharpness. "Anyway there I was. I'd used up more energy than usual and I had nothing to take. I didn't make it to the hospital."

"I didn't know the details but I imagined something like that. You're lucky we found you and even more so that we were able to discover your particular absorbics in the dispensary mess."

"Right both times—but you didn't find my absorption capsules. They weren't there. Never are. I have to go directly to the lab to get them. Of course I couldn't expect you to know that."

"Then what are you doing here, alive?" he asked, frowning. "The wrong thing should have killed you."

"I'm not a true deficient, you know. It's not that my body fails to produce glandular substances. What I lack is food and water and anything that's composed mostly of that will do, providing it's in a form I can assimilate. When you slapped me and held me up I saw someone else's capsule but I knew it would do. That person has trouble with a number of blood sugars and several fluids—not what I require for a complete diet—but it brought me out of the hunger shock."

It was not ordinary hunger which had caused her to stumble and be unable to get up; this was acute, a trauma which affected her whole organism. And because it was such a constant threat, unconsciously or not, she had prepared for it. Deficients knew each other better than any other group. They were aware which prescription could in an emergency be substituted for their own. It was unlikely to be used—but that knowledge had paid off for Jeriann.

The house ticked on as he sat watching her. That was another peculiarity of the place, aside from the lack of kitchen or any room wherein she could eat. She didn't need it and so it hadn't been built. She didn't feel hunger except negatively; it would be easy to die if she should decide to do so. And so, to reinforce her will to live, a comprehensive schedule had been imposed from above. But the most rigid personal schedule meant nothing without time. Time took the place of hunger, of the need for food, of all the savor in it.

There were clocks on the wall, inconspicuous dials or larger ones, integrated in pictures and summed up in designs. There was a huge circular chronograph on the ceiling; hourglasses and sundials were contrived in the motif on the floor—and they all seemed actually to function. And when she slept or whether she didn't, there were arrangements for that too. The house vibrated, ever so softly, but the attuned senses could hear it, feel it, in sickness and in health.

"Damn," muttered Jeriann as the vibration momentarily grew louder. She tried to say something to Docchi but her thoughts were confused and she couldn't concentrate. "Don't mind me," she said, smiling ruefully. "I was conditioned to this sort of thing. They seem to think I've got to be ready on the dot."

She could see that it wasn't very clear. "There's a clock in my head too. Everybody has one naturally but mine has been trained. Any natural beat will regulate the self-alarm, even the pounding of my heart, even if I don't think about it—but the house is more effective. *They* said I had to have it if I expected to live."

It was obvious who *they* were, the psychotechnicians who had attended her after her original accident. They were right but Docchi could see that it might become annoying.

The ticking grew in volume and the house shook and though Jeriann tried to ignore it, it would not let her be. "Time," tolled the house, though the word was unspoken, "time…time…time." To Docchi it was subdued and soft but it had a different effect on Jeriann.

"All right," she shouted to the tormenter, scrambling out of bed. She dashed into the next room, scooping up hurriedly an absorbic capsule that lay unnoticed on a shelf near the door. She was gone for some time, so long that Docchi was beginning to worry before she came out.

In the interim she had changed into street clothing and the tension that had marked her departure was gone. "I feel better," she said cheerfully. "Breakfast, such as it was, and a shower."

She sat opposite him. "I can see you're trying to figure out how I took a shower when you couldn't hear water running. Special shower. Don't ask about it."

Docchi had no intention, though he was wondering. He had his own gadgets to help him get dressed and no one was curious about them.

"You came here for something," said Jeriann. "Thanks for being polite and talking to the patient but now you can tell me what it is."

He was considering whether he should ask someone else. It was complex, too difficult to explain to Nona. Anti, who would have been best, was confined to the tank. And Jordan wouldn't do at all. That left only Jeriann, who was capable enough, *if* she was fully recovered. "Do you know Maureen?" he asked.

"I do. Can I guess what she's done now?" said Jeriann dryly.

"Your guess is probably right, except that she hasn't done it yet. I want to make certain she doesn't." He thought over Jeriann's reply. "This isn't the first time this has happened to her?"

"Of course it isn't. She's always looking for excuses. Long ago, before you came, I think, she managed to throw the stuff away and pretend she'd taken it. She concealed what she'd done for three weeks, until the doctor discovered it."

He hadn't heard this, even as a whispered legend. He'd been too busy trying to achieve new status for the accidentals to bother with gossip. He didn't know the people here as well as Jeriann did; he'd have to draw on her for detailed information. "This time it's not an excuse. The deficiency prescription isn't there for her to take."

"Nonsense," said Jeriann sharply. "I remember, thinking in that split second in the dispensary: If I were only Maureen now, the worst that could happen to me is that I'd attract attention."

He glanced at her. She hadn't thought that at all, though it was a reflection of another sort of bitterness. The girl didn't know how lucky she was in comparison to others who were seriously handicapped. "Could you go and take a look?" he asked. "Maureen said it isn't there. I understand that they do experiment occasionally. The new consignment might have got shoved aside in the excitement we had a while back—or it might be there under a different formula that Maureen can't identify." If what Jeriann said was correct, Maureen liked the idea of becoming an all-female woman. To her it might seem an anodyne, surcease from disappointment and things that hadn't gone right.

"Sure, I'll go," said Jeriann. Her cheerfulness had diminished while he spoke. Until now she hadn't actually realized there was no longer Earth to signal to in event of an emergency. "It's true they experiment. And maybe they didn't send the last shipment during our mix-up." She tossed her head, recovering her buoyancy rapidly. "Oh well, I'll go and take a look. I know the hospital pretty well."

"Good." Docchi got up.

"Wait for me," said Jeriann, going to a drawer and taking things out. She slipped a watch on her arm; there was another in the rather wide belt she wore. She selected a series of absorption capsules and dropped them into pouches on the belt that appeared to be merely ornamental until he saw what went into it. "Lunch, a drink, and an extra one for emergency," she explained laconically.

"I should think you'd require more fluid."

She looked at him disturbingly. "I would, if I had normal metabolism. But remember I don't need fluid for the digestive process. And then to further reduce the intake they've included an antiperspirant in what I do get."

He followed her to the door, where she turned around and looked back at the place she lived in. It was a small, curious house, completely arranged for the kind of person she was.

"Are you going to the hospital with me?" she asked.

"No, there's some work I've got to do near here."

"Well, then, thanks for saving my life." She slipped her arms around him and kissed him, quickly but satisfactorily. Her lips were cool and dry. Very smooth but dry; her touch was like silk. That was because of her skin.

She smiled and opened the door. "See you," she said as they parted. She never once looked back though he did. He was glad, because she might have waved and it would have been impossible to return it.

Twice, now, within an hour, he thought as he went along. Maureen of course he could dismiss since she would respond to anything that was remotely male. It was not at all the same reaction from Jeriann, and it pleased him that it wasn't.

Their environment had changed. Life on the asteroid had undergone a not so subtle transformation now that there were no longer any normals around to be compared with, to make the disastrous self-comparison to. They could begin to behave healthily and sensibly. It was nice that Jeriann had kissed him and liked it. It was the first installment of freedom.

The second installment was going to be harder—to keep that freedom at a level that meant something. He frowned heavily as he thought of what had to be done.

He was late. Except for Anti, who was absent and always would be, everyone he knew was there. In addition there were many others who hardly ever attended. It was a good sign that they were coming out and mingling; before they had seldom left their houses. Docchi spotted Jeriann but there wasn't a vacant seat near her. He sat down toward the rear.

Jordan rapped for silence. "Are there any questions?"

At the front a man stood up. Docchi remembered him from months ago, a Jack or Jed Webber. Jed it was, a quiet fellow with pale blue eyes and almost colorless blond hair. Docchi had never heard him say anything but he was speaking now, emerging from his self-imposed shell. "Yes," said Webber. "I want to know where we're going."

Jordan rapped again. "Out of order. Not on the subject. Anyway the question's not important."

"I think it is," said the man, shuffling his body awkwardly. He was not exact in his movements because he'd been sliced very nearly down the middle. Except for his head he was half man and half machine. Unlike others who'd been injured past regeneration, he could use his composite body with some degree of skill because there was one arm and one leg to which the motion of his mechanical limbs could be coordinated. His skill wasn't as great as it could have been because he hadn't practiced. The specter of the ideal human body had hindered him greatly in the past. "You don't know where we're going," insisted the man in a high voice. "We're just moving but you don't know where."

Docchi got up. "I can answer that question. It should be answered. We're going to Centauri, either Alpha or Proxima, whichever is most suitable. Is there some place else you wanted to go?"

The reply was drowned for a few seconds by an appreciative rumble but Webber was stubborn and waited until the noise died down. He swayed on his feet and pointed at Nona. "I suppose you asked her," he said. Nona smiled dreamily as attention turned to her.

"No. It would be a joke if we did and we're not interested in playing tricks on ourselves. You've forgotten one thing, that we do have a telescope."

"A small one, built as a hobby," Webber said. His voice was uncertain, as wobbly as his body was.

"True, but it's better than Galileo had." He hoped Webber wouldn't point out that Galileo hadn't tried to plot a voyage across space with his instrument.

Actually there was something strange about the few observations he'd made. He had reconstructed their path to the best of his ability—not a bad guess since no records had been kept. At the time they had left Sol they hadn't been heading directly toward the Centauris. Nona must have used their tangential motion to take them out of the system as fast as she could and later had looped back toward their present destination. The sketchy charts Docchi had, indicated the Centauris by plus or minus a few degrees, all the accuracy he could expect from the telescope. It was in the stars themselves that he had detected changes he couldn't account for.

At the far side a woman stood. Jordan nodded to her. "I wasn't asked for my opinion about all this," she said defiantly. "I don't like it. I want to go back."

Jordan cocked his head humorously. "You should have told the guards this while they were here. They'd have been glad to take you with them."

"I certainly wouldn't leave with them," she said in surprise. "Look how they acted while they were here."

"I'm afraid you're out of luck. We can't turn back because of you."

"Don't tell me we're marooned here," said the woman vehemently. "The guards left a couple of scout ships, didn't they? Why can't we take those back to Earth?"

"For the same reason *they* didn't," said Jordan patiently, "The range of the scouts is limited, it wouldn't reach then and it won't do it now."

"Pshaw," said the woman. "You're just arguing, Docchi said the gravity generator in each ship could be changed to a drive without much work—something about adding a little star encyclopedia unit. I think that's what he said."

Docchi started. Had he said that? He must have for the woman to have remembered it. He shouldn't have made such a statement, first because it wasn't so. He had made the possibility of return to Earth seem too easy.

There was another reason he regretted his rash explanation and it was the opposite of the first: inadvertently he might have blurted out the secret of the drive. It was possible to talk too much.

"I'm not the only one," the woman was insisting. She'd found a point and wouldn't let go. "There are plenty of others who feel as I do and they'll say so if they're not afraid. Who wants to go on for years and years, never reaching any place?"

"Look at the stars." A voice ahead of Docchi answered her.

It was Webber again, the meek little man who never spoke.

"I don't *want* to look at the stars," she said violently. "I never want to see anything but the sun. *Our* sun. It was good enough for mankind and I certainly don't care to change it."

"That's because you don't know," said Webber confidently.

"You're afraid and you don't need to be. When I said look at the stars I meant that those ahead of us are brighter than the ones behind. Do you know what that means?"

Docchi nodded exultantly to himself; they'd found their astronomer. He himself had noticed the first part of what Webber remarked on; he hadn't thought to turn the telescope in the opposite direction because he wasn't interested in where they'd been. The apparent brightness of the Centauri system was much greater than it should have been—that's what he hadn't been able to account for. He could now. It was surprising how much power the gravity drive could deliver.

"We're approaching the speed of light," went on Webber. "It won't take decades to reach a star. We'll be there in a few years."

The woman turned and glared but could find nothing to say. She wasn't convinced, but she sat down to cover her confusion. Around her people began to whisper, their voices rising with excitement. They'd lived long enough at the rim of the system to know what stellar distances meant and how much speed could affect their voyage.

Jordan rapped them into silence. "I've tried to get you to talk on the subject but you've resolutely refrained. Therefore you'll have to vote on it without discussion."

The vote took place, whatever it was. Docchi was unable to discover what and so he didn't participate. When the count was over Jordan gaveled sharply. "Motion carried. That's all. Meeting adjourned."

Before Docchi could protest, people were leaving, carrying him part of the way with them. He reached the wall and stood there until traffic subsided, afterwards making his way to Jordan who was talking happily to Jeriann.

"We did it," said Jordan, grinning as he came up.

"Did what? All I heard were people complaining. We had to depend on someone from the floor to smack them down. Seems to me there were a lot of important things to discuss."

"Seem to me we covered everything, which you would have known if you had got here on time," said Jordan, still grinning, "This is Jeriann's idea. It was what we were voting on."

Twisting his head Docchi read the sheet Jordan laid in front of him. It was a resolution of some sort, which he gathered from the usual whereases. He scanned it once and was halfway through again before he caught the import.

"The wages aren't high," remarked Jordan. "Survival *if* we do our job well, grousing if we don't. Otherwise we can keep on doing just what we have been." He picked up the sheet and read from it. "Whereas we are bound together by a common condition and destination—ain't that nice?—and have a common plan—" Jordan looked up. "Since you're the one they're talking about when they refer to the head of the planning committee, just what the hell *is* our plan?"

There were innumerable small goals that had to be reached before they could consider themselves self-sufficient, and to some extent Docchi was capable of summarizing them. But when it came to a final statement of aims he could only feel his way. Docchi didn't know either.

CHAPTER NINE

JERIANN came into the office. "I've got it down to twenty," she said briskly.

"What?" said Docchi absently. Management details were unfamiliar to him and he was trying to pick them up as he went along. The scattered records were in order but some were still unaccounted for. "Oh. The deficiency biologicals. Good. How did you do it?"

"I asked them."

"And they knew? It's surprising. I'd expect them to be familiar with their standard treatment. But not something that's entirely new."

Jeriann smiled faintly. "I'm not that good. I did find out what they used to get and then scrounged around in storage until I found supplies. If the old stuff kept them healthy once it should do so now."

He hadn't thought of that, but then he wasn't accustomed to considering the same things a doctor would. Any trained person would know that sulfa hadn't been discarded with the discovery of penicillin, nor penicillin with the advent of the neo-biotics. Docchi studied her covertly; Jeriann was a competent woman, and an attractive one.

"Of the remaining twenty we don't have biologicals for I've determined we can make what eleven need."

Only nine who were left out. It was a remarkable advance over a few days ago when there were forty-two. Nine for whom so far they could do nothing. It was queer how he worried about them more as the number diminished. Somehow it had greater significance now that he could remember each face distinctly. "And Maureen?" he inquired.

Instinctively Jeriann touched the decorative belt that was so much more than what it seemed. "I'm afraid I misjudged her. I couldn't locate a thing for her."

"You're sure she didn't destroy her prescription?"

"I don't see what difference it makes as long as we don't have it," said Jeriann. "But yes, I'm sure. Once something is brought in it's simply not possible for a person as ignorant of the system as she is to track down and destroy every entry relating to it."

"All right. I believe you." He glanced down at the list she'd given him. The actual figures weren't as optimistic as her report had been.

"Wait. I notice you say here that out of twenty that we don't have supplies for that we can synthesize biologicals for eleven."

She sat down. "That's what I said. How else can we get them? We've got the equipment. The asteroid never did depend on Earth for very many of our biologicals."

He knew vaguely how the medical equipment functioned, rather like the commonplace food synthesizers. "We don't have anyone with experience."

Jeriann shrugged, "I'm not a technician but I used to help out when there was nothing else to do. I expected to run it."

The light flashed on his desk but Docchi ignored it. "Have you thought what an infinitesimal error means?" he asked.

"Of course." He was struck by her calmness. "One atom hooked in the wrong place and instead of a substance the body must have it becomes a deadly poison. I've talked it over with the deficients. They agreed to it. This way they know they have a chance."

"We'll do something," he acknowledged. "Pick out the worst and work for their deficiency. Check with me before you give them anything."

"I've selected them," she said. "There are four extreme cases. They won't collapse today or tomorrow. Perhaps not in a week. But we can't let them get close."

"Agreed." The light kept flashing annoyingly in his eyes. Another complaint. Nodding at Jeriann, Docchi nudged the switch and glanced at the screen. "Anything wrong?" he asked.

It was Webber. "Nothing much. Jordan and I just bumped into an old acquaintance, I suppose we'd better bring him in."

"Cameron," exclaimed Docchi as Webber moved aside, revealing the man behind him.

The doctor's clothing was rumpled and he hadn't shaved but he was calm and assured. "You seem to be running things now," he said. "I'd like a chance to talk with you."

Docchi didn't answer directly. "Where did you find him, Webber?"

"He was living out in the open near a stream which, I imagine, was his water supply. We were checking some of the stuff the guards didn't wreck when we spotted him. We saw bushes move and went over to investigate, figuring it might be a geepee at loose ends. There was our man."

"Did he give you any trouble?"

Webber shrugged. "He wasn't exactly glad to see us. But he must have known there was no place to hide because he didn't actually try to get away."

"That's your interpretation," said Cameron, his face beside Webber. "The truth is I wanted to make sure you had no way of sending me back with the general's forces. I was taking plenty of time."

From beyond the screen Jordan snorted.

Cameron continued. "There was no use going back to Earth. My career wasn't exactly ruined—but you can appreciate the difficulties I'd have. Anyway a doctor is trained to take the most urgent cases, and I thought they were here. I'm sorry only that I had to be discovered. It spoiled the entry I was going to make."

Jeriann's face showed what she thought. Relief, and was there something else? The thought was distasteful if only because it indicated there was now a normal human present. The deadly comparison was back with them.

But it was more than that—how much more was up to him to find out. Docchi kept his emotions far away. It would hardly do to let Cameron know what he thought. "Well, there's work to do, if that's what you want. Come up as soon as you can get here."

Cameron cocked his head, "If they'll let me."

"They'll let you." Docchi switched off the screen and turned to see Jeriann getting up.

"Don't leave. I want you to check on him."

"Why should we check?" she asked in surprise.

Another one who accepted the doctor at face value. There would be plenty of others like her. Perhaps Cameron *had* remained for the reasons he'd given. If so it ought to be easy to prove. "Did I say we'd have to watch him? I didn't mean quite that. Cameron's here and we intend to use him. At the same time we must admit that he has many conventional ideas. We'll have to give him our slant on what we need."

She sat down. "I don't want to waste your time or his."

"You're not." Docchi pretended to be busy while they waited. He had to learn whether his suspicions were unfounded, Cameron may have stayed in the best medical tradition. But there was another tradition less honorable and it was an equal possibility.

It was better not to say anything to Jeriann. She respected the doctor but she wouldn't be blinded by that attitude. She'd report any untoward thing she saw. And she was attractive. Sooner than anyone—else save Nona, who couldn't communicate—she'd learn what the doctor's true motives were.

Docchi found himself studying her. She didn't have to be that anxious. He wished she weren't so eager for the doctor to arrive.

Cameron shook his head. "Don't let your enthusiasm run away with you. I can help the deficients but if new treatments are developed it will probably be the result of ideas you people have."

"What about the list? Can we synthesize for them?"

"I haven't studied it and I'm not familiar with the medical history of everyone here. I do know three of the eleven that Jeriann's selected and in each one she's exactly right. It's merely a matter of testing the preparations, I'll check but I'm sure she can do it as well as I can."

It was nice to know that they were doing all right by themselves, that they'd have gotten along without the doctor. It helped that he was here but they'd have survived anyway. "Can you do anything for Maureen?" asked Docchi.

"I don't remember her. I'll have to look it up."

"The records aren't in the best condition."

"Guards?" Docchi noted that Cameron scowled. Either he was a good actor or he was sincere. "I tried to get the general to restrain them but he wouldn't listen."

"No harm done, I suppose," said Docchi. He wanted to forget as much of that episode as he could. "However I can tell you what's wrong with Maureen. No male hormones."

"I remember." Cameron pondered. "I've never had anything to do with her. Most of her treatment came direct from Earth. I don't know. I really can't say."

"Most glands are paired. Can't you transplant one, or part of one, from some of us? We'll get donors."

"Offhand I'd say that if it were possible it would have been done long ago. For reasons that aren't understood transplants aren't always effective. Sometimes the body acts to dissolve foreign tissue or, if there's irritation, grow a tumor around it."

"That's why she's still a deficient?"

"It's my guess. They tried transplants but had to cut them out." Cameron turned to Jeriann. "Do we have equipment for synthetic hormones?"

"Maybe. I never prepared any."

The doctor leaned over the desk, flipping through the files until he came to the section he wanted. "Some test animals. Probably not enough," he said after studying it briefly. "I'll do something to keep her quiet until I can figure out a substitute."

"No experiments on us, Cameron."

He smiled wryly. "The history of medicine is a long series of experiments. If it weren't for that we'd still be in the stone age, medically speaking."

Docchi shrugged. "Suit yourself. Do what you can with Maureen."

"What about Anti?"

"We haven't had time to think about her."

"I'll see what I can do. If I stumble on anything that seems beneficial I'll let you know." Cameron turned to leave and Jeriann went with him.

Docchi watched him go. The doctor was an asset they hadn't counted on. His presence would help silence the objections of those who agreed with the woman at the meeting but hadn't said anything yet. This was the temporary advantage.

But there was still the doubt. Cameron might have stayed at the general's request. A few serious illnesses—or a death here and there—might influence them to turn back. Somehow Docchi couldn't credit the doctor with such intentions.

Then what? Well, the doctor might have remained with them on a long, long chance. A gamble, but he was the kind who took risks.

It was not suspicion alone that made Docchi suddenly tired and morose. He wished he could call Jeriann back on some pretext. She'd gone and she hadn't looked his way when she left.

Anti bobbed gently in the acid. "What's the contraption?"

"An idea of mine," said Jordan, lowering the coils carefully so the acid didn't splash.

Anti looked at it judicially. "Maybe next time you'll think of something better."

"Don't be nasty," said Jordan as the coils reached the surface of the liquid and began to submerge. "Cameron thinks it will work."

"My faith is shaken."

"It isn't a question of faith and anyway he's as good a doctor as we've ever had." Jordan kept lowering until the mechanism reached the bottom. A single cable over the side of the tank was the only thing visible. Jordan wiped his hands on the grass. "I was thinking about radiation when this thing occurred to me."

"Would you believe it? Once I was young and radiant myself."

"It's not the same thing."

"Don't think I wouldn't trade."

"You won't have to," said Jordan. "This is my idea, not the doctor's. He merely confirmed it."

"In that case it's bound to work."

Jordan pulled a tuft of grass loose and tossed it into the tank. It disappeared in a soundless blaze. To conform with what was expected of her, Anti blinked. "Don't be so afraid we're going to fail that you can't listen to what I have to say. Do you want to be cured and not know why? I've run my legs off to make this gadget."

"A figure of speech," commented Anti.

"A figure of speech," agreed Jordan. "To begin with we discovered that when you were exposed to space the cold caused the fungus flesh to die back faster than it grew. Right?"

"The fungus came from Venus," said Anti. "It's only natural it wouldn't grow well in the cold."

"The origin doesn't have anything to do with it. Normally it doesn't grow in flesh and it had to make concessions to live in the human body, the biggest one being adaptation to body temperature. At the same time the body cells tried to outgrow it but the faster they grew the more there was for the fungus to live in. A sort of an inimical symbiosis."

"If you can imagine inimical symbiosis," said Anti. "I can't."

"You haven't tried very hard. Anyway, there seems to be a ratio between the amount of fungus in one connected mass and the vigor. The more there is the faster it grows, and conversely."

"Such a pleasant reference," said Anti. "Mass. Still it's an accurate description of me, though I can think of a better one. Lump." She swam, splashing ponderously toward the edge of the tank. "Are you trying to say that if I can ever get below a certain point my body will be able to keep the fungus in check?"

"Exactly."

"What's wrong with the treatment we discovered? Give me an oxygen helmet and tie me to a cable and let me float outside the dome."

"You wouldn't float as long as the gravity's on. Besides, we can do it better. In space you lose heat solely by radiation. Radiation depends on surface and the larger a body is the more surface it had in proportion."

"Convection is what you meant," said Anti. "Acid alone helps, but a *cold* acid would combine treatments."

"A very cold acid. Supercold."

Anti nodded and nodded and then stopped. "A fine piece of reasoning except for one thing. When the temperature is decreased chemical activity slows down."

"That's the triumph of my gadget," said Jordan. "It's not only a refrigerant coil but electronically it steps up ionizations as the temperature is lowered. We sacrifice neither effect."

Soundlessly Anti sank below the surface and remained there for some time. When she came up acid trickled over her face. "I had to think. It's been so long since I dared hope," she said. "When can I walk?"

"I didn't say you would," said Jordan hastily. "There may be a lower limit beyond which it's dangerous to continue the cold acid treatment."

"Then what's the use?" said Anti. "I'm not interested in merely reducing. I'll still be bigger than a house. I want to get around."

"This is the first step," explained Jordan patiently. "After this is successful we'll think of something else."

"What language," said Anti. "The first step when obviously I'm nowhere near taking one. Can't you turn off the gravity?"

If they did it would hinder others, and the odds were nearly a thousand to one. Of course they might compromise, a short gravityless period at intervals. It would be unsatisfactory to everyone but it might give Anti the encouragement she needed.

Besides, he was unsure they could turn off the gravity without also turning off the drive. Their momentum would carry them along at the same speed they had been going. But was it wise to tamper with a mechanism that till now was functioning so smoothly and was so important?

Jordan shook his head. "I said we'd think of something else and we will. Continue with this treatment and watch your weight go down."

"Don't think I'm not aware of your cheerful intentions," said Anti. "How can you possibly weigh me as long as I have to stay in the tank?"

"The same way Archimedes did—fluid displacement. I've rigged up a scale so you can keep track of what's happening." He didn't tell her what the scale was calibrated in. Absolute figures were disheartening. It was only the progress which counted.

Anti looked at the dial near the edge of the tank. "I thought it was just another gadget." When Jordan didn't answer she looked for him. "Hey, don't leave me to freeze in this cold goop."

"You're not cold and you know it. You can't feel a thing."

"Don't be so frank," she grumbled. "Hardly anyone comes to talk to me. I like company."

"Sure, but I've got to get busy on that other idea." He didn't have one but he looked very wise and it had the desired effect.

"Guess I can't stop you," grumbled Anti. "Tell someone to come and visit with me."

Again she looked long at the dial. It was a pleasant surprise to find she was not so far from average that she could be weighed. Jordan was a gadgeteer but sometimes his contraptions worked and once in a while his ventures in psychology were extraordinarily shrewd.

For instance, the dial.

She imagined she could feel her toes tingling from the cold—if she still had toes. Soon they would emerge from the fungus flesh in which they were buried. She felt she was shedding.

What did they have that made anything seem possible? Jordan, the sometimes wonderful gadgeteer. Docchi, a competent engineer but no more than that. Unsure of himself personally he had a passion for correcting inequalities. And then there was Cameron, a good doctor who was trying to realign his principles. He wouldn't have made it except that he had a powerful attraction ahead of him. Lord knows what he saw in Nona, or she in him.

And lastly there was Nona herself, to whom big miracles came easier than small ones. There was a fragile grandeur about her but she knew nothing at all of the human body, especially her own.

And this is what they relied on. It was strikingly little to balance against the forces of Earth, which had failed them. And yet it was enough; the accidentals would not fail.

It didn't matter what the resources were as long as they weren't aimed in the right direction. She didn't have figures on the conquest of cancer but the one-time scourge of mankind could have vanished far sooner if the cost of one insignificant political gesture had been spent instead to wipe out the disease.

Perhaps this was one answer. They were struggling not to make beautiful men and women still more beautiful but to restore those who were less than perfect to some sort of usefulness, especially in their own evaluation.

The lights in the dome dimmed appreciably. It was the lengthening shadows which made the needle on the dial that Anti was watching quiver and seem to turn downward.

Jordan rode the repair robot away from the tank. It was more than had ever been done for Anti but it wasn't enough. A fifty percent reduction and she still wouldn't be able to walk. He'd have to check with anyone who had ideas of what to do. He didn't have much hope there; nobody but himself had given much thought to Anti recently.

The machine he was on wasn't functioning properly. Nothing definite, it just wasn't. He was sensitive enough to notice this through his preoccupation with other problems. It was sluggish to his touch. It was not unexpected; there was a lot of equipment that was supposed to be foolproof and wasn't, any number of machines built to last forever which didn't.

Once it would have been easy to blame technicians for failure to keep the robots in proper condition. Now he couldn't because he was that technician, the only one. Nona kept the big stuff working and Docchi helped out with anything else when he could find them. But minor machines were important too and this was his province. Robot repair units affected gross corrections on themselves but weren't capable of detecting defects in the basic repair circuit. This was his responsibility.

He stopped the squat machine and opened it. There was nothing wrong that he could see. Some other time he'd work it over thoroughly. He climbed back on and touched the controls he added for his own use.

For a while nothing happened and then an extensible started flailing. It was not what he'd signaled for. He shoved the lever in the opposite direction and though it didn't stop the gyrations of the extensible it did start the treads. The machine rumbled away at greater than ordinary speed. Jordan would have fallen off if an extensible hadn't steadied him.

Momentarily he wondered; the last response was not within the machine's capacity. It was built to repair other machines and, within limits, itself. It had no knowledge of the frailties of the human body. He wondered at this and then forgot it completely.

The robot lurched heavily, narrowly missing one of the columns that supported the dome. A collision at this speed—well, no, the column wouldn't have been greatly damaged.

Hastily Jordan reached to shut it off. There was a shower of sparks and the handle grew hot and sputtered. The grip flashed, fusing, visibly becoming inoperative.

The robot no longer faltered. Jordan wasn't in immediate danger. He could always swing off, slide off, or fall. But he ought to stop it before it wrecked itself or, worse, the dome.

The dome enclosed a good part of the asteroid but it came to an end somewhere, curving downward and joining the ground at a flexible seal. Naturally it was protected against collision and naturally the protection wasn't complete. It was conceivable that an uncontrolled robot could break through. Jordan clutched an extensible as the machine jolted and rocked. The nearest place it could damage the dome was miles away. He'd disable it long before it got there.

He steadied himself and reached for the panel, prying it open. He thrust his hand in and the lid slammed shut on his fingers. He yelled and pulled loose, leaving part of his skin inside. The lid was firmly closed.

He glowered at the machine. It was an accident that a wildly moving extensible clamped the lid down as he reached inside. He didn't like those kinds of accidents; the element of purpose was very strong.

He hesitated whether he should disable the machine. It was valuable equipment and they wouldn't get more like it. It would have to last for the duration. "Easy does it," he muttered but it wasn't easy. His hand slid back to the toaster—and it wasn't there. The sensible thing was to suppose that it had been jolted loose. The machine couldn't think in complex terms.

Or could it? He glanced down; there were indications the robot had been sliced into and he thought he knew who had done it. It was probably the one he and Docchi had disabled long ago on their escape from the asteroid. It had been repaired since and the technician who had done so had altered the circuits.

The essential thing was to stop it before it caused real damage. He suspected that, with a number of extensibles curled firmly around him, there was no danger he'd fall off. Maybe he couldn't get off if he wanted to.

He wished he'd encounter someone. He hated to admit it but he needed help. In the distance he saw people and shouted. They knew him; he was the person who rode the robot. They waved gaily and said something unintelligible as he sped by. It was irritating that they didn't see anything amiss.

The edge of the dome loomed up. They'd been going longer than he'd thought. He squirmed uneasily; he should have gotten off long ago and used something else to intercept the errant machine. A geepee, if he'd had sense enough to get one, could run it down and smash it. His only excuse was that he hadn't wanted to destroy valuable machinery.

With tremendous effort he tore himself loose and using the power of his overdeveloped arms he threw himself off. He covered his head and rolled along the ground in a tight ball. He was free.

But not for long. The treads whining in reverse, the robot whirled, scooping him up as it passed by. This time it didn't pause as it headed toward the edge of the dome. It was all his fault. The dome would seal itself after the robot plunged through, but not without loss of air—and one good mechanic.

The machine churned on but surprisingly didn't plow heedlessly into the curved transparent wall. The extensibles felt the surface, the speed was checked and the direction changed. The robot moved parallel with the edge of the dome. It had a better sense of self-preservation than was common with robots of this type.

It felt the wall as it rolled along. There was nothing noteworthy about the surface, smooth, hard, and slightly curved. Another extensible emerged from the squat body; the tip flashed a light toward the outside.

It was strange out there. Jordan hadn't often seen it; not many people came to look out. When the asteroid was in the solar system jagged rocks had gleamed in the sharp light of the sun. But now the landscape was always dark except when some curious person wanted to remind himself what the rest of his world was like. It was a torn and crumpled sight the robot's light displayed, as if some giant had risen and tossed aside the rocks he slept in. But not completely rumpled; here and there were smooth areas that some vast engine might have planed flat—or the same giant had straightened out with a swipe of his hand before departing.

The robot flicked off the light and turned away. Jordan breathed with relief when he saw where it was going, toward the central repair depot to which all robots returned periodically. It would slide into a stall and stop. He would get off. And he would see to it that the robot was thoroughly checked over before it was called out again.

The entrance slot was extremely wide and equally low; it wasn't built for passengers on the robots. Momentarily the thought flashed across his mind that he should let himself be scraped off. But it seemed a precipitous way to dismount and anyway the machine would soon stop and he could get off more conventionally. Instinct won and Jordan flattened himself as they swept under the gate. He could feel the masonry twitching at his clothing.

The slot opened into a circular space in which other robots were stationed in stalls. In the center were bins of spare parts, Jordan called out, not too hopefully. Robots were assigned from here on a broadcast band; he didn't think there were facilities for responding to the human voice.

His machine headed toward a stall at the rear. This far from the entrance the light was dim. Jordan wondered why there was any light at all; robots didn't need it. Upon reflection he decided it was a concession to human limitations.

But the machine didn't slow down as he expected. It rumbled between walls, turned at a sharp angle—and the parking slot was not what it had seemed. They were in a passageway, narrow and even more dimly lighted. That it was lighted at all indicated it wasn't a chance fissure. It had been built long ago and forgotten.

This was serious. Where was the machine going and when would it stop? He hoped it would stop. An outcropping in the passageway loomed ahead of him; he flung himself flat. A sharp projection grazed his ear. The tunnel wound on through solid rock. He was lost by the time it ended.

There were no true directions on the asteroid. Toward the sun or away from it; toward the hospital or the rocket dome. These were the principle orientations and the main one had been left behind—the sun. He didn't know where he was except that it was somewhere under the main dome. He was sure of this because he was still alive. There was air.

The passageway terminated in a large cavern. Once he saw it he relaxed. It was a laboratory and a workshop and he knew whose. There was only one person who would disassemble nine general purpose robots and arrange their headpieces in a neat row on a stone slab. Their eyes revolved slowly as the machine rumbled farther in. He stared back; the intensity with which they gazed at him was uncomfortable. How long Nona had had this workshop he didn't know. Perhaps it was here she'd hidden from the guards.

Nine pair of eyes followed their progress as the machine rolled across the floor. Jordan glared back. He could see that they were not merely in a row, that they were hooked together by a complex circuitry that wove an indefinable pattern between them. The purpose was obscure.

A repair robot was an idiot outside the one thing it was built to do. A general purpose robot, the geepee, was a higher type. It was a moron. Were nine morons brighter than one? With men, not necessarily; stupidity was often merely compounded. But with mechanical brains, using modules of computation, the combination might constitute an accurate data evaluating system.

Jordan squirmed to get a better glimpse of the heads on the slab— and fell off the machine that held him captive. He was free.

His first impulse was to scurry away. When he remembered how far he had to go and by what labyrinth route he decided to wait. Something better might come up. He raised himself and rubbed fine gravel off his cheek. Dust irritated his nose; he sneezed. Eighteen eyes glowered at him.

The repair robot ignored him. Having brought him so far and clung possessively, now it refused to notice him. On the bench there was something new to interest it. The unshakable directive around which it was built had taken over: there was a machine which should be fixed.

What? A mechanism of some sort. Not the nine heads. The repair robot raised a visual stalk and scanned. Jordan craned but couldn't see to the top of the stone bench. Extending other stalks the robot began working up high on the unknown something.

His own curiosity was aroused. Jordan swung to the bench and, gripping the edge, hoisted himself up. Parts of disassembled geepees and other electronic devices were scattered over the slab. He inched carefully along until he could see what his robot, microsenses clicking furiously, was busy with.

It was disappointing. He had expected to find a complicated machine and instead it was nothing at all—a strand of woven wire with a rectangular metal piece at one end. A belt with a buckle on it. This was what fascinated the repair robot.

Jordan went closer. The robot hummed and shook, extensibles racing through the scattered parts which it sorted and laid aside for other stalks to add to the end of the slender strand. It worked on, from time to time stopping to buzz inquisitively. When nothing happened after these outbursts it resumed activity. The pattern was clear: the belt was not functioning properly and the robot was busy repairing it.

Gradually it slowed and the pauses became longer. It clattered loudly and sputtered, extensibles waving uncontrollably until they seemed to freeze. The directive completely frustrated, the robot whined once and then was silent. It was motionless.

Jordan reached for the object, ready to swing away if there was any objection. There wasn't. He examined it closely; it was not a belt. And the rectangular metal piece was not a buckle though it could serve as one. Actually it was a mechanism of some kind, though what it was supposed to do he couldn't tell.

It was one of Nona's experiments. Of that there was little doubt. The strands were not wires but microparts fastened together and woven into an intricate pattern. Jordan snorted; the robot hadn't improved on what Nona had wrought.

He inspected it thoroughly. He could see where the robot had begun to add parts. Methodically he unhooked the surplus components. If Nona had thought they should be on there she would have attached them. They didn't belong.

When he was down to the original mechanism he looked at it perplexedly. It was designed to be worn as a belt. He fastened it around his waist and touched the stud.

By now he had some idea of what it was intended for. It was not surprising that it worked perfectly.

He expected that it would. Nona seldom failed. What Jordan didn't notice and would never discover—no one would—was that there were three minute parts that the robot had added, almost too small for the human eye to see. And those three parts were indispensable. Without them the belt would not function at all. For the lack of them Nona had discarded the idea as unworkable.

CHAPTER TEN

JED WEBBER came in noisily. His left foot was heavy and his left arm swung more than it should. Otherwise there wasn't much that remained of the timid awkward man of weeks ago.

Docchi looked up. "Did my calculations check?"

Webber grinned. "I thought they would but I wanted to be sure. It's one of the Centauris."

"Is that as close as you can come?"

"With that telescope it is. It's pretty wobbly. Who made it, anyway?"

"I did."

Webber grinned again. "In that case it's pretty damned good." With difficulty Webber kept himself from looking down but Docchi could see that his real foot was wriggling.

"Thanks. Did you get an estimate of the speed?"

Webber grunted. "Not a spectroscope on the place, and without one how can I measure the light shift?" He rubbed his arm slowly. "Unless you made one of those too and have it stored away."

"I don't. I made the telescope when I first came here. I didn't see that it proved anything even to myself so I stopped." Docchi thought briefly, "There's an analyzer in the medical lab. You can borrow it but don't change it in any way. We can't risk ruining the only means we have of checking our synthetics."

"We don't have to know how fast we're going. We'll get there just as soon. I'll look into that analyzer after my work period. There's a chance it will do what I want it to."

"What you're doing is work. You don't have to put in more hours than anyone else."

Webber smiled unhappily. "Oh—I'm as lazy as the next person. We're shorthanded in hard labor. I thought I'd fill in for a while."

The reference was what he'd expect from Webber, not at all subtle. "You mean that there's criticism over the shortage of geepees?"

"I didn't want to say anything—but yes, there is."

"I've heard the same complaint. You're not revealing something I don't know." Docchi leaned back. "To you it seems like ingratitude and I suppose it is. More than anyone else Nona is responsible for what we've achieved. I don't object to anything she wants—twice as

113

many geepees if she needs them and we have them. We'll get it back in ways we didn't expect."

"I agree. But not everyone feels the same way."

"It doesn't hurt. In times of hardship everyone complains, and they may as well direct it at her. Actually it's a measure of how important they feel she is—and the accusations are so ill-founded they can't believe them themselves."

Webber got up. For the first time, since he entered, the mechanical and muscular halves of his body failed to coordinate. "You're right. I thought if I had something to tell them they'd be less uncertain."

"Perhaps they would, for a while. I'm not keeping secrets. The truth is I don't know what she's using the geepees for."

If the explanation failed to be completely convincing it was because Webber didn't want to believe. There were others like him. He didn't blame anyone for wanting an accounting for every piece of equipment on the asteroid. And yet the attitude was an advantage. Discontent, real or fancied, wouldn't become a problem as long as it was openly displayed. There would be time to worry if Webber didn't mention his dissatisfaction. Docchi watched him leave and then bent over his work.

A few hours and a score of unimportant details later Cameron hurried in. "Need a couple of lab workers," he said on entering.

"I thought Jeriann was doing all right."

"She is—indispensable. We can't have that. Suppose she should get sick? I want her to teach someone else the synthesizers. She's got too much on her hands."

Docchi hooked his knee on a corner of the desk and tilted the chair back. "Sounds reasonable. Do you have anyone in mind?"

"Jeriann says two women have worked with her in the past. She won't have to start from scratch. She'll give you their names." Cameron rifled the files and jotted down the information. He folded the sheet, stuffing it in his pocket. "Here's something for you. We've reduced the unsolved deficients to three. All the rest we can synthesize for."

From forty-two to nine and now it was three. It was all the progress they could hope for, and much of it was due to Cameron. He had misjudged the doctor's reasons for staying and he was thankful he could admit it to himself. The man was sincere—and he was also very fond of Nona.

Coupled with an increased food supply the major hazards were vanishing. Power, of course, never had been a problem and never would be. There was only one small doubt that remained and though there was no basis for it he couldn't get it out of his mind. He wished there was some way to reassure himself.

"We weren't able to replace everything the deficients need," Cameron was saying. "However they'll get along on what we manufacture."

"Then they're still deficients?"

"Hardly," said Cameron. "The body's more versatile than you think. Long ago it was learned that certain vitamins can be created in the body from simpler substances.

"In several cases we're depending on an analogous process.

We supply simple compounds and depend on the body to put it together. Afterwards, when we checked, the body did create the new substance."

"Good. When will you take the remaining three off the emergency list?"

"Two are minor. It doesn't matter when we get to them as long as it's within the next few years."

He didn't have to be told who the third was. Maureen. He'd all but forgotten her. It was the doctor's responsibility, but he didn't feel that way.

"She's not causing trouble," emphasized Cameron. "Daily she is growing more feminine and we'd have positive proof of it except that we've taken steps."

"Confinement?"

"No, except the solitude of her mind. Hypnotics. We tell her she's getting the regular injections and it's these which cause her to want to be left alone."

It was more stringent than he cared for but he didn't have a better suggestion. "How long can she continue on hypnotics?"

"Depends. The reaction varies with the person. She can tolerate quite a bit more."

Docchi's face darkened. "You said you can't transfer tissue from any of us. Is that also true of hormones concentrated from blood donations?"

"Let's put it this way: blood won't help Maureen at all. We can't extract the complete hormone spectrum from blood, the basic factors she must have to utilize the rest just don't exist there. If I thought it would help I'd have asked for donations long ago."

Docchi tried to shut out the pictures that were coming fast. Maureen alone in a room in which she had darkened the windows so she wouldn't look outside. The door would swing open at the touch of her hand, but she would never touch it. The lock was intangible and hence unbreakable. It would break when her mind broke.

"That's all you've planned," said Docchi, "wait and see what happens?"

"Hardly. I'm having Jeriann work solely on synthesizing those hormone fractions we can't extract from blood. If she gets even a few we'll call for blood and between the two sources we'll have Maureen out of trouble."

Docchi refrained from asking what chance of success Jeriann had. It might be better not to know. Before he could question the doctor further Jordan wandered in, buoyant and cheerful. Tacitly they let the subject of Maureen drop.

"Where have you been the last few days?" said Cameron. "I've been wanting you to fix some of my equipment."

"I've been busy tearing down a robot."

"That's important but the hospital comes first," said Docchi.

"Not before this one," said Jordan. "It was erratic and I had to get out those faulty circuits before it decided to look into a nuclear pile. If I'd let it go there might be no robot, power plant or asteroid. Not to mention a hospital."

"You're exaggerating."

"No I'm not. You should have seen it. It had more curiosity than—well, Anti."

"Or you?" suggested Docchi, smiling faintly at the man's good nature. "Get to the doctor's equipment when you can."

"I'm not in a real hurry," said Cameron. "By the way, I saw Anti yesterday. She's coming along nicely with your treatment, looking almost human."

"She always did seem human to me," said Jordan.

"Sorry. No offense."

"Sure, I know. It was a compliment." The tension left Jordan again; he was relaxed and easy. "Anyway, you should see her today. Better yet. I don't have to rig the scale in her favor. I can let her read the honest figures."

"Good. But don't overdo the encouragement. It will make it harder when she finds she won't be walking for years."

"She'll be up long before you think," said Jordan mildly but the doctor chuckled at the wrong time and the mildness vanished. Jordan had come to tell them but now he couldn't. Cameron thought he was good and so he was but he forgot he wasn't dealing with ordinary people. His rules just didn't apply to Anti, nor to Nona, Jordan, or even the spectacularly useless robot. The doctor didn't understand and because of that he'd have to wait, Docchi too.

"I discovered where Nona does most of her work these days," Jordan muttered. He described where it was, omitting the details of how he got there. He was also careful not to mention anything he saw.

Cameron looked out the window as Jordan talked. "Glad you told me," he said. "I've been meaning to see what I could do for her. It might help if I watched her working."

"Very ordinary," said Jordan. "She putters around—but things fall together when she touches them."

"I imagine. I've seen great surgeons operate." Cameron gathered up his notes and left.

Jordan lingered for a while trying to make up his mind whether to tell Docchi what he had refrained from discussing while the doctor was present. He wanted to, but the longer he kept it to himself the harder it was to share. Eventually Docchi tired of chatting and bent over his work and Jordan wandered out, his secret still safe, too safe.

Docchi stopped foggily when he was alone again. Cameron would soon be trying to help Nona. Somebody had to and he, Docchi, couldn't. It was enough to settle all the prosaic details that must be attended to if the place were to function properly.

It was a relief to know that he'd no longer be concerned about her. Nevertheless a certain grayness descended that didn't lift until Jeriann came in to check on a patient's file.

CHAPTER ELEVEN

IN THE beginning there was silence and it never changed. No sound came to break the stillness. Darkness changed to light with regularity or not, but in the particular universe in which she lived there was never any noise nor any conversation, and music was unknown. She didn't miss it.

There were also machines in the universe in which she dwelt and these too observed a dichotomy. Some machines were warm and soft and this distinguished them from those which were hard and cool. The warm ones started themselves when they were very small. Later they grew up but they didn't know how they did it. Neither did she. Once she was little and she didn't remember doing anything to change it, but it did change.

The hard machines she knew more about. They didn't always have picture receptors on top. Some were blind and some saw more than she did, though not quite in the same way. She could never tell by looking at them which was apt to do which.

(There was a stupid little running machine that she had discovered once that was perpetually scurrying about looking for things to do. It would never have survived on Earth because there was an unexpected flaw in it. She herself had sensed the fault and started to fix it only to realize that here was an unexpected stroke of luck. Curiosity circuits there were by the million but they were all mechanical and what they produced could be strictly predicted. But this was unique. A deviation in the manufacturing process, a slight change in the density of the material, whatever it was something extraordinarily fine had been put together and it would take a hundred years of chance to duplicate it.)

(Midway she had changed her mind and instead had altered the machine to encourage the basic sensitivity. She hadn't seen it recently. She hoped someone who didn't understand hadn't undone her work.)

The known order crumbled under the touch into something that was strange. But where sight itself would not suffice, it was possible to touch reality, to soak it into the skin, like understanding which cometh slowly to the growing mind. But what was understanding? Parts of it were always left out and she could venture toward it only a little way.

She twisted the head on the bench. The silence was unchanging, (What was silence?) Other heads on the bench didn't move; they weren't supposed to. Once they had been attached to clumsy machines and could move about with a stiff degree of freedom. They couldn't now, though they could twist the light receptors in whichever direction suited them.

But they didn't know where to look.

She herself couldn't see the thing that was approaching. It was because her eyes were imperfect. Lenses were pliable and nerve endings were huge things, too gross to catch the instant infinitesimal signals. Or perhaps it was permeability—force bounced on distant impenetrability and bounded back to and through her senses.

She'd have to align the heads to help them help her, string them together for what reinforcement they offered each other. And still they wouldn't see because what they depended on for seeing was too slow. By itself the hookup wouldn't correct their sight.

But nearby was a fast mind though a lazy one. It liked routine once the meaning of it was made clear. And it worked with instantaneity. Blind itself it could fingertip touch the incredible impulses and interpret what it felt for those who had eyes. It would join with her, reluctantly but surely if she made it interesting, a game at which it could always win. And winning wouldn't be difficult for it, not against these nine circuit bound minds, even if it was true that they did augment one another. Singly there were stupid and even added they were not much better. Their virtue was that they were electronic.

(Alone) Were there intangible machines? Sometimes she thought there might be. People twisted their mouth and (not because they were smiling) to indicate that they too understood. She could touch the air coming out but the impulses had no meaning. It was not like vibrations machines set up, harmonics that told of the unseen structure. There was nothing mechanical that could be concealed from harmonics— there were no hard and fast secrets. But what came out of mouths was senseless. It told nothing, or if it did have meaning her hands and her skin were unable to relay the interpretation further. (People were soft machines and they did not ring true. It was difficult to understand.)

Her hands were usually quite capable. (Now) she wove wires so fine that only occasional light was caught and brilliantly reflected. Each strand led somewhere. She removed panels from the robots' heads and grouped them closer. They were beginning to shake off their incomplete individuality. They were no longer separate mechanisms, each of which could only grope for a small fragment of reality. They were merging, becoming larger and stronger. There was more to be done to them but she couldn't do it.

As light as her touch was it was too inaccurate for what must follow. There were objects smaller than her eye could see, movements finer than her muscles could control. She summoned a repair machine whose microsenses were adequate to begin with. She would like to have the one she repaired some time ago (actually it was quite smart) but it had disappeared and she didn't know where to find it. However this one would do.

It was set merely to repair what was already built, but what she wanted was not yet made. She changed the instructions; they were not to her liking anyway.

She delved into the machine and set the problem. The statement of it was complex and she wasn't sure how much data the robot aide would need. When she finished it stood there thrumming. It didn't move.

She waited but nothing happened. The robot, whose senses were far finer than her own, remained frozen and baffled. Impatiently she restated the problem, rephased it so that it could reach every part of the circuit almost instantly. Where it was complex she simplified, reducing it at last to an order the robot could act on. It began to work, slowly at first.

It copied exactly a circuit she had made previously. After she approved it started another, like the first but much smaller, attaching it in series. Satisfied it was obeying instructions, she left it. It would continue to make those circuits, each one progressively smaller, the final one delicate enough to contact the gravity computer.

Meanwhile there was her own work. It wouldn't suffice that the geepees be linked with the gravity computer. They would then see what she had discovered long ago—but it was people who had to be shown. Their eyes were even less sensitive than hers.

Fortunately this was the easiest part. She went to the screen and began to alter it. It could be made to scan what the gravity computer passed on to the geepee heads. A row of dominos, each of which would topple if the first were struck, and the screen was the last of the series.

"Hello," said a voice. "So this is where you always are. What a dreary place to work."

She didn't hear the voice. She felt the footsteps and the air brushing against her skin. She turned around, letting her hands continue, deft and sure. She didn't need to see what she was doing. The smile was involuntary.

He leaned against the wall, watching her. It was embarrassing the way she gazed back. He wished she could say something but then he'd always wished it. He'd had a thesis once (hadn't he?), that for mechanics deafness wasn't a handicap considering how noisy machines were. A deaf person could withstand a concentration of sound the average man would find intolerable. And there was no need for such a person to talk since there was no one who could hear.

The connections in her hands grew swiftly. She felt that she could work better while he was near. Why was this?

"What do you respond to?" he said gruffly. "Diagrams, blueprints? If so I'll have to learn to draw the damnedest things." He laughed uncertainly. "Come on, help me a little bit. I've got some ideas that might help you break out of your shell if you'd try to respond."

He fixed things too, warm soft mechanisms. She didn't know, but she thought it was a higher skill than hers. He was not as adept as she was, though he could learn to be. There was so much more he could do if he would realize. His mouth was a handicap. He moved it often when he should be thinking.

"Listen, robot face, I left a career for you. Do you think they wouldn't take me back? The Medicouncil wouldn't like it but I'd have been a popular hero. Sometimes they want their heroes to fail. Besides from their viewpoint it was the best possible solution. Now they don't have to think of people like you out on that god-forsaken asteroid. You're off their conscience and they don't have to have bad dreams about you."

She smiled again and it was infuriating. What he said or did had no effect. "At least show that you recognize me. Stop what you're doing. It can't be important."

He drew her to him roughly and the work fell from her hands. The connections had been done minutes before and she'd continued to hold them because she didn't want to move away from him. She was willing to let him look at her closely if he wanted. It was surprising how much he wanted to.

Later he held her away from him. "I take it back," he said softly. "You're not a robot face. There's no point of resemblance to a machine. And look, you've even discovered that you've got more than one expression."

The robot aide that had been laboring on whirred inaudibly and clacked its extensibles. It rolled away from the work bench, brushing lightly against the doctor as it did so.

Cameron glanced down blankly, not actually seeing it. "What do I do now?" he said with unexpected gloominess. "You're a child. You're as old as Jeriann, maybe as old as I am, but in this you're hardly more than a child." What was consent and how would he know when he had it? Well, no, that was not the problem—he knew, but would she? What could he explain to her? He put his arms around her and gazed thoughtfully over her head at the odds and ends of machinery she had been stringing together. The screen flickered and sprang into illumination.

He glared at it for interrupting his thoughts. It seemed to him he had just discovered something very significant and if he'd had a few more minutes he'd have been able to say it in a way he'd never forget. But there was a shape on the screen and he couldn't ignore it. The image wavered in and out of focus, growing clearer as the machine learned to hold it steady.

It was a ship.

A ship. He dropped his hands. "Don't give up on me. I'm not going to run out on you." Was it his imagination that the ship was growing larger? His throat was dry and tight. The last thing he wanted to see was a ship.

"I don't know what we can do about this, Nona, but come on. We'll see."

She leaned against the wall, showing no inclination to follow. She seemed to be disturbed but he would guess it was not about the same thing he was. "Come on," he said. "We've got to tell the others."

And still she didn't move. "I can't stay here," he muttered and kissed her. He started walking away fast so he'd be able to leave.

She could tell that he was upset by the unexpected appearance of the ship on the scanner. Perhaps he thought they were alone in space, that emptiness was lonely. He ought to have known better. She had seen it long ago, and guessed what it meant. It would have to be overcome.

What she couldn't understand was what happened to her when he touched her. Others had tried to come close and either she minded or was indifferent and they went away. But this was surely outside of her experience. She thought it meant something to touch a machine and to know therefrom what it was. But to come in contact with him and to learn all at once what he was—yes and herself too... The warm soft mechanism that she was behaved strangely—never the same way twice.

And now she was becoming confused—because she would always feel this when he was near—and she didn't mind.

She closed her eyes and could see him more clearly. (What was choice?)

Docchi walked on, carefully skirting one of the columns that supported the dome. Once it had seemed huge and unshakable and now it was remarkably slender. The dome itself was hardly adequate to keep the darkness overhead from descending. This was the dull side of their rotation; they were looking back at the way they'd come. The stars were gray and faint. "Where did you see it?" he asked after a long silence.

"In the place Jordan described. It's deep underground but I believe it's near one of the piles. I felt the wall and it was warm."

"Somewhere below the gravity computer," said Docchi. "Why there, I don't know, but Nona may have had a reason. What I want to know is: how do you account for the ship?"

"What?" said Cameron. "Oh, I leave that to you and Jordan. I can't explain it."

Docchi guessed why the doctor was less concerned than he, tried to be. Let him live with his exaltation for a while. It might not last. "Part of it's easy, how the ship came to be there."

"It isn't to me," said Cameron. "We haven't been gone long, not much more than a month."

"Six weeks to be exact. Six weeks on our calendar."

"I see, relative time. I heard we were approaching the speed of light but I didn't think we were close enough to make any difference." He glanced at his watch as if it held secrets he couldn't fathom. "How long have we actually been gone, Earth time?"

"I don't know. We haven't any figures on our acceleration rate nor our present speed."

"What are you planning to do? We can't just sit here and let them overtake us."

"I don't know. We're not helpless." Docchi's plans were vague. There was much that had to be determined before he could decide on anything. "You're certain it's one of ours? It's not an alien ship?"

The idea hadn't occurred to Cameron. He turned the image around in his mind before he answered. "I'm not familiar with ship classifications, but it's ours unless these aliens use the English language. There was a name on it. I could read part. It ended in *tory.*"

"The Victory class," said Docchi. "The biggest thing built. At one time it was intended for interstellar service, before the gravity drive fizzled."

"That's how they were able to do it," said Cameron. "I've been wondering how they were able to send a ship after us so soon, even allowing for the fact that we've been gone longer than it seems to us, maybe two or three months instead of six weeks."

He had nothing definite to go on but in Docchi's opinion the time was closer to half a year. "Right. Since the ships were already there rusting in the spaceport all they had to do was clean them up and add an information unit to the drive. They may have started work on it while we were in the solar system. When they were still looking for Nona."

The special irony was that our own discoveries were being used against them. Nona's first, the resurrected drive, and then his own not negligible contribution. Docchi himself had told them. His thoughtless remark that the drive would function without Nona had been relayed back to Earth. Vogel the engineer had probably picked it up and sent the information on. Someone would have chanced upon the idea anyway, but he had given them weeks. And a week was of incalculable importance—planets could be won or lost.

Cameron was silent as they walked on. "There's a ship but we don't know where. Let's not worry until we find where it's going."

Docchi didn't answer. That the scanner Nona had built was capable of detecting a ship between the stars indicated a tremendous range—old style. But distances had shrunk lately. There was a ship behind them and it wasn't far. Neither was it on a pleasure jaunt.

At the hospital steps they conferred briefly and then separated, Cameron leaving to find Jeriann. Docchi went into his office and tried unsuccessfully to locate Jordan.

Ultimately he gave it up. Jordan had his own ideas of what was important and lately had been mysteriously concerned with some undertaking he refused to disclose. He had even tried to conceal that there was something he was working on. Docchi switched his efforts and finally contacted Webber. At a time like this they needed what support they could get. Webber was not a substitute for Jordan but he'd do. The person he'd most have liked to have along was Anti but she couldn't leave the prison, her tank. They missed her. They always would as long as she was confined.

Docchi sat down while he waited for Webber. He needed the rest. He had been hoping that the pursuit would not begin as soon as it had. They would find some way to throw off the ship behind them—but it was not the biggest threat.

"Do you suppose she hid here when the guards were looking for her?" said Webber.

"Doesn't seem likely," said Docchi, trying to keep up. The other's composite body gave him strength he wasn't aware of. Docchi couldn't match the effortless stride, the endurance. "Guards searched here too."

They had, but how thoroughly? The asteroid had once been a planet, a world with an atmosphere, oceans, lakes, streams. Water had seeped into the ground, creating imperceptible, weaknesses in the crust. And long ago when the catastrophe came it had struck suddenly. The planet had been split with such violence that whole chunks had been hurled apart, each one intact except that the shock had enlarged on the work begun by water. Faults became underground caverns, tortuous caverns in the rock that intersected the man-made tunnel.

No matter what their orders were, the guards wouldn't have been anxious to explore too far. Under the stress of unusual gravity fissures could close again on the unwary—it was possible they'd made only a token search here.

"If we come here often there ought to be an easier way than this," said Webber as they went along.

Docchi had been thinking of it. He would be able to tell when he saw it whether it would be possible to move the scanner. If so a good place might be in gravity center. As nearly as he could tell it was almost directly overhead.

Voices sprang out of the tunnel as they neared the destination. "Don't know what's keeping them," grumbled Jordan. "Maybe we ought not to wait."

"He was looking for you," said Jeriann, her voice carrying in the stillness of the underground. "He said it was urgent for you to be here."

"A few minutes won't hurt," said Cameron. "Lucky we found you when we did or you'd have missed it."

"What do you mean, lucky?" growled Jordan. "I was on my way here when you yelled."

"Have you seen it in operation?" said Jeriann. "Cameron said you found the place."

"If I had I'd have told you. The scanner wasn't finished last time I was here. I figured Nona would let us know when she was ready."

The tunnel turned sharply and though they could hear Jordan's voice the words were indistinct. It was a quirk of acoustics because, as they travelled on, utter silence descended. They could hear nothing at all until the tunnel curved again and they entered the cavern.

He glanced around once before they were noticed. The nine geepee heads Cameron had described were almost indiscernible under the mass of circuitry that covered them. Nona had improved the scanner. He could identify some of the components but the arrangement was totally unfamiliar.

He thought he could trace the basic outline. It was a gravity device of some kind, what kind he wasn't sure. If he had thought about it previously he would have realized it practically had to be that.

"They're here," said Jeriann at his side, and he hadn't seen how she'd got there. Seconds before she'd been arguing with Jordan and now she was next to him.

Jordan looked up and Nona clipped a few connections in place. She stayed close to the doctor. "We all know what we came for so there's no need for preliminaries," said Docchi. "Cameron, can you tell Nona to start the scanner?"

"My communication is rather primitive," said Cameron with a slight smile. "However—" He had no time to say more, Nona didn't move but the scanner responded.

A shape glowed, a vague nebula, far away. It came closer and the nebula dissolved—it was a ship. There was darkness all around and yet the ship wasn't dark. The lights that streamed out of the ports couldn't account for this, there was nothing to reflect it on the hull. Radar was one explanation, a gravity radar. The impulses left the asteroid, traversed the space to the far away object and bounced back—in no time.

"It's a military ship," said Jordan. "The biggest."

The ship rocked a little or perhaps the scanner resolved the image better. The name began to swing into sight. "Tory," repeated Webber when he was able to read it. "Victory. And victory always ends with *tory.*"

"Star Victory," said Jeriann as the ship rotated and the full name grew visible. "They're premature. They haven't won yet."

"But how far away?" growled Jordan. "We ought to know the power of the screen."

The scanner wasn't calibrated and so they didn't know the distance. Later Nona might add that refinement but if she didn't there was practically no way of telling her what they wanted. Now there was merely a three quarter view, the nose of the ship and enough to make out that the rockets weren't flaring. Gravity drive of course. But they knew that.

"We've seen it," said Webber flatly. "Now what?"

"We're not going to let them take us," said Jeriann. "Docchi will think of something."

Her confidence wasn't warranted. Actually he'd done little to bring them this far. Intellectual force perhaps. He had turned discontent into something positive—and joint action had so far overcome the obstacles. But it was Nona who had given them the power to make the action worthwhile. And she was limited too—there would come an end to the seemingly endless flow of invention. There were circumstances against which no ingenuity could prevail.

At the present they needed more to go on. They knew there was a ship behind them. The relationship had to be defined. Space was vast and they might be able to elude the pursuer. They had to find out where the ship was.

They looked at Nona. She was standing close to Cameron, very close. She seemed to know what was expected of her, a mass rapport. She touched the doctor wonderingly as he smiled down at her and then she went to the scanner, working on it, changing the connections with negligent skill.

The ship wavered as she worked. It disappeared for seconds and when it came back it was rapidly approaching the viewing surface of the scanner. Closer—they touched the hull—and then they were inside, gazing out of a screen.

Jordan frowned. "They've duplicated the drive—have they duplicated her scanner?"

"I don't think so," said Docchi. "They have telescreens of short range. But there's no reason why two completely different systems can't be spliced together."

They were looking at an empty room and no one came in. Impatiently Nona touched the connections and the scene dissolved, shifted and blurred and when it cleared they were elsewhere, another screen, a different room. A broad-shouldered man hunched over a desk, muttering and scratching his scalp. He signed his name several times; one of the sheets he crumpled and discarded, first tearing out his signature. The rest of the documents he dispatched in a slot.

When he turned around they saw it was General Judd.

He reached hastily for the switch but withdrew his hand before it got there. "Well, the orphans have come back, hand in hand." He smirked with calm deliberation. "Or should I say arm in arm, Cameron?"

Docchi noticed it if no one else did. The general hadn't called Cameron a doctor. As far as the Medicouncil was concerned Cameron probably no longer was. It was the final proof, if Docchi had needed it, of which side Cameron was on.

"We have a whole new alignment," continued the general. "Cameron with Nona, and our rebellious engineer with Jeriann."

Docchi's face began to glitter but he caught the light as it surged through his veins, willing it to stop before it showed in his skin. "We haven't come back, general. We didn't think it would hurt to talk, though, if you don't mind."

"I never mind a little chat, Docchi. Always willing to hear what the other fellow has to say—as long as he comes to the point."

The general thought his position was strong enough that he could be as insulting as he wanted. He was very nearly right. "First we'd like to know what you want."

"Our terms haven't changed a bit. Turn around and go back." Judd smiled broadly, an official wolfish expression. "We don't insist you return to the same orbit. In fact it might be better if you moved the asteroid closer to Earth."

Where the Medicouncil could keep a perpetual watch. And where they would swing through the heavens forever in sight of Earth but never a part of it. "Naturally we don't accept," said Docchi. "However we don't reject negotiations completely. There are some of us who might go back for one reason or another—homesickness mostly. If you're willing we can make arrangements to transfer them to your ship."

"Ah, trouble," said the general gravely, trying to conceal his delight. "And I think I know where the trouble is. We came fully prepared for every emergency that we—or you—might meet. The Medicouncil is very thorough."

The picture of Maureen crouched in a darkened room, whimpering through clenched teeth that she didn't want ever to see anyone. The tautness as one set of muscles extended her hand toward the door and another set tore it away. And there were other images, vague now, but in time they could become threatening.

The Medicouncil had foreseen this; there were biologicals on the ship to cure Maureen. Docchi's face twitched and he hoped the general didn't notice. "I haven't checked to see how many are willing to go with you. I will, if it's satisfactory."

"Don't bother," said the general. "In case you weren't listening, I didn't say that we're a cozy little group of altruists, just anxious as hell to take over your responsibilities. The biologicals are here. You'll get them when we land a crew to make sure you do go back. My orders are very plain. We want all of you—or none."

"You know what we'll say," said Docchi. "None of us, of course." The letdown was less than he expected. He'd half known the conditions; it was consistent with all the attitudes toward accidentals— once human but now not quite. It was a typical way to ease their conscience—load the ship with every medical supply—and then refuse those in need unless they all came back. "We're getting along quite nicely without your help," he continued, and if it was less true than he liked, it was more so than the general realized. "One thing, Judd, don't try to land *without* our consent."

"So you still think we're stupid," said the general affably, at ease in the situation. *He didn't expect us to surrender,* thought Docchi. *Then why had he asked?* "We won't attempt to land until you cooperate. You will. Sooner or later you will."

"I hardly think so. We decided that a long time ago."

The general shrugged. "Suit yourself. Remember we're not vindictive, we're not trying to punish you. We do insist that you're sick and helpless. You'll have to come back and be placed under competent medical care." He glanced amusedly at Cameron.

"You don't act as if we're helpless," said Jeriann.

"Dangerously sick," said the general. "Have you ever heard of hysteria, in which the patient must be protected against himself—and he may hurt others?" He was fingering a chart on the desk, had been all the while he was talking. He examined it briefly and then looked up. "What goes on here? How can you talk across this distance?"

"It took you a long time to realize it, general. We're not right next to you." Again it was Docchi's bad habit to talk too much but there was a reason for it and this time he wasn't telling the general anything he wouldn't figure out for himself.

The general's jaw hardened and he pawed futilely at the switch. "How do we do it?" said Docchi. "It's our secret." But the general didn't reply and he wouldn't reveal the information Docchi wanted. Nona finally broke the connection at her end.

Webber breathed noisily as the image faded. He stamped the mechanical foot, echoes rolling through the cavern. "Will somebody tell me why the general's so polite? Why won't he land unless we ask him to?"

"It's not consideration," said Docchi. "The asteroid's much larger than his ship, and nearly as fast. Did you ever try to land on a stationary port?"

Webber looked abashed. "I keep forgetting we're moving."

"Sure. Aside from the fact we could smash his ship and it wouldn't inconvenience us unless it hit the dome, not a very large part of the total surface, what else can he do? Come close and try to send out men in space suits? We veer off and leave them stranded until he picks them up. If he wants to we'll play tag half way across the galaxy with him."

"So he can't land," said Webber, gaining assurance. "Why didn't I think of the reasons?"

"Because one man can't figure out everything," said Jeriann. "If there was just Nona we'd still be back in the solar system. Or Docchi by himself, or Jordan, or Anti. Together we get the answers."

So far—but it might not always hold true. Docchi was worried by the general's lack of concern. He hadn't expected to contact the accidentals but when they'd got in touch with him he wasn't startled. He knew what to do because he had been told. He wasn't a fast thinker who could improvise, his specialty was carrying out a plan.

But if Judd was not at first disconcerted he'd made up for it when he became aware they weren't using conventional communication. Docchi would have given a lot to see the chart the general had. He'd tried to provoke the officer but the ruse hadn't been effective. The general knew the distance between the ship and the asteroid, but he hadn't revealed it.

Webber walked noisily to the scanner, peering into the circuits. "The general's communication experts will be working overtime for a while," he remarked.

"For the rest of the voyage. They'll know the scanner's a gravity device but that won't help them." It was another count against them. Communication at practically unlimited range was not a prize easily given up.

But what they really wanted was Nona. Indirectly she'd given them back the gravity drive, and now this. And they would think, rightly, that there was more where these inventions came from.

He wished Anti were here to advise them. Docchi looked around to ask Jordan about her but he was already gone. Cameron was standing quietly in a corner with Nona, talking to her in a low voice while she smiled and smiled. Webber was still looking into the scanner.

Only Jeriann was waiting for him. Now that the general had mentioned it, Docchi wondered if she really was waiting for him—and for how long.

CHAPTER TWELVE

ANTI looked up at the dome. It was all she could see with comfort. Stars changed less than she would have believed. The patterns were substantially the same as on Earth. Brightness varied with rotation, that was the main difference. Now those overhead were brilliant and that meant she was facing the direction they were travelling. She wondered which was Alpha and which Proxima Centauri. She never had been able to recognize them.

She extended one arm, splashing acid. Lately there were times she had to keep moving if she didn't want to freeze. It wasn't pleasant but she could endure it for the sake of walking someday. There were degrees of helplessness and no one else, even here, was completely immobilized, confined completely to a specialized environment. She had forgotten much of the past and couldn't see far into the future. Perhaps it wasn't worth looking into.

"Quiet, you'll scare the fish."

She paddled around until she could see Jordan. "If you find fish who can live in this, throw them in. I'll welcome any kind of company."

"Maybe Cameron can mutate fish to stand the cold," suggested Jordan. "Or if that fails he can always transfer the fungus to them."

"I don't wish it on anything, even a fish."

"It wouldn't hurt. Besides, it might make them immortal."

"Thanks. I like fish, but not as playmates. They're better on a plate."

"Barbaric," said Jordan. "I prefer scientific food, synthetics. Wholly removed from the taint of the living creature. Something that didn't die in quick agony so that you could smack your lips. Germ free, compounded of balanced elements."

"Came from nature myself," said Anti. "Uncivilized though it is, I prefer nutrition from the same source."

"You're confusing yourself," commented Jordan. "Synthetics contain everything necessary for life. When was the last time Jeriann ate?"

"Longer than she cares to remember. Besides you're quibbling. She gets concentrates, which is not the same as synthetics."

"A minor point," conceded Jordan, coming closer. "However I didn't intend to talk about food."

"I don't care what it is as long as you talk. I need conversation too."

"There's Nona," began Jordan.

"Exceptions, exceptions. What do I care except that I get tired of staring up at nothing? Sometimes I wish they'd planted the tank at the entrance to the hospital. People'd have to stop and talk."

"For a while I was thinking of that."

"No you don't," said Anti. "There are useful things that have to be done."

"I abandoned the idea when I considered what your viewpoint would be. But we did move the tank once."

"Never again. Anyway geepees are scarce and who else could do it?"

"I could," said Jordan. He added quickly: "It's a joke." He swung along the tank until he was as close as he could get without toppling in. "Instead of something you'd forget once I left, I brought a gift."

"What is it? I can't see from this angle."

"It's a belt."

"You doll. It's beautiful."

"No it's not—merely wonderful."

"I know. Save it for me, till later. It will go swoosh if acid touches it."

"It positively will not react. I took care of that. There are some metals that are just about inert. It wasn't easy to cover it but I did."

"You made it for me. You shouldn't have."

Jordan puzzled himself with it. He hadn't much to do with it. At the most he'd made a protective covering for it. Nona was solely responsible for the way it functioned. And there was no doubt whom she intended it for; that was why he hadn't hesitated taking it. And yet, why hadn't she turned it over to Anti? It was working perfectly the first time he saw it.

The logical answer was that it wasn't in operating condition, that she couldn't make it work and had laid it aside for further inspiration. But this led to nonsensical conclusions involving the repair robot. He refused to accept the conclusions. "Let's say I didn't make it entirely. I added to what was existing." He swung the belt out to her.

"Are you sure it will fit? I'm quite big."

"Originally it wouldn't. I had to make it longer."

Anti examined the belt at length. "Hammered link effect. Primitive but striking."

Jordan blushed. "I thought it was a pretty smooth job. I had to do it by hand."

"It is," exclaimed Anti. "You have a strong unconscious sense of design." With trepidation she lowered it in the acid and when nothing happened she fastened it. "There," she said in triumph. "The first piece of jewelry in years. I feel like a new woman."

"You are, Anti. Believe me, you are."

She laughed giddily. "It's silly, but I do believe it. It's amazing what jewelry will do for a woman."

"It's not exactly jewelry." Jordan tried to think of how to explain it. Anti was unscientific, or better—pre-scientific. "Think of it as a complicated machine that's remotely connected to your mind."

"My mind? Am I supposed to be telepathic now? Is that what it is? Can I talk with anyone, no matter at what distance they are?"

"No, you're not telepathic except well maybe in a certain way."

Jordan was silent, trying to sort the explanation. It never occurred to her that machines operated at different levels, many of them, simultaneously, electrical or electromagnetic, others more subtle. Jordan gave up. "Think of what you'd most like to do."

"It's no use, Jordan. I won't torment myself. I know how long it's going to take."

He should have kept it and demonstrated. That would have convinced her. He would never forget the first time he had worn it— and nearly frightened himself off the ceiling. He cast about for other ways but nothing else was necessary. Anti was thinking of what she'd forbidden herself to contemplate.

"There," said Jordan, his voice rough with pride. "I knew you'd get the hang of it."

"Why didn't you say so?" said Anti. "The gravity computer. My mind and *that* mind."

For a pre-scientific person she'd grasped the essentials quickly. "Jordan, maybe you should keep it," she called. "You can use it as well as I can."

"I don't need it," he said. "Nobody's heard me complaining. And you can't, or couldn't move." He gazed at her in alarm. "Come on down," he shouted. "You can't catch the stars by yourself."

"You think I can't?" said Anti. "I'll come closer to it than anyone who ever lived."

Nevertheless she obeyed his instructions, sinking slowly until her feet touched the ground. The grass crackled and smoldered, though it was green, bursting into flame where she walked as the acid dripped down. And it was walking, though her legs carried only a fraction of her real weight. The rest of the weight was destroyed for her convenience by the gravity computer as it responded continually and repeatedly to her unspoken commands.

"The doctor will be surprised," muttered Jordan.

"Not as much as I am," said Anti. "I can fly if I want, but do you know, I'd rather walk."

Docchi teetered on the chair. Not much: if he fell he had no way of stopping himself, and there was the devil's own time getting up. "I'm speechless," he said.

"So was Cameron," said Anti.

"I imagine. He didn't expect his prognosis to be disproved so soon." Docchi righted the chair. "This is the thing Jordan's been working on."

"He said he didn't have much to do with it. He would."

Anti moved warily. The acid soaked robe had stopped dripping but there was enough left to react with subdued violence if she came into contact with the wrong substance. "The best is I'm already stronger—using my muscles more. I don't have an exact way of knowing since there aren't gadgets and dials in my mind but it seems to me I can support a lot more of my weight. Maybe I can walk unaided at quarter gravity."

Docchi let the calls, of which there were several, go unattended. It was the first big personal victory for any accidental and it was heartening amidst the general uncertainties. "Fine, fine. But how long can you continue? Won't you revert?"

"Cameron says I won't. He made several tests which indicate the virulence of the fungus. He says the body conquers."

And for her it had. The biological mechanism had reached the point of strength wherein it could contain the attenuated invasion with little outside help. After some indefinite period the menace would be reduced, finally vanquished, utterly and forever. The body conquered.

"Cameron says it will be enough to sleep in the tank. I don't mind, though I won't get much sleep. I feel the cold now, though not as much as anyone else would.

"For the rest I'll increase the weight on my legs as much as I can. It's almost automatic; no buttons to push except mentally. If I get tired I think myself lighter."

The mechanism couldn't be improved on. It was a portable null gravity field that fit neatly around her and touched nothing else. And if Anti had reported Jordan's views correctly, it was impossible to build another like it because they didn't have the parts. It was an excellent device but not of great importance except to Anti. Jordan could use one too and so could a number of others though they wouldn't get it. It replaced legs and was more efficient in all respects save appearance.

There was nothing, however, that was a substitute for hands.

"Now that you're up and moving, what do you want to do?" he said. "You must be anxious to get busy."

"It's a funny thing but I'm not," she said. "It sounds queer but I want to look around. I haven't seen anything except what I could glimpse from the tank."

Docchi rocked back; he'd always thought of her as knowing more about the asteroid than anyone else. In a personal sense, she did, having been there longer than anyone he could name. It was said she may even have been responsible for the building of the asteroid, so they'd have some place to put her. It might be true. "Go ahead. Jordan will show you around. You don't have to be in a hurry to take a job."

Anti rose a few inches to show that she could. "First I want to visit the laboratory Nona has. I want to see the ship that's after us. I know they haven't given up just because they can't land."

He felt so too though he hadn't figured out what they could do. "Let me know if anything occurs to you."

When she left, walking by preference, the responsibilities came back, Maureen and other deficients with various degrees of disability, the ship with undetermined resources behind them, stars and planets ahead of them, unknown or vaguely guessed at, mysterious. They'd reach their goal but all of the accidentals might not survive.

Anti alone was better off but there were others who were not. It was depressing at times, so much freedom and so little to show for it. Docchi went back to work but the image of the ship kept rising up out of the countless important and unimportant decisions he had to make. What did they plan to do?

Late the following day Anti returned. She marched in determinedly and sat down. It was no longer remarkable that a few chairs would fit her. She'd never be mistaken for someone else, but her bulk had diminished considerably and her weight was whatever she wanted. That the chair didn't collapse in a soggy mass or burst into flame was an indication that Jordan had found a way to neutralize the acid that clung to her without reducing the medical effectiveness. "Nice place we have," she remarked. "Didn't realize it was so pretty."

"There are others who disagree."

"They don't really see it. The only thing I don't like is the ship."

"Neither do I. What do you think?"

"Well—" Anti hesitated. "What did it look like to you?"

He described it as he remembered, answering the questions with which she kept interrupting. After he finished she was silent, nodding to herself as if he wasn't there. "You know what I think," she said. "You saw it three quarters, from the front. When I looked it was flatter. They're gaining."

Docchi glanced out the window. "Anti, they can't land here unless we let them—and we won't. What else can they do?"

"It's a military ship. They've got the force to stop us."

"Not without shattering the dome, or blowing the place apart. And they won't. You don't cure a sick person by killing him, and for their own peace of mind they've convinced themselves that we're sick."

"So we're safe there," commented Anti dubiously. "They figured at first they'd sneak up and land before we knew it. The scanner squashed that. But they had other plans from the very beginning, what they'd do if we discovered them in time." She nodded and nodded. "Well, if it was me and I couldn't stop somebody, I'd try to get where they're going before they did. It ties right in, doesn't it? They don't want us to contact aliens. All they have to do is get there first."

Of course. It was very plain, but anxiety had prevented his seeing it. Fearfulness was often next door to stupidity. Whoever got there first controlled the situation even more than Anti realized. He began to suspect the depth of preparation that was against them, the intense fury and careful planning they had to overcome. Mankind was capable of more hatred for its own kind than it ever expended against outsiders. Methodically Docchi began kicking open switches.

"You're right, Anti," he said. "But I think there are ways to see that they don't get there first." He was lying blithely, perhaps as much because he didn't want to face what he foresaw. "If those don't work, and there's a chance they won't, we have an unexpected ally."

"Who?"

"Not who, what. Distance." It was a most preposterous untruth. "If we don't get there in time we'll let them have both of the Centauris. We'll go on to the next star."

"You can always think of some way out," said Anti as tiny lights began to flash on the panel. The flickering confusion there matched his emotions.

"Jordan?" he said urgently when the latter appeared on the screen. And after that there was Webber and anyone else who knew something about electronics or could be taught with a minimum of instruction. They were willing to drive themselves to exhaustion but there was no substitute for technical superiority.

"Now don't worry," said Anti after he'd finished summoning everyone who could help. "I have a feeling they can't stop us no matter what they do."

"That so?" he said. "Which toe tells you that, or is it an ache in your bones? Think it will rain tomorrow?"

"Don't laugh," said Anti, rising and leaving with him as he hurried out. "I have confidence in what we're able to do together."

It was a good thing someone did.

"Maureen's getting worse," said Jeriann. "I need more power." There was a tiny bead of sweat on her temple, the first Docchi had seen since ordinarily she didn't perspire.

"How much worse? I'd like to see her."

Jeriann made a final adjustment on the machine but didn't straighten up immediately as if it disturbed her to contemplate what went on in her own mind. She snapped the synthesizer on and turned around, brushing the hair away from her eyes. "Do you think your diagnosis is better than Cameron's?"

"I wasn't doubting his ability."

"You'll have to take our word for it. I can see her because I'm a woman and she hardly reacts to me. Cameron can visit her because she's been conditioned to accept him. Even so he has to take precautions. The hypnotics control only the surface of her mind."

"What precautions?"

"Sprays that plasticize his skin. By now her senses are far keener than ours. The doctor has a cosmetic technician recreate his face, something impersonal with which she had no association."

"I'll take your word for it. I don't want to see her under those conditions. But you didn't answer my question: how much worse?"

The smock was clearly a laboratory garment to protect the wearer from chemical irritation and the chemicals from human contamination. It was only incidental there was a certain light in which it was almost transparent. Jeriann became aware she was standing in such a light and swished the smock angrily around her and moved out of the illumination. "I can tell you this: neither Cameron nor I will be responsible for keeping her alive longer than three weeks, *unless I get that power.*"

"Is this what Cameron said?"

"It's my own idea. I know more about this machine than he does. But you can ask him. He'll back me up."

Docchi didn't doubt her but there was more to think of than the fate of one individual. "You're just guessing, aren't you? There's a chance, if you experiment wildly enough, you'll find the right compounds."

"Please," said Jeriann, "It will only be for a few weeks. Less than that if it works the way I think it will."

"What about the other deficients? They need biologicals too."

"They can wait and Maureen can't."

Reluctantly he gave consent. "Then you can have all the power you need, for the next few days anyway. After that we'll see."

"You're a dear." Jeriann walked through the lab, inspecting it critically from every angle. "Of course I'll need help. Part of the trouble is that we can't get enough power to the machine, we're not using it to the full capacity. With larger power connections we'll be able to turn out stuff we haven't touched on before."

He shook his head. "That wasn't in the bargain. You can have all the power the existing lines will take. But we can't spare men to install new lines. The technicians we have are busy elsewhere."

"It's such a little thing," she coaxed. "The machine's not a sledge hammer that smashes molecules apart and then crushes them into a new chemical alignment. It's a keen instrument, an ultramicrosize knife that slits delicately here and there and then slides the separated atoms together to form a different molecule."

"I'm not arguing about power," he said adamantly. "I said you can have it and you can. Trained men you can't. I'll see if I can spare them after what they're working on is finished."

She stopped as if she'd stumbled into a taut wire she hadn't noticed. She looked at him thoughtfully and strolled back to the synthesizer, under the light that shone down and provocatively through the smock. She wore other clothing but that too seemed almost to vanish. "For me, won't you? Just a few men for a few days. It means a lot to Maureen."

"I can't let you have technicians now," he said obstinately.

She glanced at him curiously, sauntering closer as if to get a better look. "I forgot. Cameron has Nona, hasn't he? They're going to get married as soon as he can figure out a simple ceremony. And now you hate women, don't you? That's why you won't give Maureen the same chance you'd give a man."

He rocked back under the cold hatred. He had no idea she was capable of such venom. "You're reading into my emotions something that was never there. I'm glad Nona found someone she can respond to. But why are you so concerned with Maureen? You never liked her."

"What rationalization," she said bitterly. "It makes no difference what I thought about her. She's going to die if I don't help her, and I will. I'd expect the same from anyone else."

"Jeriann," he said but she was gone, tearing the smock off and thrusting in on a hook, leaving him alone beside a machine that alternately hummed and purred in oily accents. He stared at it with complete lack of interest as the cycle changed. The synthesizer grunted with satisfied pride and three drops of a colorless fluid were discharged into a retort.

If there was no other way they could save Maureen by contacting the expedition behind them. They had the supplies Jeriann was trying vainly to duplicate. But that was surrender and the only alternative was to go ahead as planned.

Docchi left the laboratory, taking the long way around to avoid the doctor's office. Cameron wouldn't put the same pressure on him that Jeriann had—no one could. Why did she have to think he was responsible?

CHAPTER THIRTEEN

THE dimensions of the place were fear, panic and loneliness. It was no-time or all-time, the endless instant of survival—or less. It was light or it wasn't, the illumination of the closed mind, the intellect turned in on itself, perception curled backward while it reached for the outside world. It was a universe which neither existed nor would ever quite vanish.

And there wasn't a sound. To the distorted senses, wavering and uncertain, sounds could be masculine. "Yes?" said Maureen poutingly. "Where are you now?" But she couldn't hear what she said. So she stopped speaking.

It was forbidden.

The bloodstream left her heart and had no path but to return deviously. It travelled darkly with many branches, pounding, flushed with oxygen from the lung machines. The mind was turned inward. The body was turned inward. Life had no place to go. It was out of balance.

Her feet touched the floor and she got out of bed. The flesh was heavy. The tube in her chest whistled with exertion. There was oxygen, too much of it, but there was no substitute for the regulative substances her body didn't have. She was falling apart, pulled apart by the wild dissimilar tendencies of all her cells.

She kept on walking until she lunged against a wall. Her nose splayed to one side but her veins weren't ready to bleed. There was nothing to tell them to let out the red drops. She fell down and got up, walking on, banging against the wall.

She could never find anyone she knew. After a while she realized the person she missed most was herself.

Why was it light without being light and dark with no darkness? Her eyes had forgotten they were supposed to see. She sat down in the middle of the floor and began plucking at the hospital gown, pulling it apart thread by thread. Her mind said she didn't feel what she touched but she didn't believe everything. She practiced playing tricks on her thoughts. There were so many tricks to play and such few thoughts.

She sat there, pretending to listen to something that nobody said. She waved her fingers languidly and closed her eyes with deep regret, lips curved for the kiss that wasn't given.

Cameron came in and hurried out after one glimpse, calling for Jeriann. The deterioration was proceeding more rapidly than he expected. There were not three weeks left. It might be less than three days.

Webber nodded and went on working, aware that Anti was watching the coordination of his dissimilar arms and legs. It didn't disturb the rhythm of his movements. Anti moved to the other side to get a better view of what he was doing and as she did so remembered what she'd come for.

"So that's why I couldn't get a book. What's wrong?"

"Nothing. We're tearing it down to move it."

"Why move it? This is where the books are."

He bent over the mechanism, disconnecting it. "I don't know. You'll have to ask Docchi."

He knew but was too engrossed to stop. Jordan could tell her but he wasn't here. She wandered through the library but found no one who could or would give her information. What made it worse was, with the librarian torn apart, there wasn't a book available.

She was curiously perturbed. She knew where she could find Docchi, at gravity center where he had taken over the quarters formerly occupied by Vogel. More and more the asteroid was beginning to resemble a ship and if there was a definite control area it was located in gravity center.

The first thing she saw when she entered the low structure—most of the gravity installation was underground—was the scanner. It had changed; the last trace of the makeshift origin had disappeared. It was metal encased and dials and switches replaced connections formerly made by hand. These alterations were Nona's but bringing it here was Docchi's idea. Anti frowned contemplatively; it wasn't far in straight distances from where Nona had originally constructed it, but the labor involved in carrying it through miles of tunnels and then overland to where it was now standing—that was considerable effort. It didn't square with what Jeriann had told her.

She found Docchi a few stories below the entrance level, somewhere near the actual gravity computers. He looked up and then wriggled his head out of the harness. "Have you come to help, Anti?"

"Nope. I've got a complaint."

His smile wasn't appreciative. "The headquarters for that are in the other division."

She ignored the reference to Jeriann. "I'd help if I could but I'm ignorant. And you're keeping me from learning."

"The library?"

"Of course. I can't get a single book."

He looked at the design he'd been working on and then reluctantly stepped out of the machine which enabled him to put his ideas on paper.

"Don't stop drawing because of me," said Anti.

"It was nearly done. Jordan can carry on from there." He sat down while Anti remained standing, balancing an imaginary basket of fruit on her head. The years in the tank had ruined her posture.

"I'm sorry we had to take the librarian but you can still get books. I've figured out a formula."

"First I have to be a mathematician and then I've got to crawl back in the stacks? There must be places no one can get to, especially tapes and music."

"That's the way it is. We'll have to go over the whole setup, relocate the stacks and train human librarians."

"Seems like a waste when what we had was working perfectly."

"We had to do it if we want to get to Centauri before they do." He jerked his head to indicate out there.

142

"But what good is it? The librarian is just a—" She closed her mouth.

"Just a memory system? That's what we need to duplicate the drive they have. Of course the librarian remembers the wrong thing but we're changing that."

"Can't we do it in some other way?"

"Not in time with the facilities we have. Maybe Nona could but the rest of us are just humans."

"Well, what's wrong with her?"

"Nothing. If you can get her interested in building a control unit I'll step aside."

"Why build it? She *is* the control."

"Now she is, but there are a number of reasons why a mechanical control is better. For one thing we don't know how much of her attention it requires. The drive may not function at all when she isn't consciously thinking about it."

"But the gravity never stops."

"True, but does it apply to acceleration? We can't measure that."

"You're working on a lot of suppositions—it may do this—it may not do that."

"We don't have to guess at one thing, Anti. The expedition is gaining on us. And they are using a mechanical control."

Anti looked over at the drawing Docchi had made. A bunch of squiggles. "You know more about it than I do. If it's your opinion that this is what we should have, then we ought to. To me it seems that another kind of control won't make much difference."

"Review what we have. A nuclear pile that supplies all the power, a set of gravity coils, and three computers. One computer figures the gravity for the asteroid. Another calculates the propulsive force. The third, we think, actuates the scanner. Nona may rotate the duties among the computers and the unit we're building will do the same.

"But this is what we can do that Nona doesn't: we'll cut everything to a minimum except the drive. Gravity, light, heat, all the personal conveniences will be cut to the least we can stand."

Anti rose a few inches and thought herself back to the floor. "This is what you'll do if it works the way you imagine."

"It will, Anti." Docchi's face was set. "Nona's too considerate. As long as she has it she won't impose the sacrifices we're glad to make ourselves. We're taking it out of her hands."

If they needed somebody to make hard decisions, Docchi was the man. It was a crusade with him and he was willing to drive everyone the same as himself. Anti looked at his face and decided against the question she'd come to ask. "Sounds grim, but you're right. We're willing if there's a chance we'll get there first. What can I do to help?"

"Reorganize the library. Get assistants to reach in the places too small for you. Collect the medical texts first. Cameron may need them."

"A thankless job," muttered Anti. "I started out to read a book."

Docchi smiled. "I thought you had enough of sedentary life."

"I have, but not enough of books. Picture and music tapes were easy to get in the tank but they didn't make acid proof books. Limited demand, I suppose."

"Here's the formula I've worked out. Books are selected according to subject and author, filed according to size and date received." He went over the procedure until she had it straight. "I guess I can do it," she said dubiously. "But why not start at one end and go through to the other side of the stacks?"

"You've got to segregate the medical references first."

Belated compensation because he had refused Jeriann? Perhaps, but he was not that simple. If anything it was just recognition of what came first in importance. "A tedious job," she grumbled as she started to leave.

"It is. But, except for what we are as persons and what we create in the future, it's the total of our human heritage. It's the last we'll get."

"Sometimes I believe—" said Anti. "Oh, never mind what a huge old woman thinks." She went out the door and when she came back seconds later Docchi was again drawing.

"Yes, Anti?"

"You can start cutting down on me. I won't mind."

"When it's necessary I'll take you up on it. I don't think it will be. It doesn't take much power to run the computers and they're always functioning anyway. And when we drop to quarter gravity, which is the minimum we'll go, you won't actually need your gadget. You see, you're not holding us back."

"Just the same if it will help I'll stay in the tank."

His face glittered and his eyes strayed back to the work. "If it's necessary I'll ask you," he repeated.

Anti left again, secure in the knowledge that he would do as he said. In his own way Docchi was as ruthless as Judd. But the purpose was different and therefore the comparison not accurate. Strength was not easy to define.

The librarian resembled an angular metallic squid spread out to dry on the floor. Docchi picked his way through the wiry tentacles, scrutinizing the work of the crew. He squatted near Webber, watching him splice and adjust the components, briefly, giving advice and then moving on to the next man. The librarian was dormant but to Docchi's practiced eye it was nearly ready to be recalled the semi-life of a memory machine.

Jordan came swinging in. Docchi heard him and turned. He knew who it was by the sound but seemed disappointed to find his judgment confirmed. "The star chart drum is finished," said Jordan, pausing at the tangle of wires. "Most of the observed data on the neighboring stars is included. Of course all the locations are figured from Earth."

"It's all right. The computers won't mind making the conversions." With his foot Docchi nudged a tool toward him that Webber was reaching for. "What about the crossover relays?"

"Done too, waiting to be tied in. Guaranteed to switch from one computer to the other before even they realize what's happening."

"Good. The next thing is the impulse recognition hunter. Last night I thought of a way to make the selection tighter. Here, I'll show you." Docchi went to a diagram strewn desk and waited while Jordan pawed through the sheets for him. "There it is," he said when Jordan uncovered it.

Jordan studied it in silence. "Can't make it," he said at last.

"Why not? It's not difficult."

"Yeah. But we can't manage the delivery from Earth. Don't have all the parts here." Jordan scratched his chest. "Tell you what. Think I can rob nonessential stuff and put together something like this." He took a pencil and began to sketch rapidly.

"It'll do," said Docchi, finally approving it after a number of changes.

Jordan scratched in the alterations. "Why so tight?" he complained, folding the sheet and tucking it away. "The computers don't have to be controlled so tight. They never have disobeyed."

"I know, and I'm not going to give them a chance. Every watt we allot must be used on the drive and for no other purpose."

Privately Jordan doubted it was necessary. When he thought of the great nuclear pile that warmed the heart of the asteroid and drove them on he didn't see how a mere ship, no matter how efficient, could surpass them. True, the ship was travelling faster now but that was because they weren't exerting their full energies. And when they did— Jordan shrugged and creased the paper again, swinging away.

At the door he swerved to miss Jeriann. "Hi," he said, hurrying a little faster. It was none of his concern what went on but he didn't have to be around when it blew up.

Jeriann returned the greeting and stood at the entrance. "May I come in?"

"Certainly. There's no sign it's restricted to electronic technicians."

Webber winked at her and bent his head over his work, Docchi was expressionless. "I want to talk to you," she said.

"About Maureen? I've heard. Go ahead."

She'd hoped he'd suggest a more private place but it was evident he didn't want to be alone with her. She didn't altogether blame him. "What I asked for the other day wasn't very realistic. It was mostly my fault. I had at least a month to think of getting a larger power supply to the machine but I thought I could get along without it. It was my own short-sightedness and I had no reason to expect you to drop what you're doing."

"You don't have to apologize. We're all trying to do our best—and various needs do conflict. Actually I might have found some way to run the extra power line if I hadn't been sure it was an act of pure desperation, that you had no idea of what you were going to do with it when you got it."

What made it worse was that he was right. The impulse had been irrational, the feeling that there must be something that would help. He should have said he was at fault too, that he should have built the command unit months ago. It made no difference he hadn't known there was a ship behind them. He should have said it.

"It's over," she said. "We've done what we could. I thought you'd like to see her while there's time."

"I can't leave for another ten hours. None of us can. We've got to get it wrapped up if it's going to be of any use at all," said Docchi, looking at what remained to be done. "Wait. You said I can see her. Sounds to me like she's better." He scanned her face hopefully.

She shook her head. "It doesn't mean that. We've stopped using hypnotics because they're no longer effective. Heavy sedatives, extremely heavy, are the only things that keep her from jumping up and running out to die."

His face was sallow. This was one of the times his slender shoulderless body seemed frailer than it was. "I'll come as soon as I can get away. We're near the finish line on this." He turned and walked past Webber to the far end of the room, bending over a technician's work to examine it.

She was trying to tell him and all he had to do was half listen. Nobody blamed either of them. Maureen wouldn't, if she were capable of any kind of judgment. From his position among the tangled tentacles of the mechanical squid, seemingly strangled by the motionless machinery, Webber winked soberly at her. Jeriann bit her lip and hurried out. Her eyes burned but that was all. Her body was protected against unnecessary fluid loss.

It wasn't possible to drive the technicians. They weren't very skilled and the work was delicate. From the beginning they had known the importance of what they were doing and they were already at their top speed and above that no increase in productivity could be achieved. When he said ten hours Docchi optimistically thought eighteen.

And yet they were done in nine. Not because it would help Maureen—they knew it wouldn't. But because—well, why? Nobody asked for explanations. They made no mistakes; nothing had to be torn down and built again. And the less skilled men, those who puttered from one instruction to the next, stalling between orders, now seemed to anticipate what they would be told and to complete the work before it was given to them. They learned fast and what they didn't know how to do was done right anyway.

The wires ceased to resemble tentacles and were neatly arranged in the cabinet of the command unit, formerly the librarian, which was then moved against the wall. Calling in Jordan and discussing it with him, Docchi left the remainder of the work in his capable hands.

He was tired all over, inside and out. He didn't want to see anyone die, not someone he had been partly responsible for sentencing, whatever the circumstances. He walked along in the semi-twilight, wishing there was a cool breeze. He hadn't ordered one and so it was missing. Before long there wouldn't be any power to spare for circulation of the air.

Anti met him at the hospital steps, going up with him. "I've been waiting. I didn't want to go in alone."

He talked to her briefly and they went on in silence. The asteroid was being diminished, perhaps already had been. They all had first-hand knowledge of what death was—at one time or another they'd brushed very near to it—but they were not accustomed to losing the encounter. One of their own kind, who should live for hundreds of years, would not.

Jeriann heard them and came outside of the hushed room. "I don't know what to say," she whispered. "Oh yes I do. I wish I had your face, Docchi. You would see it shining."

Whatever she thought, her face was shining, though not in the same way. He looked into her eyes but they were not easy to read. "You did it," he whispered.

"I don't know why I'm talking so low," she said, raising her voice. "It doesn't hurt now. No, I didn't have anything to do with it. Come in and see her."

Maureen was sleeping. Her breathing was light but regular as the lung machines responded normally. Her skin was waxen but it was not unhealthy. The wrinkles of strain had fallen away and her face was relaxed in the beauty of survival.

"Go ahead and talk," said Cameron from the corner as he bent over an analyzer. "I shot her full of dope. I guess I didn't have to—she'll sleep now no matter what you do."

"Thanks, doctor," said Docchi. "We're lucky to have you."

"Not half as lucky as I am to be here. Damnedest thing I ever saw. My colleagues wouldn't believe it." Carefully he closed the analyzer and rolled it away. "I forget I no longer have colleagues."

"The more remarkable. Your efforts alone."

"I guess you don't understand. I had nothing to do with it," said Cameron. "I was an interested and awed spectator but nothing more. The person who saved Maureen was Maureen herself."

"Now how could she?" said Anti. "She lacked male hormones and the bodily processes were out of control, upset, running away with themselves." She raised a few inches from the floor to get a better glimpse of the patient. The best refutation of Anti's argument was Maureen herself.

"It couldn't happen to anyone but an accidental," began Jeriann, but Cameron cut her off.

His voice was cool and dry, that of a lecturer. It was the only chance he'd get to share his discovery. "You know why you're biocompensators: the severe injury, and later pulling through with the help of medical science, developing the extraordinary resistance I spoke of. You had to have it or you didn't live. And the resistance remained after the injury was gone.

"In Maureen's case every function began to be disturbed after the supply of hormones was cut off. It got worse as we were unable to manufacture what she needed. She developed a raging fever and was in a constant state of hallucination. In an earlier era she would have been a mass of cancerous tissue. Fortunately we are now able to control cancer quite simply.

"At any rate she was rapidly reaching the state where there was no coordination at all. Death should have been the result—but the body stepped in."

"Yes, but how?" said Anti.

"I don't know but I'm going to find out," said Cameron. "Last time I tested all the normal hormones were present. Somehow, out of tissues that weren't adapted to it, her body built up new organs and glands that supply her with the substances she needs to live."

Cell by cell the body had refused to die. Organs, nerves and tissues had fought the enveloping chaos. The body as a whole and in parts tried to survive but it was not adapted to conditions. So it adapted.

Nerves forged new paths in places they had never gone before because there was nothing at the end which they could attach to. But by the time they arrived at their destination certain specialized cells had changed their specialty. All cells in the adult body derived from an original one and they remembered though it was long ago. In the endless cellular generations since conception, in the continual microscopic death and rebirth that constitutes the life process, the cells had changed much—but in extremity the change was not irreversible.

Here a nerve began to fatten its stringy length; it was the beginning of what was later to become a long missing gland. Elsewhere a muscle seemed to encyst, adhering to another stray cell, changing both of them, working toward the definite goal.

From the brink the body turned and began the slow march toward health. What was missing it learned to replace and what could not be replaced it found substitutes for. Cell by cell, with organs and tissues and nerves, the body had fought its own great battle—and won.

"Spontaneous reconstruction," commented the doctor, touching the forehead of the patient he had not been able to help, merely observe. "It begins where our artificial regenerative processes leave off. I think—oh never mind. There's a lot of development to be done and I don't want to promise anybody something I can't deliver." He eyed Docchi's armless body speculatively.

Webber came in, noisily clanking his mechanical arm and leg. "Heard the good news," he said cheerfully. "Finished my work so I came over." He glanced admiringly at Maureen. "Say, I didn't remember she looked like that."

She was a pleasant sight and not merely because she'd fought off death. Her lips were full and color was returning to her face and the shape under the sheets was provocatively curved.

"Tomorrow or the next day she can leave the hospital for a few hours," said Cameron. "The new functions are growing stronger by the minute. Now she needs to get out after the long confinement."

"I'll volunteer to take her for a walk," said Webber.

"You will not," said Jeriann. "For the next few weeks she sees only women. Physiologically she's sound again but mentally she's still the complete female. You'll visit her when she's normal but not before."

"Guess I'll have to wait," said Webber, but he looked pleased.

She lingered outside while Webber left, seeking an opportunity to talk to Docchi. "I wanted to see you," she said as soon as they were alone.

"Any time. You know where I'll be."

"I know, and always working too."

"It's got to be done," he said doggedly.

"Sure. I know. I'll come over when I can." But she wouldn't, not until he gave her some encouragement. He had not forgiven the scene in the lab. Cameron called then and she went inside to her patient.

Docchi went back to gravity center, thoughts crowding through his mind. Little victories, though the life or death of a woman was not insignificant, were achieved without much effort. But that which meant something to everyone on the asteroid was more difficult. Where, in relation to their own position, was the ship that was striving to reach the Centauri group before they did?

CHAPTER FOURTEEN

"I'M COLD," said Jeriann.

"Put on more clothes," said Docchi grimly.

"That's not a nice thing to say to a girl with a figure as pretty as hers," said Anti.

"She can go to hydroponics," suggested Jordan. "It's warmer there and we've had to allow lights."

"But it's a lot smaller than it was and too many have crowded in. I don't want to be crushed," said Jeriann. She wouldn't have left even if it hadn't been true.

"Have to cut down," said Anti. "Meanwhile, what do we eat? Synthetics." She snorted.

"Synthetics are pure," said Jordan. His enthusiasm was less than it had been. A steady diet had begun to alter his opinion.

"Pure what?" said Anti, but received no reply. She looked over the circle huddled around the scanner. Nona was curled near Cameron, sleeping peacefully. Docchi leaned forward with uncomfortable intensity. Jeriann was beside him but he didn't seem to notice her. "How long does this go on?" said Anti. "I'm getting tired of freezing in the dark." Actually she didn't mind it; cold that would kill others still bothered her hardly at all.

"Until we know," said Docchi. "All the way to Centauri if it takes that long."

"How can we know?"

"We'll find out as soon as we measure relative speeds," answered Docchi. "The scanner is similar to radar but it uses gravity, which makes things rather difficult. We can't send out an impulse and see how long it takes to get back because it travels instantaneously as far as we're concerned."

"Then there isn't any way? They seem to know how fast we're going."

"Better astronomical equipment," said Docchi. "We're a bigger object and they were able to measure our light shift, until we stopped illuminating the whole dome."

"And now they can't tell because they can seldom see us?"

"The contrary, if they're on their toes. They should guess that we're putting most of the power into the drive."

"Then how can we find out?" said Anti.

"Triangulation," said Docchi. "When we first saw them it was from the front. In past weeks they've crept up until they're nearly broadside. Now I hope they'll drop back. It may take weeks to tell, especially if our speeds are almost evenly matched."

"And if we don't gain?"

"With our power?" interrupted Jordan, ceasing to tune the scanner. "But, all right, we don't gain. We'll get there first because we're still a little ahead of them.

"If there are no aliens there's no question of interstellar law. They'll have to hunt us down over an entire planet and maybe blast us off. I don't think sentiment will let them actually harm us. If there are aliens, what are they going to do? We've told our story first."

The asteroid seemed to leap ahead as all but the most necessary functions were curtailed and additional power was channeled into the drive. There was no sense of motion, merely of tension as the unmistakable vibration increased. In the darkness through the darkness they hurtled. Sleeping or waking Docchi remained near the scanner, as if his presence would somehow cause the ship to recede. It didn't.

Across the silence the race went on intently. Weeks passed and Anti walked with increased assurance as her weight diminished and her strength grew greater. Maureen recovered and was released from the hospital. She disappeared frequently mostly with Webber, and no one questioned where they went.

Jeriann came when she could get away from her hospital work. She came at night because it was usually night now though occasionally lights were turned on for short periods and warmth was allowed to filter through the dome. They couldn't risk killing the plants on which they depended for part of their oxygen supply.

"Good thing you're here," said Docchi once when she entered. "I want you to make some adjustments." She followed him to the next room where the former librarian was now the command unit presiding over their destiny.

"There," he said gloomily as she changed a number of settings slightly. "That's as good as I can do."

"How good is it?"

"Faster than we've gone before. I don't know the exact speed."

"Faster than with Nona?"

"I think so. Of course I don't know what she could have gotten out of it if she'd tried—but she always seemed to hold something back."

She would rather not have asked but the answer was on his face. "But it's not good enough?"

He sat down near the command unit. "They found out what we were doing and increased their own speed. It's slightly greater than ours."

"Well, why do we do it?" she said. "It takes more and more power to add another mile per second as we approach the speed of light. But that holds true for them too."

He tried to frown away the problem she posed. "Sure, but it doesn't matter to them as long as they can match anything we do."

"But they'd just as soon not. They're inconvenienced the same as we are when they have to divert too much power. They're better organized and it's not so bad, but still they have to do without their ordinary comforts. I don't see any point in tormenting ourselves. Let's turn on the lights and warm up the place. They'll do the same when they see it."

"Maybe they will," he said grudgingly. He was not going to accept her advice.

She tried again. "Will the scanner reach Earth?"

He shook his head. "Not quite. The range is limited. I can't give you figures but I estimate we're well over halfway to the Centauris." He got up and paced in front of the command unit. "I know what you're thinking—the appeal to the people of Earth. We tried it once. You know where it got us."

He had turned and didn't notice her. "I wasn't thinking of that at all. I was wondering how close we are. We might get in touch with the aliens."

He whirled around. "Say that again. Did you really say that?"

"Of course there may not *be* any aliens," murmured Jeriann.

"Doesn't matter, or I don't think it does. I'll have to figure it out, but I'm sure it will figure." His face flashed once. "Get Jordan, will you? I'll be at the scanner."

Gravity center was virtually a shaft that extended underground toward the center of the asteroid. At the bottom, shielded and re-shielded, sealed off and impregnable, was the nuclear pile. Nearly half way down a horizontal shaft branched off, leading to the gravity coils which were anchored to solid rock.

Much higher, near the surface, were the gravity computers. Physical access to them was equally difficult. There were connections so that electrical impulses could reach them, otherwise the command unit could not have directed them, have taken over the control. But in every other respect they were isolated and remote.

It narrowed Jeriann's search that there were places she didn't have to look. Nevertheless she passed him twice, going up and down, before she saw him curled up inconspicuously beside a machine whose function she didn't know.

"Now what does he want?" grumbled Jordan, rubbing his eyes. "He won't rest and he won't let anyone else get a few minutes sleep."

"He's hardest on you," she said. "You're his hands. He wants you to operate the scanner."

"Well, his hands are getting mighty tired," growled Jordan. But his sleepiness disappeared and he followed swiftly after her.

Docchi was standing at the scanner, his face furrowed as if thought alone would move dials. He inclined his head toward the image. "Take the ship off," he said impatiently. "I've hypnotized myself with it. We don't need to keep staring at it."

The ship vanished. "Now what?"

"They'll beat us to the stars. Let them. We don't have to be first. A planet of our own will do." Doubt and hope struggled for Docchi's face and Jeriann couldn't say which won. "Explore the Centauri system," he said.

"Both of them?"

"The nearest one first. After that we'll see."

A bright star slid to the center of the scanner. It flickered and then grew brighter, blazing out as they visually approached it. They were within a few million miles as the solar prominences lashed out blindingly. Jeriann could feel the heat. For the first time in weeks she was warm. "Cut the focus," called Docchi. "You'll burn out the scanner."

The sun softened and dimmed but remained where it was as the strength of the field was reduced. Jordan awaited instructions.

"Now that I'm sure we can reach it, we'll get the asteroid back to normal. Later we'll resume exploration," said Docchi. He started toward the command unit to make alterations and then saw that, though Jordan was following him, Jeriann wasn't. "Can't you stay?" he asked.

She indicated the empty belt. "I used my last absorption capsule."

She had no right to be happy merely because he was less brusque than usual. On her way home a facsimile of sunshine began blazing down from the dome. The grass was crisp and sere but it would revive.

The race didn't end because the ship and asteroid were no longer constantly accelerating. Whatever the general thought of it and however he modified his own plans, as far as the accidentals were concerned the emphasis had merely shifted. Exploration. It didn't matter who got to the system first—it was who found the inhabited or inhabitable planets.

The ship had slightly more speed even when, by mutual consent, both cut the strength of the drive. Slowly it pulled level and then began to creep ahead. But the scanner nullified the advantage. The astronomical equipment of the ship, superior though it was, was not adequate to observe the planets in detail from this distance. Before the ship could locate planets and catalogue the characteristics it would ultimately have to slow down and waste days or weeks searching the specks of light to decide which were worth closer investigation.

With the mass sensitive scanner there was no such problem. Six planets for Alpha and seven for Proxima with, for a while, the possibility that one or two more might be on the far side of the respective suns. Within weeks, relative to the asteroid, much longer for stationary objects, that possibility was eliminated. Six and seven planets there were and no more.

In one respect the scanner wasn't perfect, Nona was shown where it failed to perform satisfactorily and, after looking it over with mild curiosity, took it completely apart, altering a number of circuits. When she reassembled it again it had exactly the same limitations.

Jordan switched it on and brought the planet in focus. He changed the dial setting and the image blurred, scattering a coruscating rainbow of brilliant light. Once again he patiently adjusted the dials and the planet returned to normal. "That's as close as we can get," he said. "I'd estimate about fifty thousand miles out."

"Try the fourth planet, the Saturn type," suggested Docchi.

Minus rings but with several satellites a large planet replaced the smaller one they had been looking at. After vainly trying to get closer Jordan gave his opinion. "A hundred and fifty thousand miles from the surface. This thing's mass sensitive, that's all-proportional to the mass. It won't resolve an image close to the surface of a planet. Notice that we couldn't get nearer than a few million miles of the sun—but we could slide right into a little thing like a ship."

Reluctantly Docchi nodded. "We'll have to be satisfied with it as it is. Nevertheless I think it can be made to approach the surface of any mass, even the sun."

"Nona couldn't do it," said Jordan.

Docchi smiled. "I think she's more interested in her husband at the moment. Besides, what did she have to work with? Odds and ends of parts that really aren't suited for what they have to do. It would be different if she had an unlimited supply of gravity generating parts, or could get what she needs made to order."

"What you want is a whole new science," said Jordan.

"Why not? We've got the beginning of it," said Docchi. Meanwhile the search went on. Each planet was scrutinized as closely as the scanner would allow. The images were photographed, enlarged and studied, pored over by everyone who could show some experience in topographical work. Two inhabitable planets were discovered, one in each star system.

It was somewhat disappointing that there was no trace of an alien civilization on either world or on any of the planets.

Jeriann looked up from the photograph. "I can't see anything. Clouds...nothing but clouds."

Jordan shrugged. "Methane probably. It was the best I could get. What do you want to see?"

"I think we should get a good look at the surface before we rule out aliens."

"Still after the aliens." Docchi smiled tolerantly. "You'll have to wait till the next system, or the next."

"I think she wants to find them because it's one of the reasons normals didn't want us to go."

"A little," confessed Jeriann. "They refused us because of what aliens might think when they saw us."

"Ever reflect it's exactly what they might think?"

Jeriann was startled and before she could reply Jordan produced another argument. "We're better off without them. Where would we be if those two planets were settled, spilling over with strange creatures that could outthink us without untwining their tails?"

Jeriann flushed. "You're teasing me because I don't know much about astronomy. You're not very good inside a medical lab." She stared hard at the photograph. "I still think you're wrong to conclude there aren't any aliens just because they don't show up on planets we can live on."

Jordan rested his huge hand on the disc of the planet she was studying. "Ever hear of Jupiter, Saturn, or Uranus?"

"I'm not that ignorant."

"I didn't mean you were," said Jordan. "But man's actually landed on two of those planets and though we haven't got to Jupiter we have sent down a little remote controlled ship. There's *nothing* on all three of the big planets, not even microscopic life. The latest theory is that there's some kind of life over most of the universe but that intelligence will have to show up under conditions similar to those that evolved us. Of course we're willing to be convinced, but—"

He crumpled the photograph. "Nevertheless I'll try to get a better picture of the Alpha Centauri version of Saturn."

"Stop quarreling," said Anti. "I think it's nice that there are two planets, neither of which has anyone to lay prior claim to it. Which one shall we take?"

"I'll take the Proxima planet," said Jordan as he went back to the scanner.

"Do we have to choose now?" asked Jeriann.

"We should," said Docchi. "The advantage we have is very small; we have to exploit it. Ideally we ought not to decelerate until the last minute and at the end of that period we should find ourselves in a perfect thousand mile orbit around the planet." He glanced at the model of the system they'd constructed. "Myself, I'm for the second Alpha planet."

Anti snorted. "That thing? It's nothing but a hotter edition of Mars."

"Mars isn't bad, Anti. People live on it. Besides, it isn't Mars. It's hotter, warmer than Earth in fact. Dry, but there are two small oceans and several mountain chains and on the shady side of the hills there seem to be trees. We can live comfortably there."

"I thought of something else," said Jeriann. "They'll head straight for the planet that will support the biggest populations. Let them have the prize—we don't need it."

"I had that in mind," said Docchi. "It will give us more time to get safely established. Once we're on, there's nothing much they can do."

The deceleration began soon and went off smoothly. In less than a subjective year since they left Earth they entered the Alpha system. But they were not the first humans to arrive. The official expedition in the Star Victory preceded them by several days. The difference was that the accidentals knew exactly where they were going and actually arrived at the planet while the other ship was still cautiously investigating the outer orbits.

"It doesn't matter," said Anti as they gathered by the scanner, discussing it. "In principle we're responsible for what they've done. They can have the glory. What we came for was a place to live in peace."

"And we'll get it," said Docchi. In the last few weeks his uneasiness, never very deep, had come to the surface. The knowledge of how narrow a margin they had was frightening.

Outside the planet filled the dome. It was actually quite small but it was close and covered most of the sky. Now that they were near they could see that only superficially did it resemble Mars. There were mountains and several large streams and it wasn't as barren as at first they had thought.

"I wish I could land, or we could go closer," said Anti.

There was no answer for that. Anti's personal null gravity field would function only so long as it was in contact with the gravity computer, which in effect it was an extension of. She wasn't yet strong enough to stand on the surface of their new home. As for the other, the asteroid was quite large and it wasn't advisable to risk a nearer approach.

Webber came in, grinning hugely and rattling his arm and leg more than necessary. "The first load's on. When do we peel off?"

"Whenever you're ready. The rocket dome is on automatic. Take off and it'll open for you."

"It's safe to leave?"

"If you're the rocket pilot you say you are. It's an ordinary landing. The scouts the general left us are in fair condition."

"Don't worry about me. I meant, will the expedition interfere?"

"Last time we checked the ship was nosing around the outer planets."

"Good stupid old Judd. It's nice that we can depend on him to proceed with the utmost of military caution—and arrive at his goal too late."

It was not quite fair to the general, who was shrewd enough when it came to things he had been trained to deal with. From the military standpoint he had to check every possibility before going on to the next. He was the official representative of the entire solar system and he did not dare act as hastily as the accidentals could. His responsibilities held him back. But there were other times in which unimaginative obedience to higher authority would carry the day.

"Be careful," warned Docchi. "Don't let anyone go out until the air and soil and water have been tested and re-tested and approved."

"The doctor thinks we can handle any virus, bacteria, parasite, or anything else you can name that shows up. It's not the first strange world man has landed on."

"This is not the solar system," said Docchi. "You may have to restrain Cameron if he's overly anxious to show Nona what the new world is like."

"For that reason you—" Webber stopped, glancing away from Docchi's face. "It's too bad you can't go. You ought to have some first to your name."

"Don't concern yourself. I'll get there one of these days. Somebody's got to be up here at this end."

"And I'll make certain nothing goes wrong down there." Webber shifted uncomfortably but the mood didn't last. "I'll be back in a week for the next load. Once we get settled things will speed up."

"We'll be waiting," called Jordan as Webber left.

There was tension before the rocket lifted and sluiced through the dome locks. It didn't abate as the swatch of light flared across the darkness and faded against the bright illumination of the planetary disc. It was only when they were able to observe the successful landing on the selected site and the radio response came in. "All clear. A bit shaken up on the way down but no damage except to my ego. I think I got all the rusty rocketry out of my system. We're waiting while tests come in. We'll let you know before we go out."

"Now I can breathe," said Anti. "A place of our own. Just let the general come and try to take us off."

"Why not? He has weapons, which we don't. There's nothing to stop him from landing down there and capturing them. I won't feel safe until we have a real settlement going and can defend it. And then I'm not sure."

"Now, Jeriann," admonished Anti.

"They'll obey their own laws," said Docchi. "Planets outside the solar system that aren't claimed by others belong to those who first settle them. They passed that long ago as an incentive to interstellar travel. The moment we landed we became independent. To molest us now would be a clear violation of everything they believe in."

"I hope you're right," said Jeriann. "I hope you are."

Anti was gazing out the window at the arch of the dome through which she could see the edge of the planet, ruddy, with a small sparkling green and gold ocean turned toward them. She got to her feet. "I'm going outside and see the world before it slips away. I was wrong. It's not like Mars. Much prettier."

Docchi was busy for a moment as Anti and Jordan left and when the work was finished and he turned around he saw that Jeriann had remained with him. Without realizing what she was doing she was fingering the empty spaces on her belt. It wasn't conspicuous but like him she wore her infirmity on the outside where everyone could see.

"I'm sorry you couldn't go first," she said, touching the one remaining capsule.

"First or later isn't important. But why not be sorry you weren't first?"

"Well, there are things to be done and oh, I don't know."

She was disturbed for some reason he could not guess. The sight of their world seemed to upset her as much as it did him, but with different effects. "It's the same with me. But now the worst is over." Docchi sat motionless. "Jeriann."

"Yes?"

"Once I said I'd come to see you when I could."

"You promised, but you never came."

"The promise was to myself. I can come to see you now. Am I still invited?"

"Why do you ask a question like that?" said Jeriann. "You know, don't you? You know what I'll say."

First they registered and then they left the Hall of Records, walking slowly, watching the planet roll over the dome, disappearing by degrees. It was out of sight, the last patch vanishing as they reached her dwelling. And inside, where time was waiting everywhere, the remainder of it on the floor, peering down from the ceiling and ticking with soft persistence in the walls, they quite forgot time for a while.

They slept dreamlessly. It was nearly morning before he became restless and awakened. It was not the rhythmical noises that were intended to keep her informed of the schedule that bothered him.

He lay there and tried to determine where the sound came from. He could feel her body next to his, warm and wonderful. He couldn't get back to sleep and he couldn't ignore what was happening.

He moved and touched her. She was quivering. "Are you laughing or crying?" he whispered.

"I can't cry so I've got to be laughing," she answered. "It's funny. I was lying here thinking about it. I suppose I can cook, I don't know. It's been a long time."

"Is that all?" He chuckled. "Don't give it another thought, I understand how you feel about it."

"Do you? I don't think so." She squirmed closer and put her arms around him. "That's what's so funny. There's no food here and nothing to cook it on. Not only that, there never will be. You've got yourself a prize woman."

"I think so too. I'm satisfied," he said. "Can't you feel my arms around you?"

She would never be able to convince him that she could.

CHAPTER FIFTEEN

NOW that Cameron was gone there was much more to be done in the hospital. Jeriann rushed to get through but small errors plagued her, nullifying a good part of her work. Finally she forced herself to be more careful, checking the biologicals with extreme caution.

"I hear," said Maureen, sauntering in, "the nuptials were informal, catch as catch can."

"No ceremony," said Jeriann. "We stopped in and registered and went on to my place."

"What's the difference as long as you're sure of him," said Maureen.

"I'm not. I'm sure of me."

Maureen looked at her critically. "In your case it's good enough," she said with a trace of envy as she leaned against the machine.

"Don't," said Jeriann sharply. "This thing is an art, not a science. The heat of your hand will alter the product."

"Well, all right," said Maureen crossly. "If I had something worthwhile to do I wouldn't be so nervous."

"I think it can be arranged," said Jeriann, smiling. "How would you like to be a colonist?"

"On the next ship? Maybe."

"It would be exciting. Also you'd be near Webber." Jeriann made a delicate adjustment.

"I haven't made up my mind about him," said Maureen airily. "He's virile though."

"He clanks a lot, if that's what you mean."

"At least he doesn't pretend he's carrying the world on his shoulders without any—" Maureen stopped. "I guess I shouldn't say that in front of you."

"You shouldn't," agreed Jeriann. "Nowhere I'll be apt to hear it. Now why don't you see Jordan about getting on the next ship?"

After that the work went smoothly and she soon found she'd completed the day's quota and part of the next. She continued longer until she had tomorrow free. They had the whole day off to do what they liked, if she could persuade him to rest. She was humming when she went out and it was clear evening and there was a beautiful silver fleck in the sky.

Only it was not beautiful because it was a ship—and it was not their ship.

And neither was it the Star Victory. She'd watched it so often on the scanner that every line of it was etched in her mind.

She hurried to gravity center, every step an effort. Why couldn't they have been discovered later? She would have preferred an alien ship, anything to this. Where had it come from?

Jordan was waiting at the entrance. "I knew you'd be here. You saw the scout?"

It was simple if she had thought about it. The Star Victory was large and carried auxiliary landing craft. "When did it come?"

"Less than an hour ago. Go on in. I'll wait for Anti."

Docchi was leaning against the command unit. The telescreen on the opposite wall was glowing but there was nothing on it except harsh white glare. "I tried to get you at the hospital as soon as they stopped talking. You'd just left."

"They didn't call until they got close?"

A smile had died on his face and the corpse of it was still there. "They nailed us dead. We should have had someone checking on the scanner. It works turned away from the planet. I guess it wouldn't have done any good though—there was just too much space to cover. First thing we knew they were on the telescreen. Jordan went outside, and there they were."

She was thinking of the people on the planet. The asteroid couldn't abandon them. She hoped the scout didn't know how vulnerable they were. "What did they say?"

"The general sent an urgent message. He asked us not to land on this or any other planet."

"He *asked* us?" The general was accustomed to commanding. His face was illuminated with the weak radiance of his veins.

"I didn't tell them we had landed and I don't think they observed it." He stopped to recall what she said and the effort was painful. "Oh yes, the general asked us. Below the cloud banks he discovered an alien civilization on the Saturn type planet and is negotiating with them. Naturally they'd regard it as a hostile act on the part of mankind if we occupied a planet in their system without first asking."

Jeriann touched the absorption capsules without feeling them. "Aliens!"

"You were right, though you had no right to be. Not that it would have made any difference what we thought. As long as the general was cruising around the planet we wouldn't have dared investigate."

It didn't pay to generalize on what they learned from one planet, in one system. When man had journeyed throughout the galaxy there would still be surprises waiting for him when he came to the other side. "Let the expedition worry about hostile acts," said Jeriann. "If the aliens break off negotiations, so much the better for us."

"You forget we didn't come solely for ourselves. We hoped to make ourselves useful to mankind. What kind of disservice is that, to embroil humanity in a war with the first aliens we meet?" His face was flaring and white and the smile gone.

"Don't," whispered Jeriann. "I'm afraid of lightning—yours most of all. I expect to hear thunder and be struck dead."

"I'm sorry," he said. "We have a right to think of ourselves but not exclusively of ourselves."

"I mean, do they care? If they live on that planet they can't want this. They couldn't survive under such different conditions. Astronomical observations must be difficult with so many clouds, and without space travel are we sure the aliens even know about this world?"

He blinked wearily. "We took a chance. We had to. They have space travel. The general wouldn't be so anxious not to offend them if they were inferior to our own civilization."

"But we didn't see their ships."

"Again we weren't looking in the right place. There's nothing in this system they travel to. But there is a comparable planet in Proxima, and in recent months they've been on opposite sides of the respective suns. They wait for more favorable positions."

It was not luck that had favored the general. Theory said there should be intelligent life in the Centauri system and it further indicated that it would be found on an Earth type planet. It was half correct, and the wrong half had fallen against the accidentals. Stubbornly insisting on following the plan laid down by his superiors, the general had won.

"What are we going to do?" said Jeriann. "There are hostages down there."

"We'll get them back," said Docchi. "Nobody can stop us."

"Can we? Their ships are faster than ours."

"They can't use their speed close to a planet. And the expedition won't be aggressive in someone else's backyard. We can't land without breaking up the asteroid but we'll go near enough so they won't be able to intercept our ship."

It was a daring maneuver. The bulk of the asteroid could be used to cut off any attempt to overtake their returning ship. "There's Roche's limit," said Jeriann.

"Doesn't apply. We're not a simple planetoidal mass. We'll clamp the heaviest gravity we're capable of and, barring something unforeseen, we can hold the crust together at a distance of ten to twenty miles of the surface."

She understood; they'd take the risk if necessary but it ought to be avoided, because it was a risk. Nobody knew what solid tides would be set in the crust of the asteroid as the result of an external gravity field.

"And then what?" she said. "We get them back and then what?" Her hands were heavy. The silver mote overhead, shining in the light of Alpha, was implacable.

"What else is there?" said Docchi with an attempt at cheerfulness. "We'll get them back, every person, and then we'll go on. To the next star and the next, and if we have to, the one after that. Somewhere we'll find a place."

Jeriann touched him wonderingly. "I love you for saying that. I love you anyway, but particularly for saying that."

He seemed to shrink, flaming where she touched him, fiery fingertips on his face. "You know?" he said dully.

"Yes. For quite a while now. Anti suspects too. I think we all do. This was our last chance, wasn't it?"

He couldn't look at her. "We shouldn't have stopped. The next star surely would have been the place."

"Place," said Jeriann. "It wasn't your fault. Why do you suppose we were so eager to agree with you? We knew the longer we went on the more we were at a disadvantage."

It was so drearily obvious that nearly everyone had some inkling of the truth. The Star Victory was not the only ship of its class; some were rusting in the spaceyards and some were in use as interplanetary freighters. And if the Star Victory could be converted easily, why not the others?

A new drive to replace the obsolete one? Order it and with a little switching around in the manufacturing plants, diverting it from other uses, it was delivered tomorrow and completely installed the day after that. The command unit the accidentals had labored so long to alter? Every dinky little office had as good and in many cases all that was required was changing the information spools. And thousands of crews were available, already trained, used to working together. It wouldn't be hard to recruit them and add a few officers at the top and a staff of linguists and scientists.

Nona had given them the one thing they needed and now mankind was exploding into space. There was no end in sight. The whole neighboring sphere of space that enveloped the solar system was due for immediate exploration.

And the accidentals hadn't been forgotten. They were not the objective, wealth was: planets to be claimed and occupied or mined, civilizations to be contacted with whom products and techniques and entire new sciences could be exchanged.

If they were lucky enough to get away from the Centauri system at the next star they'd find other ships waiting, doing business with the natives, if there were any; if not, establishing firm little colonies on everything that was capable of supporting human life. They were surrounded, overwhelmed by numbers. It was no wonder the general hadn't been perturbed at the failure of his plan to land unnoticed on the asteroid. He knew what had been slow in occurring to them. For them there was no next star.

Docchi gazed in sick defeat at Jeriann. There was no need to talk. There was nothing to say.

The asteroid was rolling toward twilight as Anti came in. "What are we doing about those insolent pirates? They have no jurisdiction here. We ought to aim the asteroid at them. We can smash them." She saw their faces and the words stopped. "I was hoping—but I guess we can't hide it among ourselves," she said.

"It's no use," said Docchi heavily. "We'll have to go down and take them off the planet."

"How will they know? We can't get a beam down with a whole planet in the way," said Anti. "Let's wait till morning so we can tell them to be ready."

"I don't know," said Docchi indecisively.

"None of us know anything," said Anti fiercely. "Go home and get some sleep. We'll think of something by morning."

After they were gone Anti went outside. Looking up she could see the scout, still visible, glistening in the light of Alpha. It was much brighter than the stars that had been watching them.

Cameron tried to be detached and objective. "Do they know we're here?"

"I don't think so. They'd have been upset if they had any idea."

"Seems likely," agreed the doctor. "We left as they were approaching. But we took off from the face nearest the planet and they came in from the opposite side. The asteroid acted as a screen."

"Probably," agreed Docchi with indifference. "How soon can you be ready?"

"Do we have to come up immediately?"

Docchi shrugged. "I can shove the scout out of the way. I don't know what will happen if and when the Star Victory gets here."

"It's too big to maneuver close to the surface of the planet."

"Perhaps. But it carries other scouts it can launch."

Cameron grimaced. "Two or three fast little ships would be difficult to brush away. But do we have to let them get close?"

"How can we stop them? Better come up while you can."

Cameron was fighting it, not recognizing the odds. "The scanner will work, won't it?" questioned the doctor.

"Turned away from the planet, yes."

"That's what I meant. Keep it trained on the alien world. If the Star Victory comes out of the clouds and heads this way you'll know it in plenty of time to scoop us up."

It could be done but why jeopardize themselves further? He wanted to refuse but Jeriann was pressing close to him, whispering. "Do—you have any reason for wanting to stay?" he asked reluctantly.

"You see right through me, don't you?" said Cameron. "No, there's no real reason except this, Nona's interested in this world and wants to stay."

It was as valid as anything else he could have said. That they had come so far, if only to fail at the final step, was due almost entirely to her efforts. She deserved some reward, though it was only the satisfaction of mild curiosity. "Wait," he said suspiciously. "Are you sure you know what she wants? We're sometimes able to tell her what we want, but never the other way around."

"But I know—" The doctor stopped and looked at him wildly, his face flooded with sudden exaltation which gradually faded. "I do know," he said at last. "For a moment I thought it was telepathy. But I guess not. I'm not a computer." He glanced out of the viewport at a world they couldn't see.

"Thank you for bringing it to my attention, Docchi," he said when he faced them again. "It's just interest. For the first time she has someone she wants to understand—me—and a world outside she longs to visit. The combination is strong enough to stimulate her mind—and she's bright enough to learn anything she decides she has to."

Cameron rubbed his hand across his face and he was tired too. "Let us stay here as long as you can without endangering yourselves, I want to work with her under these surroundings. I think now, looking back at the way she's behaved these last few days, I can make a start at teaching her to read."

"It must be a lovely place if she likes it so well," said Jeriann, "Maybe you can turn the screen of your ship so we can see what it's like outside."

"No," said Docchi hoarsely. "Don't waste time taking apart the ship. Get busy with her, teach her what you can. Take her outside if it's safe, but don't go far. We may call suddenly." He lowered his voice as he went on talking and at the end was no louder than usual.

"I understand," said Cameron, "Don't worry about us. Something may come out of it."

"It's worse for them," said Jeriann when the screen darkened. "They've seen it and then they'll have to come back. It won't be anything we'll have to shove deep in our memories."

He didn't know. He didn't know at all. "I need your help," he said, going into the scanner room. Under his direction Jeriann made adjustments and brought the alien world in view. Cloud swathed and mysterious, a strange civilization hidden under the impenetrable atmosphere, it rolled on through space.

"We'll take turns," he said, "The minute anything bright comes up we'll get busy."

"I hate them," said Jeriann.

"Who?"

"The aliens. If it weren't for them we'd have a clear claim on the planet."

"But they didn't do anything," he said. "They're merely protecting their own interests. We'd do the same." Nevertheless he hated the aliens too.

Jeriann was shaking him. She had to shout before he started and woke up. "They've left," she said. "We've got to hurry."

He was tired and didn't want to move. It was very unimportant, "Are you sure it was the Star Victory you saw? It may have been a satellite."

"It was the ship—at least it was using rockets."

He got out of bed and let her help him dress. Usually he refused her aid. "Rockets? But the Star Victory doesn't have any." Of course it did; it was part of the obsolete equipment that hadn't been removed because there wasn't time. Besides, it was an excellent reverse source of propulsion.

"I don't care. That's what I saw," said Jeriann.

"Where are Jordan and Anti?"

"I've called them. They'll be there."

He finished dressing and they hurried to the scanner. There was no mistake; it was the ship, but there was no bright tail behind. They were using the gravity drive. He watched it grimly.

"But they were," said Jeriann. "There's nothing wrong with my eyesight. They were using rockets."

He withheld comment. Rockets weren't nearly as efficient as the gravity drive, particularly near a large planet. Yet Jeriann said she saw it. He hoped she hadn't.

Anti and Jordan came in almost simultaneously and joined the vigil. Minutes passed in silence and then the brief orange flower blossomed again.

"See," said Jeriann.

"Now why are they doing that?" growled Jordan, "They were doing fine without it."

"Maybe they need more speed," suggested Anti.

Jordan grunted. "Wouldn't add ten percent."

"But if they needed ten percent, if they were in trouble—"

"They are in trouble," said Jeriann. "It's a signal."

This was a version he could accept—if there weren't better explanations. Swiftly Docchi made mental approximations. "At the rate they're going they'll be here in half a day. They can't reach us with their telescreen until they're nearly here. Shall we go inside and see what's wrong with them?"

They looked at each other, and looked, until Anti answered. "What's a few minutes?" she said. "We've plenty of time to pick up our people. We can be gone before they get close."

Could they? That was what he didn't know. Taking an asteroid near the surface of a planet had never been tried and there were no rules. He'd have to feel it out as he went along, ready to turn away at the first indication of overload. Docchi looked at Jeriann, who nodded imperceptibly.

"I think we're in agreement," said Jordan, touching the dials.

General Judd was waiting for them. "There you are," he said enigmatically. "I hoped you'd understand."

"I'm afraid we don't. You'll have to explain."

"Still the old flamethrower, I see," said the general brusquely. "Mainly I wanted to make sure you didn't run when you saw us coming. My psychologists assured me you'd be a sucker for anything that looked like distress. I've got new respect for them." He chuckled.

"Now that we've been suckered, as you so kindly put it, please tell us what you want."

"I'm coming to—" The general's face reddened and his eyes bulged and he started coughing. The air wheezed stranglingly in and out of his lungs until finally he was able to control the spasm. He grabbed a tissue and wiped his face with it. "Designs are no good," he said. "Ship, spacesuits, everything. Meant to hold pressure from the inside and down there it's in the other direction—and it's really pressure. Gets into everything. Not very much but it fries your lungs. Remember that."

"We will. Get to the point, general."

The general looked at Docchi thoughtfully and seemed satisfied with what he saw. "Don't be impatient. What I have to say is complicated and you'll have to get the background. Are you interested?"

"I am," said Anti.

"Good," said the general, not waiting for the others to signify. "Well, we landed. We went in on the gravity drive and possibly it was a mistake but I don't see what else we could have done—rockets wouldn't have held us. Anyway they had their instruments out and we think they could tell what we were using."

"What were they like, the aliens?" asked Jeriann.

The general seemed to regard that as unimportant information. He glanced appreciatively at Jeriann, but ignored her question. "Funny thing. They didn't ask *us* about our drive and, of course, we didn't tell them. As nearly as we can tell they have something like it—about in the stage of development ours was a few years ago. Theirs will take them to Proxima because it's relatively close but it's no good beyond that." The general thought about what he'd just said. "Well, their drive wouldn't work at real interstellar distance—which is why they haven't visited us—but unfortunately we must have given them a clue. They know ours works and in no time they'll have it figured out."

"Sort of suspicious, aren't you?" said Anti.

"Lord, yes," said the general. "Do you know what land surface their planet has, what a population it will support? Two planets against three, but theirs are so much bigger. It balances off a little that we have a better drive and our reproduction rate can be higher than theirs."

"I take it you didn't tell them about Jupiter and Saturn?" said Jordan.

"No point bringing *that* up," said the general, apprehensive at the mere thought. "Oh they have things we want. Two very attractive planets, and they're wizards at high pressure chemistry and organics— you'd expect them to be—but the exchange was hardly worth it." The general sat motionless, recalling the scenes on that strange planet.

"They *could* be very dangerous. It was imperative that we establish some sort of friendly contact. Naturally we told them about you."

"Naturally," said Docchi dryly. "You were four light years from home and you weren't dealing with uncivilized natives."

"Nothing derogatory, you understand," said the general hastily.

"I'm sure," said Docchi. "general, some time ago I asked what you wanted. Much as we appreciate your friendly conversation—and the friendliness is quite unexpected—unless you can tell us what you're after in the next few minutes we'll have to conclude that your sole objective is to hold us here while you get closer."

"Don't do anything rash," said the general, as concerned as Docchi had ever seen him. "You see it was a stalemate. We were a little afraid of them and they didn't trust us and both sides were noncommittal. We didn't show each other a thing. But there had to be a solution."

"General, I warned you."

"Can't you see?" half-shouted the general, rising up. "I thought you were smart. We're going home and we may as well unload our surplus supplies. You'll need them. It will be about nine years before anyone gets back." He shoved the chair aside and concentrated steadily on Jeriann, the one normal human among them.

"This is what we decided," he said. "You get the planet for the next fifteen or twenty years, longer if they approve. Meanwhile all trade between us passes through you." He jammed his hands in his pockets. "There. Do you accept?"

"Do we accept?" said Anti. "He asks us."

"I see you do," said the general with gloomy satisfaction. "It was their suggestion. They want to study you at length to see what makes humans behave. Naturally you'll be keeping your eyes open." He swallowed and conquered the incipient cough. "Now if you'll turn off this beastly little gadget and let me have some privacy I'll talk to you when we get there."

Jordan reached for the scanner but was not quite soon enough. The general thought he was alone when he wasn't. "Those damned butterflies. Trillions of them." His face twisted.

CHAPTER SIXTEEN

THEY went walking in the night. Stars were out but they didn't notice. They had found a star to belong to and weren't looking for others. "Which one?" said Jeriann, turning her head.

"I can't point. Anyway I don't know," said Docchi. "I can get it for you on the scanner."

Jeriann laughed. "Never mind. I don't need to see their planet. They'll come soon enough."

"Almost too soon. I keep wondering what they're actually like."

"Me too," said Jeriann. "I don't even know how big they are. Sure I saw them on the screen for a short time, but it's not like meeting them. Large butterflies is what I first thought, but the resemblance fades as you continue looking. And, what is their size? There was nothing familiar to judge them against."

"Wingspread is a better measure, said Docchi. "The general said eight feet but I think he was overly impressed by the flat expanse of their bodies." In a while he added thoughtfully, "But it was not their height I was thinking of."

"I know," said Jeriann. She frowned. "Why did they choose us? They could have had the general's expedition. Instead they asked for us. Why?"

They went on in silence, past the acid tank. They looked in. It was empty. Now they had better use for the chemicals. "How is this for a reason?" said Jeriann as they strolled away.

"Still on the aliens?"

"Why not? We've got to learn how they think."

Docchi smiled and through the darkness she could see the faint luminosity of his lips and where his eyes crinkled. "We do, but in the absence of anything positive all I can apply is self-interest. And I don't see how they benefit by having us."

"I do," said Jeriann. "It's because we're normal." She hurried on before Docchi could protest. "Don't try to talk me down until I explain. When they contacted us yesterday and said they'd be here in about three weeks, on an official visit, did you notice which one was prettiest?"

"I figured that much out myself," said Docchi. "At least in the beginning we look very much alike to them, as they do to us. Appearance doesn't count."

"True, but that was not my point. I haven't reached it. When you looked at the—uh—butterfly that spoke to you in that high squeaky voice you were wondering how he learned our language so well in such a short time. You were thinking: are they all as smart? Can I trust him?"

"We've got to trust them," said Docchi grimly. "We're a long way from support. And they did ask us to stay."

"But trust all of them, every individual butterfly, under any circumstance? Or just some?"

"We're dealing with a government," said Docchi. "We aren't concerned with individuals. There must be deviations in what they're like. Some won't be trustworthy." He paused. "But of course a government is a reflection of what its citizens are." He paused again, came to a dead stop. "And so, for the aliens, we are average humans."

"That's what I meant," said Jeriann. "A *cross section* of what they'd find on Earth. But of course they can't go to Earth and see for themselves—not yet. And so they had to make the best choice of what was at hand."

They started walking again and Docchi leaned against her. "I think you're right. The general's expedition, all specialists and experts, including the military, who are specialists of another kind, was not a representative group. The butterflies could study them forever but they wouldn't get a true picture.

"But they had to know exactly what humans are like, what their potentialities are, and how they live together. And so they took us."

"It seems strange," said Jeriann, sliding her arm around him. "Until now I've never thought of us as normal. But even if the aliens had refused both of us and asked for another group of colonists they wouldn't have done as well. Colonists for a special planet are specially selected—hardiest, strongest, most aggressive or discontented—there would always be something to throw them off.

"But accidents cut across everything, age, intelligence, sex, occupation. Name it and it's here. We're the only representative group that ever left Earth or ever will."

"It's odd," agreed Docchi. "But it doesn't match what happens when we meet our first aliens. It's nothing like anyone imagined. Here we stand, face to face across the stars. There is no competition for inhabitable planets since our definitions are mutually exclusive. But we are afraid; neither side wants war. And so we go ahead cautiously, looking for signs in the other that will reassure us."

"I don't know," said Jeriann. "We're being tested. Will we measure up?"

"We won't fail. In spite of what we may seem to some of our own people, we're average men and women—and man hasn't stopped climbing upward since that day somebody built the first fire."

Jeriann squeezed him and they slowed. In their wandering they had come to gravity center. They looked at each other and decided to go in. Jeriann opened the door and there was a light down the hall. They went to it and looked in.

Jordan was in front of the scanner, scowling at it in fierce concentration. "I hope those idiots got it down straight," he muttered back at them.

"Don't be so concerned. You took it apart for them, didn't you?"

"Yeah, but it doesn't mean I made them understand." He wiped his forehead. "However, even if they don't know what it's all about, somebody ought to be able to build another. It'll work if they use a little sense."

Docchi smiled. "Don't discount what gravity experts know. After they get through thinking over the ideas in those circuits they'll doll up the scanner and before you know it they'll have a machine that can reach us from Earth."

"That'll be the day," said Jordan. "Let's hope they don't. It's bad enough they know we're here—but if they have to look at us too..." He shook his head.

"You're wrong," said Anti, coming in and sitting down. "Won't be that way at all." She bent and began rubbing her legs. "My poor feet. I've been walking around for the longest time—full weight too."

"Why won't it?" said Jordan. "Remember what happened the last time we got in touch with them."

"Not the same people," said Anti. "There were always some, like the doctor who didn't think we had to be beautiful to talk to us or be near. We'll get more of that kind. They don't have to call unless they want to."

"And last time we weren't anybody, less than a thousand and not an important person in the lot. Now we're representatives to the Centauri system."

"Profit," said Jordan. "You think they won't be able to afford to show their feelings. I wish I could agree. But even with the gravity drive they can't carry much between here and Earth. In the next fifty years the trade that goes out of here won't make one person rich."

"I disagree. Ideas don't weigh much and there'll be lots of those flying back and forth. And was there ever anything more valuable?" Anti smiled. "But there's more. *We* won't be the same. Only yesterday Cameron said he saw Nona looking worriedly at a book. It won't be long before she gets the idea and wham—new books."

"She was never the one who had trouble. Anyway, she'll never speak."

"She doesn't have to as long as she can write—and get some idea of what we're saying."

"Then she's all right and that will make the doctor happy." Jordan was dubious. "But what of us—Docchi, Jeriann, me—the rest?"

Anti leaned back and slid off her sandals, wriggling her toes in voluptuously and looking at them with wondering pleasure. "Me? I don't plan to dance again, but in a year or so I'll get around. The doctor expects Docchi to have arms in the next three or four years if the principle he discovered with Maureen works out.

"And even you, Jordan, may be kicking again, though it will take longer. Say four or five years for you."

"I'll kick," scoffed Jordan, but his disbelief wasn't as strong as it had been.

"Sure you will," said Anti. "It may not be as quick as we expect. Of course if we learn anything from interchange of science with the aliens the time may be shortened. Cameron says they're bound to help us advance, just as we'll aid them. He's cautious though, and doesn't want to figure that in until it actually occurs."

"I'll believe it when..." said Docchi. "But you didn't mention Jeriann. Or do you consider her already normal?"

Anti frowned at her toes and slipped her feet into the sandals. "No, I don't. She seems to be in nearly perfect health. But don't believe everything you see."

"Darling," said Jeriann. "When did I have my last capsule? I don't have any with me."

"An hour or so ago."

"Are you sure? My time sense keeps warning me."

"If you think we should let's go and get one."

"She knows," said Anti. "I heard the doctor telling her that her case looked easy but wasn't. She'll be the last."

"Wait," called Docchi who scarcely heard what Anti was saying. He hurried out into the hall after Jeriann. He was gone a few minutes, and when he came back there was a handprint flaming and furious on his face.

He looked at Anti dully. "I didn't say anything. I told her to wait and I'd go with her."

"She can't help it," said Anti. "I thought it was time you knew."

"What is there to know?" he said bitterly. "She's upset because she can't eat. Compared to some of us it's merely an inconvenience. I resent her childishness."

"It was always there for you to see but you never looked close enough," sighed Anti. "How many times has she had to control herself."

"But I never said anything—"

"I know what you said," answered Anti. "When she had *her* accident it was a very hot day. She was a young girl and was busy playing and didn't realize how badly she wanted it until she started for the fountain. She was struck down before she reached it. Now—what was it you told her?"

"A drink," he said, staring at Anti in dismay. "I told her—"

"Twenty years of thirst. But you knew there was nothing that is even moist in her house. The shower spouts fine dry particles. And she had no pictures that show lakes or rivers. Go find her."

Water. It was life because it came before life. There were creatures that could exist quite comfortably without light. There were some that died in the half strength of the sun, to whom the visible spectrum and beyond was inimical. There were others that didn't need oxygen, anaerobic microorganisms which perished in the free atmosphere because of the presence of a substance commonly considered necessary for living things.

But there was nothing that could exist without water. Life on Earth originated there and to it must always return. It was the cradle of the first cell, and the mother too. There were minute cells that lived motionless and free floating in water long before any living thing learned to swim through its droplet universe. Before there were fins or hands and feet, eyes to respond to light, and an orifice to eat and shape fine noises with—there was water. And any living creature that had a mouth from time to time might refresh its lips with the common and precious fluid.

Except Jeriann.

The psychotechnicians knew they could condition her and so it had been done. She could not drink, would not. She would resist if it were forced upon her, struggle until her bones broke. But even the psycho technicians who had created the mental block hadn't completely trusted it. And so a place had been built for her in which she would not be reminded of water, the one thing she never got enough of.

Because the habit of life was strong and water meant survival. This was not something she imagined. It was buried in the memory of the cells, deeper than any mind, going back to the beginning. Twenty years of never enough.

Docchi stumbled out. It was neither light nor dawn when he found her. The side of the asteroid was turned away from the sun but though the planet was rising brightly and filled much of the sky there were still deep shadows within the dome. "I've been waiting for you," she said quietly as he came near. Her face reflected the planet shine.

"Jeriann," he said.

"Look at it," she said.

"I see."

"But you're looking at me." She turned his head toward the planet. "There. If you look closely you can see sunlight sparkling on the ocean. Isn't it beautiful?"

"Someday you'll lie on the beach and let the waves wash over you."

"Someday" she said.

THE END

If you've enjoyed this book, you will not want to miss these terrific titles…

ARMCHAIR SCI-FI & HORROR DOUBLE NOVELS, $12.95 each

D-131   **COSMIC KILL** by Robert Silverberg
BEYOND THE END OF SPACE by John W. Campbell

D-132   **THE DARK OTHER** by Stanley Weinbaum)
WITCH OF THE DEMON SEAS by Poul Anderson

D-133   **PLANET OF THE SMALL MEN** by Murray Leinster
MASTERS OF SPACE by E. E. "Doc" Smith & E. Everett Evans

D-134   **BEFORE THE ASTEROIDS** by Harl Vincent
SIXTH GLACIER, THE by Marius

D-135   **AFTER WORLD'S END** by Jack Williamson
THE FLOATING ROBOT by David Wright O'Brien

D-136   **NINE WORLDS WEST** by Paul W. Fairman
FRONTIERS BEYOND THE SUN by Rog Phillips

D-137   **THE COSMIC KINGS** by Edmond Hamilton
LONE STAR PLANET by H. Beam Piper & John J. McGuire

D-138   **BEYOND THE DARKNESS** by S. J. Byrne
THE FIRELESS AGE by David H. Keller, M. D.

D-139   **FLAME JEWEL OF THE ANCIENTS** by Edwin L. Graber
THE PIRATE PLANET by Charles W. Diffin

D-140   **ADDRESS: CENTAURI** by F. L. Wallace
IF THESE BE GODS by Algis Budrys

ARMCHAIR SCIENCE FICTION & HORROR CLASSICS, $12.95 each

C-58   **THE WITCHING NIGHT**
by Leslie Waller

C-59   **SEARCH THE SKY**
by Frederick Pohl and C. M. Kornbluth

C-60   **INTRIGUE ON THE UPPER LEVEL**
by Thomas Tempel Hoyne

ARMCHAIR SCI-FI & HORROR GEMS SERIES, $12.95 each

G-15   **SCIENCE FICTION GEMS, Vol. Eight**
Keith Laumer and others

G-16   **HORROR GEMS, Vol. Eight**
Algernon Blackwood and others

LEAVING NEW YORK, DESTINATION...VENUS?

When you board an airliner for a flight from New York to Los Angeles, you don't expect to end up on another planet. But that's exactly what happened to the crew and passengers of Flight 106. The flight had seemed so ordinary. The pilot received his green light from ground control; the takeoff went very smoothly; and there had been no turbulence to deal with. Fifteen minutes after boarding, the stewardess was getting to know her passengers in her usual, cheery manner. Everything seemed A-okay.

But an abrupt mid-air collision changed the lives of all on board, who suddenly found themselves in the custody of alien forces from another world. These alien captors proclaimed that return to Earth was impossible—their new home would soon be the planet Venus. But there were two on board who had other ideas. Sammy Walters and Sue Painter were two Earthlings bound and determined to find a way back to their home planet. The only question was...how?

CAST OF CHARACTERS

SAMMY WALTERS

Flying was his life, and a certain girl was his obsession; he was determined to protect Sue Painter—even from an alien threat.

SUE PAINTER

She was an exceptional passenger attendant, but she never dreamed her plane would be struck by a flying saucer.

DUFFY SCOTT

Scott was an experienced pilot, but bored with life—until he unexpectedly met up with some incoming pilots from Venus.

MRS. ELSTON

This widow, on her way to L.A. to bury her only child, had lost interest in life...until she found herself on the way to a new planet!

LEMUEL TOLLIVER

He claimed to have been taken to Venus, and even wrote a book about it. But what did the Venerians have to say about it?

WILLIAM BLAKE HUNTINGFORD

As a war-time newsman, he'd had a lot to report...but a collision with a flying saucer could be his greatest story.

PAUL HOLLOWAY

He may not have been socially adept, but he was one of the best flight engineers in the world.

IF THESE
BE GODS

By
ALGIS BUDRYS

ARMCHAIR FICTION
PO Box 4369, Medford, Oregon 97504

CHAPTER ONE

FLIGHT One-Oh-Six, *Inter-Sky Airlines,* New York to Los Angeles, was a DC-7B with twenty-odd thousand hours logged flight time. She was due for another thousand hour check at Los Angeles, when she got there, and on this mild Summer morning while she sat at the head of Runway Two at La Guardia, her engines running up for takeoff, no one knew she would never make it.

Her captain was Duffy Scott, a stocky, white-haired, weather-tanned little man with deep creases around his eyes, machine gun scars on one leg, eyes as pale as glacier ice, and flight time that included Curtiss P-6E's. He had just put down the instrument test checklist, with its scarlet ISA logotype in the upper left hand corner, and he was reflecting, as he always did at this time, on what time had done to what had once been a bold and venturesome trade.

When Duffy Scott had been a young daredevil fresh out of Kelly Field, ISA had been *Interstate Airways;* a company operating largely out of its founder's battered hat, with its corporate assets tied up in two sheet-iron Ford tri-motors and a schedule calling for regular flights between Newark and Boston.

Somewhere along the line, the Fords had been replaced. Sometime during the '30s, the founder had sold out to a board of directors. The offices had moved into their own building in downtown New York, and the schedule had grown. Sometime during World War II, it had become necessary to torture syntax into providing a new name to fit the initials. And somewhere between 1925 and 1958, Duffy Scott had lost that bright Kelly Field gleam and turned into a settled, leathery man who didn't even very much mind drawing a monotonously regular paycheck for wheeling a four-motored passenger train over the same ribbon of sky for month after month after year.

Except that he sometimes grew a little more withdrawn than usual, and stared unseeingly over the barricade of instruments in his cockpit and wished that something—something not too serious—would come along to jolt his routine just a little.

THE co-pilot was a slim young man with a butch haircut. His name was Sammy Walters. He showed no signs of having any nerves in his system at all, and he was thinking about a girl.

The flight engineer was a tall man named Paul Holloway, who had learned his trade in the Army Air Corps after coming off a Kansas farm. He was inclined toward being a lone wolf, and even though he had been in one ISA crew or another for eight years, no one knew him very well. He was incessantly reading technical magazines and engineering journals, and these seemed to take up a major part of his off time. He was remarked upon as being a man who neither smoked nor drank, nor, even though he was almost as handsome as pilots were supposed to be, paid any attention whatsoever to women. At the moment he was making his first plots on the fuel consumption graph, and mildly regretting not having stayed in the Air Force, now that the rocket program was really showing signs of coming to a head.

"Green light, Duff," the copilot said to the captain.

Duffy Scott released the wheel brakes. Sammy Walters advanced the throttles, and the aircraft began to roll. It gathered speed into the wind, and at 9:10 A.M. Wednesday, August 27, 1958, *Inter-Sky Airlines* Flight 106 left the ground for the last time.

THE passenger list was small—down to the point where ISA was losing money on the flight. All the airlines were having a touch of that trouble this summer. There had been a run of crashes in June and July. Most of them had been billed as "mysterious" by the newspapers. The Civil Aeronautics Board inspectors had gone to work and patiently pinned down the various causes, but their findings inevitably were released long after the crashes were dead as news, and therefore new "mysterious" crashes continued to appear on Page One while the various explanations for the old ones ran back among the discount house advertisements.

It was also a peak summer for flying saucer sightings, and the two factors inevitably became connected in the public mind. There was talk of doing something about the interplanetary menace in the air. Airline public relations firms worked hard to knock it down, but air travel fell off nevertheless.

Airline personnel went on about the business of working at their trade. The industry was big enough, and the true percentage of accidents was small enough, so that very few of them actually knew or had heard of the crewmen in the downed aircraft. Accidents were something that happened, that usually happened in bunches for no good reason, and that would inevitably stop happening as unaccountably as they began. Meanwhile, flight like ISA 106 ran very light.

Inter-Sky Airlines would never have assigned as big an aircraft as a DC-7B to Flight 106 if ISA's main shops had not been at Los Angeles and if the plane weren't due for a check. ISA *had* managed to wangle through an agreement with the aircrew union and assign only one passenger attendant to the flight. This was Sue Painter—a black-haired, willowy girl with pleasant features who was debating marrying a junior executive at the Los Angeles offices of a TV network, and who sometimes wondered, though not seriously, if she shouldn't quit flying and try getting into the movies.

She might, or she might not, have made it—she was attractive without being beautiful, and she was good to look at without having a spectacular body. She had only an average potential as an actress. She was probably ISA's best passenger attendant.

Now that 106 was airborne and on course, she came down the aisle to check on her passengers. She was faced with the problem of making a handful of people feel at home in the face of scores of empty seats. She expected to solve the problem, even though most of the passengers were presently scattered far apart, and she set about doing so. She had already memorized the passenger list and matched names to faces when she checked seat belts back at La Guardia. Now she came to the first occupied seat and bent over it.

"Everything all right, Mrs. Elston?" she smiled at the worried, gray-haired woman who sat stiffly upright, her swollen ankles pinched by the high tops of her black leather shoes. "Here—let me open your seat belt for you. It's quite all right now—we're well off the ground."

MRS. Elston looked quickly down at her lap. "Oh, I'm sorry—I forgot." She smiled wanly at Sue Painter as though she didn't expect to be believed when she said, "I'm not nervous about flying, really. I was just thinking of something else." Her eyes, under the rim of her plain dark bonnet, suddenly filled with tears which did not quite run down her furrowed cheeks. With a perceptible shock, Sue Painter realized that Mrs. Elston was even much older than she had seemed—or perhaps she only appeared to be.

"You see," Mrs. Elston said in a soft voice, "I'm going to attend my only child's funeral. I'm a widow, and Thomas was all the family I had. His company sent him to Los Angeles a year ago, and he died of a heart attack last night." She sank back as Sue Painter gently opened the belt and folded the two halves out of the way. "I always have been afraid of flying," she sighed. "But I'm not afraid anymore. I've outlived a fine husband and a wonderful son. It's hard to understand—a strong, robust man like my Joseph was dying in his prime, and now Thomas...It's more than I can puzzle out. I've never been a particularly strong person. I only had one child...the doctors told me I couldn't have any more after Thomas...and yet—I'm alive, and they're gone. I wouldn't be afraid if we crashed, Miss." She turned her face toward the window, and looked out at the dazzlingly bright southern horizon. Her lips quivered, and she put a crumpled white handkerchief to her cheeks. "I—I might even welcome it," she whispered.

"There now, Mrs. Elston," Sue Painter said. "I've been flying for five years, over three hundred thousand miles. And I've never been in a plane that had so much trouble as a burned-out light bulb." She realized as she said it that she might have thought of something better than Set

Speech #38, but Mrs. Elston had touched her so deeply that her presence of mind had been completely destroyed.

Mrs. Elston hadn't taken it the wrong way. She turned back from the window and put the handkerchief away in her patent leather handbag. She smiled up at Sue in the same wan fashion she had before.

"I'm sorry, Miss. I know it embarrasses people to have me talk that way. There isn't anything you can say to a person who wants to die, is there! People don't want to die. Not young people. Not a pretty girl like you. They don't have any way of coming to grips with a person who feels the way I do. To tell you the truth, I'm a little bit bewildered myself." She reached out and patted Sue's hand. "But don't you worry about me. I'll be all right."

SUE Painter said something—she scarcely heard herself, and could not remember a moment later, what it was and moved on to the next passenger. It had been her thought, when she began her tour of the cabin, to find out enough about each passenger so that she could introduce those with kindred interests to each other. Who could she introduce to Mrs. Elston?

She wanted desperately to do *something*—to somehow help fill the grieving void in Mrs. Elston's life. But there was nothing she could think of. Mrs. Elston's life was behind her. There was no time left in it for anything new. Young Sue Painter thought how terrible it was to live so close to dying.

THE next passenger was a smallish man in a salt-and-pepper sharkskin double breasted suit; he wore his jacket unbuttoned, revealing a matching vest with a watch chain that crossed his little potbelly. He had gray-black hair, receding from his temples to the back of his skull but still growing, from the center of his forehead and the sides of his head. It was brushed straight back, in a carefully groomed trident, and, together with the thin little mustache and the tortoise-shell glasses, gave Mr. Percival Guild the appearance of a small town chamber of commerce president.

Sue Painter had regained her customary composure. "Everything all right, Mr. Guild? Can I get you something?"

Percival Guild smiled up mechanically. "Quite all right, young lady, thank you. There is one thing—would you get me a deck of cards and a lapboard, please."

"Of course, Mr. Guild. Would you like me to find some partners for you among the passengers? You could play in the lounge—it's quite comfortable."

"No, thank you," Percival Guild said definitely. "I never play with partners. I prefer solitaire."

Percival Guild played solitaire incessantly. Unlike most solitaire players, he never varied his games. He had learned Canfield as a boy, from an uncle who was his guardian and who had died some time ago in a sanatorium. Percival Guild had lived within himself since the age of sixteen, and never played any form of cards except Canfield. He was married to a woman he scarcely noticed, and had three children he left entirely in his wife's care. Once he had stayed up two days and three nights in succession, alone in a hotel room in Minneapolis, dealing out hand after hand of Canfield. At the end of the third night, his eyes red-rimmed and his back one great aching mass, he had slipped out of the hotel, walked fourteen blocks, and there, in another hotel where he did not inquire at the desk but simply stepped into an elevator, he had cut the throat of a rival salesman who was about to win over his best account. Then he had left the same way he came, gone back to his own hotel, and begun dealing Canfield once more, waiting for the police. But, somehow, the police never came. For ten years, Percival Guild had been traveling his territories, advancing in his company, moving his family to ever better residential areas, playing Canfield, and waiting for the Minneapolis police to solve a ten-year-old murder. With the passage of time, he had begun to give up hope. But he knew there was Justice. He knew there was no way of cheating the natural order of things without losing all the savor of the game of life. If the ten years of success he had gained by cheating were not to be turned to ashes in his mouth, then somewhere, sometime, he must pay. He would pay gladly, because then all his present success would have been fairly earned.

It was all quite logical to Percival Guild. Everywhere he went, he waited for the Minneapolis police—or for any other personification of Justice. Always, just around the corner, Percival Guild expected to have an appointment with Destiny.

"Of course, Mr. Guild," Sue Painter said. "I'll bring you your cards right away."

"Thank you, Miss," Percival Guild said grimly.

CHAPTER TWO

In the forward cabin, Sammy Walters reached up and pushed his headphones more firmly against his ears. He listened for a moment, acknowledged, and tapped Duffy Scott's shoulder.

"Chicago states Distant Early Warning radar's picked up a flock of blips coming over the Pole, on course to pass over Indiana right about the time we'll be there. Wants us to report if we see anything."

Duffy Scott nodded. It was the most routine of messages. DEW was always picking up stray blips and ghost images, most of which were born in the Aurora Borealis. Even assuming the blips were unfriendlies or something else actually tangible, the various Air Force Fighter Interceptor Commands would have checked them out long before ISA Flight 106 crossed their projected path. In all of Duffy Scott's experience, none of these advisory bulletins had ever panned out. No one expected them to. They were put on the air just in case. If by any chance something from over the Pole got as far as Indiana, it would already be much too late to do anything about it.

Of course, Duffy Scott thought to himself, there was no real reason why those blips couldn't be the start of World War III. No real reason, except that he didn't believe it. Even though he had gotten the news of Pearl Harbor while pushing a DC3 over the Andes on a day every bit as peaceful as this, it was impossible to think that he, himself, of all the pilots in the air today, should become personally involved in anything so dramatic. The odds were enormously against it.

Still, *somebody* always had to be it. In the back of his mind, he felt the merest trace of tingling anticipation. Sure—he thought violently—let's get the world blown up just to give me a thrill! The anticipation disappeared, buried under common sense. ISA 106 droned westward, an hour and a half away from Indianapolis.

MIKE Hogan had been first aboard the plane at La Guardia. He had picked a seat next to a window, buckled his seat belt, leaned back, crossed his long legs, and gone to sleep. Fifteen minutes later, when Sue Painter spoke to Percival Guild two rows behind him, he came easily a wake, stretched, slipped off the belt, and lit a cigarette. He was in the habit of cat-napping, like any healthy animal, whenever he had nothing else to do. Now he felt refreshed and alive, in spite of the fact that his only other sleep in the past twenty-four hours had been a similar nap in the cab that took him straight from Winslow Dennison's cocktail party to the airport.

He thought about Dennison now, and grimaced. Dennison was the New York publicity director for A-J TV Inc., a video film series syndication company, and he had held the party as a kickoff for a campaign plugging A-J's newest product: *The Adventures of Ash Holcomb*. The series was built around a medium-clever idea; the hero was the son of Doctor Luther Holcomb, scientific genius. Dr. Holcomb supposedly had a time machine, through which his handsome, muscular son could travel to have adventures in any era, past, future, or, without the machine but with other gadgets, the present. Thus, *The Adventures of Ash Holcomb* could become a western, crime, historical, or science fiction series at any moment, depending on the latest trend, and the invincible Ash could slaughter villains and make love to beautiful women in four formats.

Mike Hogan, until two years ago, had been an ex-naval officer who had had his fill of discipline. After the Second World War he had resigned his commission, bought a car and trailer with his saved back pay, and gone where he pleased, working as a high steel construction gang foreman, a high tension lineman, or an oil driller whenever his money ran out. Before the war he had been all these things, as well as a dozen more like them. He was a broad shouldered, hard-jawed, solidly competent man with work scars on his hands, and at the moment his black hair was bleached platinum white.

Two years ago, Mike Hogan had been bossing an oil gang in Oklahoma. He had been at it for six months, and there was money in his bank account. He was ready to quit and move on.

It had happened that a movie location crew was set up in the area, getting background shots for a new two-fisted vehicle starring one of the big masculine box-office names. It had happened that the second unit director noticed Mike Hogan, and thought to himself that the studio had been having a great deal of trouble keeping the star in line. It had happened that the director, and the producer, saw their opportunity to help themselves with the studio.

So, Mike Hogan had come to Hollywood under contract to the director and the producer, and had actually made one low-budget picture. He turned out to have a reasonable amount of talent, and enough attraction to worry the box-office king a little. The box-office king signed his new contract without as much trouble as he had been planning to make. The studio then saw no reason to keep a third string substitute on its payroll, and Mike Hogan never made a Hollywood picture again.

But it had happened that Mike Hogan liked the freedom of not working from nine to five every day, six days a week, fifty-two weeks a year. Perhaps something had happened to him when he saw his name on a major studio credit. And the producer and director still held his personal contract. It happened that the producer had a connection with a TV film outfit. It happened that A-J TV needed somebody to play Ash Holcomb.

So it happened that Mike Hogan had his hair bleached, and his name changed to Lance Shawnee, and had flown to New York for Winslow Dennison's cocktail party, and now was flying back to make more Ash Holcomb episodes.

And it happened that Mike Hogan was already sick of dry Martinis and account executives. It happened that Mike Hogan was restless again, and worried that he would run to nerves and hangovers, and lose the fine control of his skills that were his pride and his freedom. He was trapped by his contracts, and beginning to feel the trap of having more money than he knew how to handle. He wanted to let the peroxide grow out of his hair, and clamber up a web of quivering steel into the clean wind that whips through the towers men build upon their Earth. He had begun looking for something, some lucky chance, that would let him escape.

IT WAS only after he heard the flight attendant speaking to someone in the seat next to him that he realized he, of all the few passengers in the aircraft, was not sitting alone.

"Everything all right, Mr. Tolliver?"

"Let me assure you, Miss, everything will be fine. There is absolutely no danger with me aboard."

Mike Hogan looked curiously at his fellow passenger.

Mr. Tolliver was a gaunt, bald man with rimless eyeglasses that he wore all during his waking hours. He wore a blue serge suit and carried a book in his lap. It was turned over to the back jacket, and the photograph reproduced there showed Mr. Tolliver, in the same suit, gravely holding a pipe and fingering a celestial globe on the desktop in front of him.

Mr. Tolliver was holding the book in such a manner that his fingers did not obscure the picture. To do that, he had to place his hand so the spine, with its title, was hidden from Mike Hogan's curious glance.

"I—I beg your pardon, Mr. Tolliver?" the bewildered flight attendant was saying. Mike Hogan had time to see she was a pleasantly attractive girl. He liked her instantly, and hoped she wasn't going to have too bad a time with Mr. Tolliver.

Mr. Tolliver smiled benignly up at her. "I know all you aviation people..." He pronounced it *aa*-viation. "...are greatly worried about the crashes. I can assure you the spacemen will do nothing to harm this aircraft. You see, I am one of their chosen people." His hand, as though accidentally, turned the book over. The front jacket showed a bell-shaped flying saucer hovering over a pastoral countryside, with classic Grecian buildings visible in the background, lightly dressed, golden-skinned people in the foreground, and alien vegetation growing in the middle distance. The title was *I Have Been To Venus,* by Lemuel Tolliver.

"Oh, I see," the flight attendant said. Fast on the uptake, Mike Hogan thought to himself. Very fast. Now she was smiling brightly at Lemuel Tolliver. "Well, Mr. Tolliver, I'm very glad you're aboard. We don't often have important authors with us."

"Oh, I'm not an author, Miss. That is, not in the usual sense of the word. This book—" He caressed the jacket with his fingertips, "—this book is only one means of bringing the spacemen's message to the people of this frightened world. I am on my way now to California to deliver a series of lectures—to address people who are willing to believe that there are things in the sky no one can explain, and to tell them that there is a better world, and a better way of life."

"Of course, Mr. Tolliver. I wish you lots of success." The flight attendant smiled again. "Is there anything I can get you? Some magazines to read?"

Lemuel Tolliver shook his head. "No, thank you, Miss. I'm quite content, thank you."

"All right," She turned to Mike Hogan. "Is there something I can get you, Mr. Shawnee?"

MIKE Hogan saw her eyes widen a fraction as she noticed the bleach in his hair. He grinned at her. "No thanks. I'll come back to the lounge later, if you've got some honest bourbon in stock. But I'm fine for now." He let his eyes linger on her blouse, and gave the grin a touch of a special twist. He had already learned that men with peroxided hair had best do that. The difficulty lay in making his interest obvious without being offensive. It was one more tightrope he was sick of walking, even though this fresh-faced girl was the first woman he'd met since he took the part who made him care whether he succeeded or not.

"We have all kinds of beverages, Mr. Shawnee. ISA does its best to assure a happy trip," the flight attendant said with her well-trained smile, and went down the aisle to see to the last passenger.

CHAPTER THREE

Sammy Walters tapped Duffy Scott's sleeve again. "Got some more on those blips. Chicago says they're still on course, altitude maybe eighty thousand, speed about 1000 but erratic." His voice grew a little puzzled. "They didn't sound worried about it."

"Fifteen miles is a lot of altitude, Sammy," Scott explained patiently. "Nobody's got an operational production bomber that'll go it. It might be missiles, but a thousand miles an hour is mighty slow for something like that. That's less than a third of a mile per second. It still might be, if they were hanging at the top of a trajectory and getting ready to come down, but then their speed would be increasing constantly, instead of jumping around. They might be correcting trajectories, which would account for *that,* but then they wouldn't be maintaining a constant course. So the only thing that fits the description would be a flock of ghost blips. Radar'll do that, sometimes—take a funny bounce, or distort, or just plain see something that isn't there. One thing's sure those blips'll peter out the same way they showed up, and nobody'll ever be able to explain it definitely. It happens pretty often, and whenever one of these crackpots hears about it, there's another flying saucer for you."

"But Chicago still wants us to look."

Duffy Scott sighed. He was sighing for a number of things, and, though he did not quite know it, one of the things was his constant refusal to make an adventure of this opportunity. "Chicago wants us to look because the DEW operators have the blips logged, and the word is in to Washington, and the word is back out from Washington to the Fighter Commands, and from the Fighter Commands to the CAB, and the CAB has sent the word to Chicago, and that's why Chicago still wants us to look." He stared out over the distances that stretched beyond the starboard wing. "Pittsburgh," he said.

"That makes us about an hour out of Indianapolis. In about an hour, you can start looking. Because Chicago sent me the word, and I'm giving the word to you. That makes it a good long chain of command—which ought to prove that you can have a good long chain without it being attached to anything."

PAUL Holloway, the Flight Engineer, sitting within easy hearing distance of Duffy Scott and Sammy Walters, almost said something. He opened his lips, and made the wet click people make when they begin to speak. But he caught himself, and the steady roar of the propellers covered the slight sound so that neither the captain nor co-pilot heard it.

Words were brimming inside Paul Holloway, as words often did. Like every man who devotes a great deal of time to silent thinking, Paul Holloway had chewed on a great many subjects and arrived at opinions on them. When those subjects were raised by someone else in his hearing, everything he had ever thought or decided on the subject came pouring into the forefront of his mind. That is why, if a silent man can only be started talking, an astonishing flood of words spills out of him.

But, curiously, this can rarely be done when the subject is very important to the man. The man is silent to begin with because he fears no one will listen, or care. If the subject is one he has spent a long time with, his deductions and conclusions come so personalized, so individual—or so it seems to him—that they could not help but be faintly ridiculous to anyone else.

So Paul Holloway almost said something to Duffy Scott, but stopped. It had been the way Duffy said 'flying saucers' that cued him, and it had been the same tone of voice that had stopped him.

Paul Holloway knew he lived on a world that was only one rolling ball on the shore of a sea of stars. Most people are willing to admit the fact, Paul Holloway *knew* it. When he looked at the sky, in the night, he was not looking up. He was looking out—out into the depths of the limitless ocean where other worlds must be, with other peoples. He had carried his knowledge further; he knew that someone out there must be capable of navigating space. To have things be any other way was to have them violate all laws of probability. To think that out of all those stars, with all those planets, not one race had spaceships—that, for Paul Holloway, was unthinkable.

He had no proof of this. He needed none. He had no proof that Mankind was the only intelligent life in the universe, either, and of the two unproven alternatives he believed the more logical one.

The thought that Man was not supreme—that Paul Holloway was not supreme—did not frighten or repel him. It made him less lonely. When he stared silently out of a control cabin window and spoke to no one, he was not withdrawing. He was going out.

He had never seen a flying saucer or anything else vaguely like one. He had no idea of whether flying saucers existed, or, if they did, where they might come from. Paul Holloway needed no tangible proofs. He had faith.

He busied himself with his fuel flowmeter and consumption graphs. He watched his instruments, read the messages they gave him, and acted in accordance. Because he was not a friendly man, his fellow crew members had only his work for a basis on which to judge him. He did that work perfectly and single-mindedly, but now his professional attention was lessened by one small fraction of a degree. Just the littlest bit, Paul Holloway was wishing Duffy Scott would get his nose rubbed in flying saucers—in the biggest, most startling squadron of alien spaceships that ever raced across Terrestrial skies.

THE last passenger was a portly man in a tweed suit. He had a beefy red face, curly iron-gray hair with patches of pink scalp shining through it, and was smoking a cigar. His name was Blake Huntingford—William Blake Huntingford, actually, but that had been dropped before his senior year at Harvard—and he was a Washington newspaper columnist at the moment. He had been machine-gunned at Cambrai, in the first large tank battle in history, and gone on to wipe out one of Von Hindenburg's mortar squads in spite of it. He had been on the wrong side in the Spanish Civil War, and he had stood in the cold surf at Dunkirk with a wounded man on each arm. He had hitched a ride in a Liberator to cover a Ploesti air strike, after he'd found no army would take him any more except as a correspondent, and he'd had to jump out over Yugoslavia after the scientifically designed Davis wing on the B-24 wrapped itself around the fuselage. He had spent the rest of the war first in a prison camp and then in a ZI hospital. He'd missed the Pacific war entirely, and he'd gone to Korea first, when that began, and gotten his newspaper accreditization second, after he'd already been shot once. He was lucky at that.

He liked to go to war with an Abercrombie and Fitch rucksack full of clean underwear, and Bols gin in orange earthenware bottles; he hated getting dirty, and, though he didn't care one way or another about liquor, he felt people expected a correspondent to be a source of supply. He had three four-star generals for friends, and two for deadly enemies. He was a pudgy, eccentric, mildly vain man who had no idea of what fear might feel like. He was on his way to Beverly Hills to see his children by his fourth wife, and then he was planning to go on to Hong Kong and see if he couldn't drift into China and take a look around. He had once fired a shot that had almost killed Duffy Scott, in an old war nobody remembered, but neither of them knew it.

At the moment, he had a bad headache, and was wondering how long it would last. The violent pain was blurring his vision, and he knuckled his right eye impatiently.

"Comfortable, Mr. Huntingford?" the pretty young flight attendant was asking him.

HE LOOKED up at her through a mist of pain, and squinted to bring her features into focus. Quite a pretty girl, he confirmed. Most men wouldn't think her as attractive as she really is—but then, most men haven't had my experience.

The flash of wry vanity made him smile at himself, and at the girl as well. "Tiptop," he said heartily in the thick Cambridge accent he had acquired sometime around 1925 and scrupulously maintained ever since. He saw no point in mentioning the headache—he could barely bring himself to believe in using antibiotics, much less aspirin—and, besides, a headache was a ridiculous malady for a man who had been shot, starved, frostbitten, beaten by prison camp guards on occasion, and who could expect more of the same for the rest of his life. He held up his cigar and said, "I hope this is all right. I know anything besides cigarettes is against regulations, but I thought, being able to sit away from anyone else the way I am, you wouldn't mind?"

"That's quite all right, Mr. Huntingford." Sue Painter suddenly peered at him for a closer look. He was staring at the end of the cigar, wide-eyed, and he had suddenly gone pale. "Is anything wrong?"

He shook his head. "NO—no, thank you, Miss," he said hastily. "I was just...thinking of something."

The answer he gave her was automatic and instinctive. It had always been his first reaction to refuse help.

It had happened while he watched. First the glowing orange end of the cigar had been outlined in a growing halo of murkiness, like oil smoke. Then the pall had spread, until the orange glow was the only dim light filtering through it. The seat in front of him, the side of the fuselage, even his hand, had all been lost in the swelling mist. Then even the last spark had wavered out, and it was as though he sat in a room full of dark, impenetrable fog.

He brought the cigar to his lips with a halting gesture, and drew on it. Hot smoke burned at his tongue, but no bright gleam of fire came to life before his eyes. He rubbed his hand over his face, and blinked, rubbed his face again.

"Are you sure everything's all right, Mr. Huntingford?"

He smiled up at the voice. "Quite fine, Miss. As a matter of fact, I did have a slight headache, but it seems to be gone, now. Wonderful things, these pressurized cabins."

He reached toward the ashtray, keeping his arm steady and purposeful. Luckily, he had remembered exactly where it was—when his fingertips touched cold curved metal, he almost sighed. He stubbed out the cigar. Even though it had hardly been smoked at all, he'd immediately become worried that it might be near burning his fingers.

The flight attendant had gone back up the aisle. Blake Huntingford sat with his hands in his lap, thinking:

It's bound to clear up again. In a little while, the pressure or whatever it was that did it will change, and it'll clear up again. I'll stop by at a doctor's in Los Angeles and have myself checked over, just in case, but it can't be anything serious. It'll clear up again.

He sat quite still, hands in his lap, staring into the fog, waiting for it to clear.

CHAPTER FOUR

In the control cabin, Sammy Walters chewed his lower lip and tapped Duffy Scott's shoulder again. "We're going to overhead the Indiana state line in about five minutes. Want me to start looking now?"

Duffy Scott sighed again. "Anything you want, Sammy."

"If you don't think it's worth bothering, I won't."

"You do what you want, Sammy."

"Damn it, you're the captain. Do you want me to start looking?"

"All right, all right—I'm the captain. Start looking."

MIKE Hogan looked over at Lemuel Tolliver, who still held the book jacket-uppermost. "Planning to read it over on the flight, were you?" he asked gently.

Lemuel Tolliver looked down quickly. "Why—why, no."

"You just carry it."

Lemuel Tolliver's watery blue eyes grew stormy behind the clear shells of his rimless glasses. "That's correct, Mr.—ah, Shawnee, was it?"

"Hogan. Michael Faraday Hogan. My father was an engineer." *My brother drives a hack*, he added to himself. *My sister takes in washing, and the baby balls the jack. And it looks like I'm never gonna cease my wanderin'.* He began to hum, silently in his mind, and almost hummed the next thing he said to Mr. Tolliver, "You wrote it, so you don't have to read it. But you always carry a copy, hmm? It's different, I must say."

Now why should I want to needle this eccentric old man? He thought to himself. If he wants to say he's been to Venus and been buddies with some nice gold-skinned Venerians who all talk like church elders, why should I mind? He's not bothering me.

The hell he isn't, he thought immediately afterward. He sticks that book in people's faces to make them think he's important, and he spreads his pap to satisfy the people who want their troubles solved for them. Saucers, nothing! Those are pie plates. Pie in the sky, from the Sweet By-And-By, and Lemuel Tolliver cuts it to the customer's taste.

Come on, Hogan—face it. You don't know what to think.

"That is correct, Mr. Hogan," Lemuel Tolliver said again. "I take copies with me wherever I go, in the hope that I will interest someone in their content." He was obviously angry at Hogan, but was also obviously doing his best to hide it. "I would like to know—I would like to know, Mr. Hogan, if you are so sure of everything that you can say the spacemen's message has no meaning for you?"

"I wouldn't know. I don't know what they're selling."

"They are selling Love, Mr. Hogan. Brotherly love, and the spiritual kinship of all The Creator Spirit's children. They are selling peace, and good will, and a better life than we misguided inhabitants of this sin-ridden world can dream of. In this book, I am trying to pass on to the world a message of hope and understanding. I was honored beyond measure when they came to my farm and chose me to be their instrument, I shall devote the remainder of my life to awakening Mankind. In this book, I describe their world, which we mistakenly call Venus, and the wonders of living in accord with The Creator Spirit. Think of how marvelous it would be if this world were to be free of war, of pestilence and famine—of avarice, and drunkenness, and drug-taking, and lechery."

Mike Hogan was humming again, "There ain't no sickness, no toil and trouble, in that fair land to which you go?"

"Exactly, Mr. Hogan. In spite of your outward mockery, I think you might well profit from reading this book." He pushed it into Mike Hogan's hands.

HOGAN raised his eyebrows. "Well, maybe." He turned it over a few times. "All right." What the hell. "I'll read it later."

"As you wish, Mr. Hogan. That will be three dollars and fifty cents, please."

"*What!*"

"Three dollars and fifty cents," Lemuel Tolliver repeated firmly. "The retail price is clearly marked on the flyleaf."

"Now, wait a minute...I've gotten a book or two from a writer before. I'll be damned if I'll pay for an author's free copy."

"My dear Mr. Hogan, that is not an author's free copy. My publisher's contract allows me a twenty-five percent royalty on each copy sold, that is true, but in return it was necessary for me to underwrite the costs of printing and binding. The publication of this book required my life's savings, and I was forced to mortgage my farm to purchase the edition after my publisher informed me it had not sold well and would be scrapped for waste paper."

"You never went to any recognized publisher, Mr. Tolliver."

"I went to whoever was willing to publish this message at all. Now I can regain my money only by selling the book myself. That will be three dollars and fifty cents, please."

HOGAN'S mouth twisted in a wry grin. He hunched forward in the seat and fished his wallet out of his hip pocket. He handed Mr. Tolliver four ones, and Mr. Tolliver scrupulously counted a quarter, two dimes and five pennies out of a snap-latch black purse.

"Thank you very much, Mr. Hogan. I'm sure you'll profit by your reading. You'll find I've autographed the flyleaf, incidentally."

Hogan opened the book, and read, "To another willing listener to the message from Lhuanna, with best regards, Lemuel Tolliver."

"Lhuanna," Mike Hogan said.

"That is the true name for the world we call Venus," Mr. Tolliver explained.

Hogan twisted around in his seat so he could look Mr. Tolliver squarely in the face. "Did you deliberately sit next to me so you could sell me this book?"

Mr. Tolliver did not answer. He ignored Mike Hogan and sat facing forward, his shoulders stiff and his withered fingers looking strangely empty in his lap.

"A lot of good this is doing me," Sammy Walters grumbled in the control compartment. ISA 106 was boring steadily through patchy overcast. Sammy could see the airspace under the clouds only in disconnected fragments. The high sun reflecting off the upturned faces of the clouds made him squint and blink, even behind his sage green glasses, and almost anything might have been in the air at or above their own level. Still, he kept looking, facing out toward the right, looking northward in the direction of the faraway Pole.

Duffy Scott snorted and kept his eyes on the instruments, as good pilots did. The day when aircraft were flown the way automobiles are driven was long past. A pilot on course, following his flight plan at his assigned altitude, might look through his windscreen once in ten minutes. The remainder of the time he paid strict attention to his hundreds of instrument dials, which were there to tell him whether he was going to stay in the air or not.

Paul Holloway had his own instruments to pay attention to. He was barely aware of what Sammy Walters was doing. The subject of alien spaceships had drifted back into its compartment in his mind, where it belonged while he tended the gauges that told him how long the plane was going to stay in the air. His actions were automatic.

SUE Painter frowned unhappily as she watched the water bubble up through the top half of the Silex. She couldn't remember ever working a flight as weird as this one. First poor Mrs. Elston, who wanted to die, and then Mr. Tolliver, who had written that book about Venus. And that rugged-looking Lance Shawnee, with the bleached hair. Lance Shawnee! She was going to find out about that phony name and the dye job if it was the last thing she did on this flight.

Sue Painter wondered if he wasn't running from the police, or something. She was grateful for Mr. Huntingford, who looked like he might be able to handle trouble, and for Mr. Guild, who looked like a sensible man even if he was so stuffy.

She turned off the burner under the Silex and let the coffee start trickling down. She began making up luncheon trays, wishing she wasn't so nervous. There was no real reason for feeling that way—it was just that on a flight that felt as funny as this one, you half expected something to happen.

PERCIVAL Guild looked down at the board. Everything was laid out, except for the three cards he held in his hand. Now, if the bottom card was the nine of clubs, then the eight of hearts and seven of spades ought to be behind it, in that order. He might be wrong. He might lose.

He turned the three cards over. The bottom card had been the nine, with the eight and seven behind it. He nodded with satisfaction, laid them down in their proper places even though there was no real need to, and methodically moved the cards in each suit, in proper order, onto their proper ace. Though, of course, there was no real need to do that, either. It was just that in moving them, he might still make a mistake and thus lose the game.

He made no mistakes, but this way he had given his invisible opponent the benefit of every possible doubt. He picked up the cards and began to shuffle them carefully. He looked up for a moment, out through his window. Birds, he thought to himself, and bent his head to watch his shuffling.

Two seats in front of Percival Guild, Mike Hogan nudged Lemuel Tolliver and pointed. "Hey—look at *that!*"

Lemuel Tolliver bent sideward, across his lap, and craned his thin neck. "N*ooo...*"

Mrs. Elston sat looking at nothing. Blake Huntingford was doing the same.

CHAPTER FIVE

Sammy Walters' thinking was conditioned by his training. *Coming out of patch cloud,* he thought. *Won't ever see us in time. Flying line ahead—the first one's the only one with a chance to see us at all. Okay. He's pulling up. Maybe...No!* Damn that second man—didn't he see his leader pull up? *Didn't* he see? What's the *matter* with a dumb knucklehead like that! *"Duff!"*

ISA 106's cabin was pressurized. When the spaceship's leading edge chopped into her, it was as though an axe had struck a vacuum bottle.

THERE were sixteen of the ships in all—four flights of four each, not that it mattered to ISA 106—and the wing commander *had* managed to pull up at the last moment and get clear. His wingman had almost made it, as well, but he had tried a banking turn instead of a straight pull up, for instinctive reasons that were irrevocably buried in the history of his childhood. It was a question of one man reacting one way to a situation, and succeeding, because he was the way he was, and of another man reacting another way, and failing. Even so, ISA 106 was not quite cut in two. She hung in the sky, still holding flying speed, though her back was broken and flying debris had seriously injured her port wing. Fire was licking back from her outboard engine nacelle, and an aileron was in the process of disintegrating. For another moment or two, she could fly, though the cabin air had blown her passenger compartment out as cleanly as an artillery shell whirling up the barrel of a cannon.

The wing commander took it all in at a glance, already far beyond the collision scene. There was the native airliner, crabbing sideward from the shock, battered ragdolls trailing from the mortal gash in her silvery hide. Over there were the ships of his wing, scattered all over the sky in confusion. He looked for his wingman's ship, and found it; he muttered a relieved oath—it was flying, still airworthy. Whether it was still vacuum tight was another matter, but that could wait.

The wing commander spun his ship around its vertical axis, using maximum aperture on his perimeter jets. He cracked his fuel feed control open as far as it would go, and literally blazed across the sky to get back to the native aircraft. Something had to be done for those people. He prayed most of them were still alive.

And now, as he reversed course, the sound of high-speed atmospheric flight caught up with him. For three hours, his flight had been outrunning the noise of its own passage, as twelve massive objects tore through the air, displacing more cubic feet of space than any lightning bolt ever spawned. It was as though an entire storm had saved its energy for one titanic bolt; as though a mountain of air had rushed to fill the emptiness it left, and, rushing, met another mountain head on.

The sound crashed against his ship, against the entire wing, against ISA 106. It echoed from the tortured ground below, and shook the air with fury. Raw, raging hammer blows lashed and raved above Indiana, and all of Hell's artillery could not have matched them.

Sue Painter had been sucked out of the service compartment and thrown out through the opening in the cabin. She had broken an arm on the edge of the service compartment door, but it was a clean simple fracture, and, given time, could heal perfectly.

Mrs. Elston had been plucked from her seat and cannoned free of the plane. Her purse followed her, knocking Lemuel Tolliver unconscious, and throwing his eyeglasses off his face. He shot out into the sky, spread-eagled and whirling. Mike Hogan followed him, pounded by the seat backs over which the rushing air hurled him. Blake Huntingford knew only that something like a near miss by a bomb had intruded on his darkness. Now he felt a great wind pulling at him, different from the one great gust that had whirled and battered him. He wondered if he might not be falling.

All of them were falling. The pressure difference between the cabin and the outside air, at ISA 106's altitude, had not been great enough to do them much physical damage. But all of them were falling.

Duffy Scott and Sammy Walters had been in their seats, which were designed to keep the pilots from being jounced about. Neither of them had his safety belt buckled, but the seat design resisted the storm of expanding air long enough to keep them near the controls. Both of them had been plucked up, finally, and thrown against the overhead instruments before they fell back. Blood was running from cuts in their heads; both of them were conscious, and both of them had their hands back on the controls. But they were falling, too.

Paul Holloway had been blown off his seat and out into the passenger cabin. Before he could travel the long distance from the forward cabin, through the crew rest compartment, and up the length of the passenger cabin, the storm inside ISA 106 was dead. He lay in the aisle, sobbing a breath. He looked up, saw Percival Guild, and sobbed again, while he fell with the dying aircraft. Disorder was all about him.

PERCIVAL Guild, with his card-player's mind, had been the only passenger to sum up something of what had happened while it was still happening. A great many things went through his mind as he covered the short distance between his seat and the gash through which the raging air was pouring. Only he clearly heard the thunder that enveloped the airplane, and only he would have interpreted it as the sound of Doom.

He saw the jagged lips of torn metal, and saw that unless he floundered now, he would pass safely between them. Somehow, in that split second, he was able to arch his neck. He was able to smile. He was serene. There was credit and debit in the order of the universe. There was logic, precision…borrowing and repayment. The Minneapolis police had come at last. Percival Guild felt an enormous blow against his throat, and wondered that so sharp an edge could still hurt so much.

DUFFY Scott hung grimly to the control yoke, 106 was trying desperately to fall off on one wing, and he fought all of her wounded weight with his arms and shoulders. He made an unintelligible sound at Sammy Walters, but the co-pilot was already cranking the trim tab controls, trying to compensate for the lost aileron. Somehow, one of them tripped the extinguisher controls on the burning engine, and the nacelle vanished in a cloud of carbon dioxide.

106 was shuddering, her tall section writhing. Her keel spar held, but was powerless to resist shearing forces. In another moment, 106 would snap apart into two unflyable masses of aircraft metal.

Duffy Scott knew it, and Sammy Walters knew it. But they went on trying. The Indianapolis field was only a few miles away. It might as well have been on another planet, but the thing to do was to keep trying. Sammy Walters feathered the propeller on the dead engine. Duffy Scott called for practically no throttle on the two sound starboard engines, and full power on the one operating portside motor, in an attempt to turn 106 without throwing strain on her rudder. They lost speed sickeningly, and hundreds of feet of altitude, but that was just as well, if they could do it without using the elevators. The starboard aileron was already set to push its wing down, to keep 106 level at all costs.

106 yawed, but refused to turn. The keel spar shrieked in agony. Duffy Scott bit through his lower lip.

"Listen—Sam: I'm going to try reversing pitch on one of the right-hand props. Get it to push, instead of pull. Maybe that'll turn us."

"Snap us in two."

Duffy Scott nodded in agony. "I know, I know. But maybe it won't."

They felt a jar under the port wingtip, and another under the starboard. They looked out.

THE WING commander now worked frantically to coordinate his spaceship's controls. He had to balance a major portion of the native airliner's massive weight against the amount of engine power he could divert to the ducted fans that kept his ship hovering, and at the same time match velocity and direction with the airliner. But it was working out. The hovering fans on the underside of his ship were whirling at such a pace that would burn out their shaft bearings very soon, but they were meanwhile pressing his spaceship against the underside of one of the airliner's wings. At the other wingtip, another of the ships from his flight was doing the same. Now a third ship moved in under the airliner's nose, and formed the third leg of a stable supporting platform. At the same time, all three spaceships as a unit were matching the airliner's forward speed and sideward yaw.

It was fantastic airmanship, even for men who had been flying as a unit for years. But the wing commander felt no satisfaction from it. Equally bad airmanship had created this situation in the first place.

He still had no time to think about things for very long. He half stood in his seat and then motioned frantically to the pair of natives in the airliner's control cabin. He hoped he would not have to resort to radio, and waste time trying to find their particular frequency. He sighed when one of the natives finally understood, and cut his power. Slowly the airliner's propellers ran down to a stop. Gradually, the interlocked spaceships and airliner lost forward motion, and came to a hovering stop in the sky. Suddenly it was still as death, with only the high altitude wind moaning over the airliner's fuselage, and the sound of metal creaking came clearly through the hulls of all four craft. The airliner's tail section trembled.

Far below them, Lemuel Tolliver's eyeglasses shattered on the ground.

CHAPTER SIX

Sammy Walters looked at Duffy Scott. "What do we do now?"

Scott shook his head wearily. "We get out of here before the whole business slips off those saucers, or whatever they are."

"They look like saucers to me."

"*All right!*" Scott yelled with sudden, nerve-torn violence. "They're saucers. Now let's get the passengers out of here, somehow."

Paul Holloway chuckled tensely behind them. He swayed against the compartment divider, holding one hand to his broken cheekbone. "Nobody in there to worry about. Everybody got blown out except for one little guy. And he's hanging there with a hunk of aluminum through his neck. Got him in the carotid, I'd say—blood all over the place. So there's just the three of us to worry about."

"Lord," Sammy Walters muttered. He wiped trickles of his own blood out of his eyes and peered out the cabin windows. "How we going to work this?"

"Climb out on the wings, I guess, and try and cross over into those saucers."

"Sounds good. It's a long way down, Duff."

"You want to stay on board and find out just how long?"

Sammy Walters shook his head quickly. "No—not me, Duff. I'm going."

"All right," Duffy Scott tried to keep on thinking. It was an effort. "I don't think those things'll take more than one of us apiece. Sammy, you try for the one on the port wing. Paul, you take starboard. I'm going to try going over the nose."

Sammy Walters turned pale. "Man, there isn't a handhold or a flat surface anywhere there, Duff. You'll slip off for sure."

"You do what I said!" Duffy Scott shrilled. "You and Paul go back in the cabin, smash a couple of windows over the wings, and get going. You leave me to do things my way. I'm the captain here, damn it!" He was terrified of what he'd have to do. The DC-7B's nose was sharply rounded, and the saucer rested under it in such a way that he would have to inch his way out to the very tip and then slide off, with thousands of feet of empty air only inches away from the only place his feet could touch. He saw the saucer's pilot beckoning him frantically, his perfectly human-looking face urgent behind the tinted glass of his flight helmet, and he knew how little time they had. There was a grinding jar as the aircraft slipped a little on the saucer's curved flanks, and the three spaceships jockeyed frantically to hold 106 steady.

Sammy and Paul were already on their way back toward the passenger cabin, moving cautiously to keep the airliner in balance. Duffy Scott crossed himself, slipped off his shoes, and used one of them to crash out the glass in a forward window. He wormed his way over the instrument panel and out through the shattered window frame. He pressed his flat palms to the gritty aluminum skin, and inched his way around. Hugging the nose with his arms and thighs, he began pushing backwards, hoping that when he felt himself slip, the saucer and not emptiness would be under his feet. He pressed his cheek against the riveted skin, and did not raise his head. The wind ruffled coldly through his uniform, and he prayed.

I'm scared, he suddenly realized. I'm scared white, I'm shaking, and sick to my stomach, and if I miss I know I'll scream and beat the air with my hands all the way down.

He pushed himself backward the final inch. He felt himself sliding irrevocably down over the steep curve of the nose tip. The ends of his fingers were bleeding. He shut his eyes.

SUDDENLY his feet were on a firm surface. Through his thin socks, he could feel the texture of the saucer's metal. He took a gulping breath and pushed himself off-balance backward. He fell onto the saucer's deck, full-length and on his back. He rolled over with infinite slowness made it, and scrabbled up the slope to the cockpit bubble. The pilot had it unlatched. Duffy Scott crawled in, wedged himself in the cramped space behind the pilot's seat, and fought the terrible sickness in his stomach. He hugged the seat back and rested his face against the cool leather. He looked up for a moment and saw Paul Holloway and Sammy Walters wave from the saucers they'd crawled out to. He lifted a hand feebly.

The stricken DC-7B was surrounded by hovering saucers. He saw that some of them had extra people in them, and realized that somehow those enormously skillful pilots had managed to match speeds with falling human beings and catch them on their broad decks. It looked, at first glance, as if everybody except that one dead passenger was accounted for.

But he couldn't be sure. He'd forgotten how many of them there were—whether he'd missed one, or forgotten to count in Sue Painter, or what. He raised his hands and began carefully counting on his fingers. Somewhere out on the nose of ISA 106, Duffy Scott had turned into an old man.

THE wing commander looked around. All of the natives were accounted for—at least, those he'd seen spewed out of the airliner. "Is there anybody left inside?" he asked the crewmember he'd picked up.

"No..." Sammy Walters said, "...except for one corpse."

"We did kill one, then?"

"You did."

The wing commander wiped a hand under the tilted faceplate of his helmet. "I'm sorry."

"Nothing you can do about it now."

"No," The wing commander wondered if his voice sounded as sick to the native as it did to him.

BUT there was no time to delay. He would have liked to recover the body, but that was out of the question. Already his instrument board was half red with trouble lights as his ship slowly came apart under the strain of supporting the airliner. And off to the north, silver arrows were buzzing up at them like angry wasps. Usually the native fighter interceptor commands could be outrun and outmaneuvered, but not when your own ship was pinned down.

"What now?" Sammy Walters asked him.

"We have to get back to our carrier ship. At least a fourth of my command isn't even airworthy any more. If I don't land them soon, they'll be in serious trouble. He did not mention that his own ship was one of the ones that might burn out their motors at any instant.

He spoke into his command microphone, and eased his ship backward, in synchronized motion with the other two ships holding ISA 106.

With a grind of scraping metal, the airliner slid free. She dropped like a stone for hundreds of feet. Then she picked up flying speed, and her nose struggled up. She flew for a moment, trembling on the verge of a spin. Then she broke apart, piece after piece plunging to Earth.

The wing commander sadly watched her fall. Then his wingman moved up into position, and the remainder of the wing came into formation. With a mumbled prayer, the wing commander fed power to his drive jets. Somehow, they held, though he heard circuit breaker after circuit breaker crack open behind the control panel. Half his ship was dead, but it would still fly forward.

The formation passed over the oncoming native interceptors at maximum acceleration, and blazed toward the mother ship hiding in the aurora borealis.

CHAPTER SEVEN

Mrs. Elston looked around at the interior of the mother ship with eyes that had no yardsticks to measure this kind of immensity. The rows of parked little saucers inside the floodlighted hangar deck looked like so many metal buttons laid out in a row on a bureau top. The girders overhead were like the arches of an enormous cathedral, and the noises; the hoot of warning sirens as service trucks dodged around the saucers, the echoes of mechanics' feet, the clang of service hatches being opened—all these were like the sounds of the biggest railroad station in the world.

The youngster who had piloted them through the opening in the mother ship's hull—the same amazing young man who had caught her in mid-air like a flapjack on a spatula—carefully lifted her down to the hangar floor. "All right now, ma'am?" he asked anxiously.

"Fine, thank you." She winced familiarly at the accustomed pain of her weight on her ankles. She looked around again, and at the young man, who was about six feet tall, had blonde hair and blue eyes, and looked as if he didn't eat as much as he should. "Is this Russia?" she asked.

The young man gravely shook his head. "No, ma'am. This is a big flying saucer—like an aircraft carrier. We're from Venus."

"Then why do you speak English?"

"So you'll be able to understand me, ma'am," he answered politely. "Now you'd better come along with me.

We've got to get off the deck so they can move our ships to the service area."

"What are you going to do with us?"

The youngster shook his head worriedly. "I don't know, ma'am. It's always a mess when something like this happens." He offered her his arm, and she took it thankfully. Walking wasn't easy with her ankles.

As they walked toward a group of people—more saucer pilots, and the rest of the passengers from the airplane, she saw—she turned her head constantly, finding something new to look at every minute.

"VENUS, huh?" Sammy Walters was saying to the wing commander. "You sure don't look it."

"There's no reason to believe the human race is restricted to one planet," the wing commander answered patiently. He felt tired clear through to his bones, and the trouble wasn't half over yet. He thought of the dead man they'd left in the airliner's cabin, and guilt sapped at him. But that was still no reason to keep this man with him in a state of mystification. The wing commander sighed. Duty meant meeting the small obligations, as well as the larger. "We estimate that human beings could live on at least half the planets we know of. You have no idea how tough the human race is, or how faithfully it propagates itself."

"But—where did it all start? Where'd we come from in the first place?"

"I don't know. The theory is we're from outside the Solar System entirely. Or else, God created our ancestors simultaneously on many planets. You have a choice of explanations—or, perhaps those're just two ways of describing the same thing."

He could understand the Earthman's natural desire to have things explained. He'd feel the same way himself. But it was wearing, nevertheless, to have to lecture on anthropology when all the time he was trying to think of what defense his wingman could bring at the court-martial. The fact that the same court would try him, and undoubtedly assign the greater part of the responsibility for the accident to him as commanding officer, was not of as much concern to him.

SUE Painter clutched her broken arm and tried not to sob. She could barely pay attention to anything around her, it hurt so much. The pilot who'd picked her up was saying comforting things about a doctor being on his way up, but that made very little impression on her.

Then she heard somebody call her name, and come running across the hangar toward her, "Sue!"

It was Sammy Walters. She'd never thought much about him one way or another, but now when he put his arm around her waist, she leaned against its warmth and felt better.

"WHAT kind of fuel do you use?" Paul Holloway was asking a pilot. "How about reaction mass? What about that hull shape—cooling surface for atmospheric entry, and heat collector for spaceflight, right? Can you give me your cruising range in miles? How does that stand up at top speed? Just one power plant, with selective linkages to your steering jets, your hovering fans, or your drive, or all three, right? How long is your pilot training program? He had completely forgotten his cheekbone. He did not even notice that it hurt him to talk.

BLAKE Huntingford had fallen through fog, wondering what had picked him up and bruised him so badly. At first he had difficulty in breathing, but that was soon over. Instead, his ears popped violently with pressure change, and a gimlet began boring into his skull, between the eyes, with unrelenting pain that felt like streaks of yellow lightning.

It became unbearable, and he opened his mouth to cry out. Then it felt as though a chisel had opened his forehead and burst a thick bubble inside. Suddenly he could see; he could see how close he was to onrushing ground. It was as though he had awakened into a nightmare.

But Blake Huntingford had never had a nightmare in his life. He studied this one with calm detachment as it moved toward its climax with furious speed. Then something nudged his arm and he forced his head around to see the leading edge of a flying saucer. It was in a flat dive, accelerating at exactly his own speed, and in all the rising universe, only he and the saucer were motionless. It edged under him, and he touched its deck as lightly as a sparrow settling on a branch. The pilot's cockpit was open, and he found handholds on its edge. Then, fifty feet above the ground, they had begun to rise together. Blake Huntingford, plastered down to the deck by a great hand of wind, had continued to study his nightmare.

But there were limits to nightmares. Once he had clambered inside the cockpit, and squeezed in behind the pilot, he had realized the simplest explanation was not the correct one.

It was actually happening, he thought. And as he stood on the mother ship's hangar deck, he still thought it. He listened intently, trying to make the most of what he could hear, for he had gone blind again as soon as he passed ten thousand feet of altitude.

MIKE Hogan cocked an eyebrow at one of the pilots. "Venus. And how are things on Lhuanna?"

"Lhuanna?" He was fazed.

Mike Hogan turned to Lemuel Tolliver, who stood beside him with his eyes watering. Without his glasses, he looked old and helpless. "Wasn't that the name for Venus, Mr. Tolliver?"

The spaceship pilot looked at Lemuel Tolliver with sudden interest. "*Lemuel* Tolliver?" A grin twitched his mouth. "I didn't recognize you from your photograph. I've read your book. Very interesting." Lemuel Tolliver shrank back, and now there were tears on his cheeks.

The pilot turned quickly to Mike Hogan. He seemed ashamed of himself, and, looking at Tolliver and thinking of what the man must be going through. Hogan felt the same way. "As a matter of fact," the Venerian said in a voice that was embarrassed for Tolliver, "we have an interesting situation coming up when you people get out in space yourselves. We don't speak English at home, of course—we have different nations, with different languages, just like you do. There must be a hundred different names for Venus—though I've got to admit I've never heard of Lhuanna being one of them—but all of them translate to just one thing. What else would it be? It's the world that was our only home for generations. It was all we knew—the lights in the sky couldn't conceivably be thought of as anything like the world. That's what we call it—the world. The ground under our feet, Earth."

THE eight people from Earth sat together in the compartment that had been given them. Duffy Scott slumped forward in his chair, his face buried in his sweaty hands. Blake Huntingford sat next to him, his hands resting on his knees, his head up, listening. Mrs. Elston was moving softly around the compartment, feeling the texture of the chair upholstery, marveling at it, and going on to the curtains at the port. She peered at everything. Even here, in this one room, there were so many things to look at.

Paul Holloway sat ignoring everything and silently putting together all the things he'd learned. New compartments in his mind were being filled, and new cross-references were being established. As he listened to his mind repeat each new fact over and over it touched, his face reflected his joy. Lemuel Tolliver, right beside him, sat stiff and withdrawn, his face gaunt. Mike Hogan felt free as air.

Sue Painter, her arm buried inside a traction splint that let her move it with only a twinge or two of mild discomfort, huddled up against Sammy Walker. "Wh—what are they going to do to us? Does anyone know? Sammy?"

"We'll be all right, Sue." He squeezed her shoulders.

"They've got to cover up," Duffy Scott said from behind his hands. He looked up, pale and worn. "They've stirred up a fuss, but it'll die down if we don't come back. It won't be forgotten, but there won't be anything to go on. If we come back, we'll all have tales to tell. So we're not going back. At the very least, they won't let us go back."

Blake Huntingford turned his head sharply toward the sound of Duffy's voice. "Shut up, man," he said crisply.

"They're not going to keep Sue here without a fight," Sammy Walters said angrily.

"Whoa, boy," Mike Hogan said, and they sat looking at each other.

CHAPTER EIGHT

The wing commander came slowly down the companionway, following the mother ship's executive officer. He was thinking of his wingman—a sharp, almost brilliant pilot, an excellent officer with an unlimited future, who had simply made one error in judgment. At a thousand miles per hour, six feet was not much of a mistake. But it had been enough. By that six feet, his wingman's career was ruined, his name disgraced, and his future stolen. In a proud, space-faring nation, a cashiered officer had very little to look forward to.

"Is this where they are?" the executive officer asked him sharply. They had stopped in front of a compartment door.

"Yes, sir. I'll open it for you." He did so mechanically, still preoccupied. The ship's captain had reserved judgment in his own case—possibly because it had been the captain himself who had ordered the training flight. No one could be quite sure where the ultimate responsibility would rest, and the entire mess was going to be carried back to the government at home.

The wing commander stepped through the doorway first, so he could announce the executive officer. He saw all their faces turn toward him, and he felt a wrench as he thought of the one dead man who had been left behind when the airliner was allowed to crash. That troubled him more than anything else. Almost any accident could be mended, and almost any wrong could be apologized for, and righted. But a man killed was a man killed, and nothing could ever redress it.

"Our executive officer would like to speak to you," he told them clumsily, and stepped aside.

The executive officer was a graying man who would be made captain of the next carrier ship built. He was a captain in everything but rank already. He carried command presence with him like an aura, and his self-assurance rested on twenty years' excellent service. The wing commander might have thought the executive was a little too unbending, but the wing commander also realized that he had only a third of his superior's experience, and might very well be wrong.

"First," the executive rapped out, "I must apologize for the unfortunate accident which has necessitated your coming here. Our entire Service holds itself responsible, and the culpable Service personnel have already been disciplined, or are in the process of so being. I trust this is satisfactory.

"Now..." he said, having gotten that finished—and why couldn't the natives learn to get out of the way when something went by? "...now we have to deal with the predicament in which we find ourselves."

Mike Hogan looked up. "What predicament is that?"

"That should be obvious. We are certainly not in a position to let you return to your planet."

Duffy Scott laughed. "Tell us something we don't know." Sammy Walters tightened his grip on Sue Painter's shoulders.

"All right," Mike Hogan said, "so we can't go back. What's the alternative?"

"You will be taken to Venus and kept there for the rest of your lives. The exact details will have to wait for a directive from higher authority, which is considering your case at the moment. But no matter how you are to be disposed of, you must be taken to Venus and never be permitted to contact your home world again."

The wing commander thought that the executive might have chosen a happier way to put it. The phrase "disposed of" had brought a wince of horror from the young woman, and a hostile grimace from the fellow holding her. All the executive officer had meant, in essence, was that until they were safely fitted into some harmless but comfortable Venerian society, their file would perforce remain open, and everyone concerned with it would not be free to go on to something else. Their nation was busy. Service personnel were constantly dealing with one problem or another. Naturally, everyone would want to get this over with. But the executive had thoughtlessly used standard officialese in describing the fact; the wing commander knew, if the executive did not, that most Earthmen would put only one meaning to being "disposed of."

It made him feel even worse to realize this. It was not enough that because of him one of their number was dead, and the rest of them were doomed to permanent exile. Now they had also been exposed to a new emotional shock.

"What do you care whether we go home or not?" Sammy Walters demanded. "You've been coming and going on Earth for years, ignoring anything we might be doing. You go for little cruises across North America, you snoop around all you want to, and you've never even admitted knowing we were alive."

"Young man," The executive officer drew himself up. "No doubt you consider your planet to be of great importance. It may very well be, to you. But it is only another human world to us, and one in an earlier stage of development than our own. Let me assure you that we have had everything you have, and have improved on it since. When and if you achieve spatial navigation for yourselves, the question of commercial and diplomatic intercourse may come up. Meanwhile, your planet serves as a convenient training site for our cadets, who must grow accustomed to dealing with foreign planets.

"However there is a difference between a native observing a man use a rifle, and that same native gaining a glimmering of what causes a rifle to function. You will assuredly never see your Earth again."

SUE Painter whimpered. It was Mike Hogan who stood up and almost accidentally got between the executive and Sammy Walters, who had been tensing himself to jump.

"Begging your pardon, my friend, but I don't think you are that far ahead of us. I haven't seen anything super-duper yet. I've seen stuff we won't have for a while, but nothing we haven't thought about. Maybe that colonial administrator tone of voice is something you picked up twenty years ago and forgot to lose?" Mike Hogan grinned pleasantly.

Some of the air went out of the executive officer, and the wing commander had difficulty restraining his smile. The Earthman had punctured the executive's logic in a vital spot.

But it didn't matter. The executive was still in the command position. Hidebound or not, he was the official face of Venus.

We're human, the wing commander thought. As human as they are. At least as human. We do our best, according to what we think is best—and still we murder and exile them, and insult them, too. It doesn't matter what I think of the executive or his opinions. I'm one of his people, and I'm tarred with the same brush. We all are. We're all Venerians to these people, no matter how much we disagree among ourselves.

The executive barely had his temper under control. "Very well. Do any of you have some plan whereby you may go home and we may be assured you will tell no one what you know, or what happened? Can you conceive of such a possibility? With reporters and government agencies demanding answers? No? I thought so. Then you're coming to Venus, whether you—or I—like it or not."

IT WAS Lemuel Tolliver who broke the silence. "I'd be anxious to go," he said. The other passengers looked at him in astonishment. "Yes. I've been thinking very hard," he went on. "It's become obvious to me that I was wrong." He seemed to be at peace with himself again. "I can't remember now that the spacemen ever said they were from Venus, I just assumed it. When they took me to their planet, I guess it looked more like what I thought Venus would look like. But it must have been Mars, all along. So I'd be very anxious to go to Venus and bring the Message to your people." He looked at the executive and the wing commander. "I can't understand you having spaceships almost as good as theirs and still never having been to Mars. I know you haven't been, or you would know peace and harmony within yourselves already. It must be the force-shield the spacemen have around their world— around Lhuanna—that keeps you away."

No one—not even the executive—said anything for a moment. Then he shrugged and said, "What of the rest of you? Whatever your reasons might be."

"Buddy," Sammy Walters said slowly, "you better make my handcuffs tight." Sue Painter clung to him wordlessly. "You try and hurt this girl, and you'll have trouble."

The wing commander saw the executive's neck veins swell. He wished the co-pilot hadn't been so vehement.

"*If* we had any desire to hurt the young lady," the executive said, "I doubt you'd be able to interfere effectively."

Sammy Walters did spring to his feet this time. He stalked toward the executive. "You try something, Buddy, and see what happens to you."

The executive looked Sammy Walters up and down. "Very well," he said. He then motioned to the wing commander. "I had hoped to arrive at a gentlemen's agreement with you people." He stepped back through the doorway, and the wing commander followed him. "You'll stay here through the duration of our voyage back. It will probably please you greatly to know that you've interrupted a training cruise involving more financial expense than your entire government spends in an entire year!" The thought made him completely furious. He slammed the door in Sammy Walker's face and locked it tight.

CHAPTER NINE

"All *right!*" Sammy Walters exploded ten minutes later. "We're stuck and we're going to stay stuck. Except maybe we won't. I'm going to try and break out of this."

"Hey, boy, don't let that stuffed shirt throw you," Mike Hogan said. "That's all he is. The rest of these birds seem pretty decent. Nobody said they had to pull us out of that crash, you know. It would have made things a lot simpler for them if they'd just let us drop and scrammed out of there."

"Nobody said they had to hit us in the first place," Walters replied.

"They didn't do it deliberately."

Sammy Walters crashed the flat of his palm down on the low table in front of him. "Talk! That's all it is—talk. Now look, I say we can break out of this and get up to the hangar deck. There's got to be some kind of saucer up there big enough to carry all of us."

"Come on, Sam," Duffy Scott said wearily. "Who flies it?"

"*I* fly it! I can fly any damn thing with airfoils, and a few without. What's more, I kept busy looking over my pilot's shoulder all the way up here. Anyhow, it's a chance. That's more than we've got once we get to Venus."

Mike Hogan said, "Look, boy—let's assume you make it to the hangar deck. Let's assume you find an eight pas-senger saucer—"

"Seven," Mr. Tolliver corrected.

"Seven. All right—you find this saucer, you get it started, you get out of the mother ship. I'll give you all of that. What do you do when every saucer on this ship takes out after you?"

"It's a chance," Sammy Walters repeated stubbornly.

"A damned lousy one."

"I think," Mrs. Elston said gently, "I would like to stay here." She was examining the lighting fixture, which was a sheet of fluorescent plastic. So many new things to look at. So much to discover. It was like being young again.

"What?" Sammy Walters exclaimed. "I can understand him, but not you. You're no crackpot. Or are you?"

"Watch your language, Sammy," Paul Holloway said in a detached voice. "I'm not going anywhere either." Then he went back into himself again, still cataloging the things he'd learned, and making places to fit what he would acquire soon.

"What's come *over* you people?" Sammy demanded. "Duffy, what're you going to do?"

Scott shook his head. "I don't care, one way or another."

Sammy Walters scowled at Hogan. "What's your play? You and the big cheese didn't do so well."

"No," Hogan said, "no, we didn't. But I can stand it if he can. See, it doesn't matter if he likes me or not. I've got trained hands to go with my itchy feet. I figure once I turn out to be useful, they'll let me be a Venusian just like the rest of them."

"Venerian," Blake Huntingford corrected.

"Funny," Hogan said, running his hand over his hair. "Ash Holcomb always says Venerian."

"For Pete's sake!" Sammy Walters cried. "You mean Sue and I are going to have to do this alone?"

"Looks like," Hogan remarked. "You do what you want, though, boy." He sat down. He was humming. Sammy Walters took Sue's hand and glared at them. Duffy Scott looked down at the floor. Blake Huntingford sat in the dark and reflected that Sammy had left him out of his plans entirely. It nettled him to be thought an old crock.

THE wing commander came silently back down the companionway, with emotions churning inside him.

He had thought this out for hours, pacing back and forth in his cabin, and now he was here. He had no idea whether what he was going to do was right or wrong. It was at least treacherous. Once an Earthman got back to his home planet with a spaceship, it would only be a matter of time before Earth erupted into the Solar System, equipped with vessels just as good as anything Venus possessed.

But what was he to do? Here were eight people, certainly convinced they were going to their deaths.

The thought of the dead passenger weighed heavily on his mind. Perhaps this would compensate, in some measure.

The hangar deck was practically deserted at this hour, he knew. The mechanics were off watch, and only a few crewmen would still be up there. Most of the ship's personnel were eating.

The long range scouts would be parked to one side of the deck, and they would hold seven people with only a little cramming. Two of the Earthmen were trained pilots. He could certainly explain the controls to one of them. Then he had only to jam the hangar roof after they were through it, and they would be safely away.

As for what would happen to him afterwards...well, that would remain to be seen.

He opened the Earthmen's compartment door, and Sammy Walters crashed a chair down on his head.

SAMMY took Sue Painter's hand. He faced the rest of the passengers. "All right then. All aboard what's coming aboard."

Blake Huntingford stood up. "I'll help you. But I need eyes. Get up, Scott."

Duffy got to his feet. "All right," he said somewhat expressionlessly.

"Good. Now," Huntingford said, "you lead the way, Sammy. Scott, give me your sleeve."

Mike Hogan then straightened up from the wing commander's body. "Well, you didn't quite kill him. I'll give you that."

Sammy paid him no attention. He stepped out into the companionway, still holding Sue Painter's hand. "Nobody out here. We're lucky. Okay, let's see—the hangar deck's *this* way."

"Lead the way," Huntingford said. "Scott—you follow them. And Sammy—just find yourself a ship for two. Scott and I'll have things to keep us busy."

Duffy Scott shrugged. There wasn't anything for him on Earth, or anywhere.

Blake Huntingford turned and faced the remaining passengers. "I don't think you'll be in any trouble. Not when you might have escaped but didn't. Good luck."

"Same to you," Mike Hogan answered gravely. Ten minutes later, he heard the alarm bells.

"Did they make it?" Blake Huntingford asked Duffy Scott.

"Yes. They got free. The kid really *can* fly."

Running feet came pounding up all the companionways toward the hangar deck. Blake Huntingford sighed. "Now—hit me between the eyes! As hard as you can. *Quick*, man!"

Duffy understood almost immediately. Huntingford's head snapped back to the force of the blow. He peered into the shadows. "Again!"

This time, the fog thinned. Floodlights swam before his eyes through a thin veil. As he rubbed his face, he began to make out watery silhouettes. Then his vision cleared a little bit more, and he could see well enough. "Come on!" He picked up two heavy wrenches and handed one to Scott. He ran to the nearest spaceship and began smashing at its undercarriage. "This'll stop them for a while! Cripple the ones in the front row, Scott. We'll give them a good tangle to straighten out."

Something like excitement ran through Duffy Scott's veins again. He brought his wrench smashing around at a stilt-like undercarriage prop, and barely got out of the way as the saucer crumpled forward. Metal tore underneath it, and Duffy grinned with satisfaction.

They ran along the row of parked ships, and the din of their work echoed and re-echoed in the hangar like a battle of war gods. Crewmen ran across the hangar floor toward them, but it was already too late. Blake Huntingford stepped up into place beside Duffy, and hefted his wrench. He was laughing aloud.

Old crock, eh? Well, perhaps, he thought. Perhaps the Venerians had doctors who could repair him. Perhaps he ought never to have started this. But Sammy Walters had made him angry, and Duffy Scott's apathy had given him something to push against. "What a way, and what a place to finish," he cried with joy. And Duffy, hearing him, recognized the fighting man's note in his voice.

Perhaps nothing else could have found one more surge of energy in the used-up husk of Duffy Scott. But Blake Huntingford had done it. They stood shoulder to shoulder, laughing, their weapons ready, as the crewmen swarmed down upon them.

FAR below them, night was falling on the western hemisphere of Earth. Sammy Walters pulled the ship out of its plunging dive, and steadied it. He reached back over his shoulder and touched Sue Painter's hair.

The sunset was before them. They flew toward it.

THE END

www.ingramcontent.com/pod-product-compliance
Lightning Source LLC
Chambersburg PA
CBHW050034180626
46810CB00002B/709